Hazel from
Ruth

✿ ✿ ✿ ✿ ✿ ✿ ✿ ✿ ✿ ✿ ✿ ✿ ✿ ✿ ✿

TACTICAL
EXERCISE

✻ ✻ ✻ ✻ ✻ ✻ ✻ ✻ ✻ ✻ ✻ ✻ ✻ ✻ ✻

BOOKS BY EVELYN WAUGH

DECLINE AND FALL
VILE BODIES
BLACK MISCHIEF
A HANDFUL OF DUST
SCOOP
PUT OUT MORE FLAGS
BRIDESHEAD REVISITED
EDMUND CAMPION
WHEN THE GOING WAS GOOD
THE LOVED ONE
SCOTT–KING'S MODERN EUROPE
HELENA
MEN AT ARMS
TACTICAL EXERCISE

✻ ✻ ✻ ✻ ✻ ✻ ✻ ✻ ✻ ✻ ✻ ✻ ✻ ✻ ✻

✻ ✻ ✻ ✻ ✻ ✻ ✻ ✻ ✻ ✻ ✻ ✻ ✻ ✻ ✻

BY EVELYN WAUGH

TACTICAL
EXERCISE

LITTLE, BROWN AND COMPANY
Boston   Toronto

✻ ✻ ✻ ✻ ✻ ✻ ✻ ✻ ✻ ✻ ✻ ✻ ✻ ✻ ✻

LIBRARY OF CONGRESS CATALOG CARD NO. 54–11123

FIRST EDITION

The author wishes to thank *Good Housekeeping* for permission
to use "The Wish" (now "Tactical Exercise") and *Town and
Country* for permission to use parts of "Work Suspended."

PRINTED IN THE UNITED STATES OF AMERICA

CONTENTS

✿ ✿ ✿ ✿ ✿ ✿ ✿ ✿ ✿ ✿ ✿ ✿ ✿ ✿ ✿

TACTICAL
EXERCISE

1910

❊ ❊ ❊ ❊ ❊ ❊ ❊ ❊ ❊ ❊ ❊ ❊ ❊ ❊ ❊

THE CURSE OF THE HORSE RACE

(Written at the age of 7 years 1 month)

CHAPTER I
Betting

I bet you 500 pounds I'll win. The speeker was Rupert a man of about 25 he had a dark bushy mistarsh and flashing eyes.

I shouldnot trust to much on your horse said Tom for ineed he had not the sum to spear.

The race was to take pleace at ten the following morning.

CHAPTER II
The Race

The next moring Tom took his seat in the gront stand while Rupert mounted Sally (which was his horse) with the others to wate for the pistol shot which would anounse the start.

The race was soon over and Rupet had lost. What was he to do could he do the deed? Yes I'll *kill* him in the night, he though

CHAPTER III

The Fire

Rupert crept stedfustly along with out a sound but as he drew his sword it squeeked a little this awoke Tom seasing a candle he lit it just at that moment Rupert struck and sent the candle flying

The candle lit the curtain Rupert trying to get away tumbled over the bed Tom maid a dash for the door and cleided with a perlisman who had come to see what was the matter and a panic took place.

CHAPTER IV

Explaind

While Tom and the peliesman were escaping through the door Rupert was adopting quite a diffrat methard of escape he puld the matris of the bed and hurled the it out of the window then jumed out he landed safe and sound on the matris then began to run for all he was worth

Now let us leave Rupert and turn to Tom and the peliesman as soon as they got out Tom told the peliesman what had hapend.

CHAPTER V

Hot on the Trail

"See there he is" said Tom "We must folow him and take him to prizen" said the peliesman.

Theres no time to spere said Tom letts get horses said the peliesman so they bort horses and and galerpin in the direcion thet had seen him go.

On they went until they were face to face with each other. the peliesman lept from his horse only to be stabed to the hart by Rupert then Tom jumped down and got Rupert a smart blow on the cheak.

CHAPTER VI

A Deadly Fight

This enraged Rupert that that he shouted and made a plung but Tom was too quick for him artfully dogeing the sword he brout his sword round on Ruperts other cheak.

Just at that moment Ruper slashed killed the peliesmans horse then lept on Toms horse and golapt off.

CHAPTER VII

The Mysterious Man

Of course ther was no chance of catching him on foot so Tom walked to the nearest inn to stay the night but it was ful up he had to share with another man.

Thou Tom was yery tired he could not sleep, their was something about the man he was he did not like he reminded him of some one he didnot know who.

Sudnly he felt something moveing on the bed looking up he saw the man fully dressed just gettimg off the bed

CHAPTER VIII

Run to Erth

Now Tom could see that the mysteraous man was Rupert. Has he come to do a merder? Or has he only cometostay the night? thees were the thoughts that rushed throu Toms head.

he lay still to what Rupert would do first he opend a cuberd and took out a small letter bag from this he too some thing wich made Toms blud turn cold it was a bistol Tom lept forward and seesed Rupert by the throught and flung him to the ground

then snaching a bit of robe from the ground he bound Rupert hand and foot.

CHAPTER IX

Hung

then Tom drest hinself then Ton took Rupert to the puliese cort Rupert was hung for killing the puliesman. I hope the story will be a leson to you never to bet.

1932

✳ ✳ ✳ ✳ ✳ ✳ ✳ ✳ ✳ ✳ ✳ ✳ ✳ ✳ ✳

CRUISE

(Letters from a young lady of leisure)

S.S. *Glory of Greece*

DARLING,

Well I said I would write and so I would have only goodness it was rough so didnt. Now everything is a bit more alright so I will tell you. Well as you know the cruise started at Monte Carlo and when Papa and all of us went to Victoria we found that the tickets didnt include the journey there so Goodness how furious he was and said he wouldnt go but Mum said of course we must go and we said that too only Papa had changed all his money into Liri or Franks on account of foreigners being so dishonest but he kept a shilling for the porter at Dover being methodical so then he had to change it back again and that set him wrong all the way to Monte Carlo and he wouldnt get me and Bertie a sleeper and wouldnt sleep himself in his through being so angry Goodness how Sad.

Then everything was much more alright the purser called him Colonel and he likes his cabin so he took Bertie to the casino and he lost and Bertie won and I think Bertie got a bit plastered at least he made a noise going to bed he's in the next cabin as if he were being sick and that was before we sailed. Bertie has got some books on Baroque art on account of his being at Oxford.

Well the first day it was rough and I got up and felt odd in the bath and the soap wouldnt work on account of salt water you see and came into breakfast and there was a list of so many things including steak and onions and there was a corking young man who said we are the only ones down may I sit here and it was going beautifully and he had steak and onions but it was no good I had to go back to bed just when he was saying there was nothing he admired so much about a girl as her being a good sailor goodness how sad.

The thing is not to have a bath and to be very slow in all movements. So next day it was Naples and we saw some Bertie churches and then that bit that got blown up in an earthquake and a poor dog killed they have a plaster cast of him goodness how sad. Papa and Bertie saw some pictures we werent allowed to see and Bill drew them for me afterwards and Miss P. tried to look too. I havent told you about Bill and Miss P. have I? Well Bill is rather old but clean looking and I don't suppose hes very old not really I mean and he's had a very disillusionary life on account of his wife who he says I wont say a word against but she gave him the raspberry with a foreigner and that makes him hate foreigners. Miss P. is called Miss Phillips and is lousy she wears a yachting cap and is a bitch. And the way she makes up to the second officer is no ones business and its clear to the meanest intelligence he hates her but its part of the rules that all sailors have to pretend to fancy the passengers. Who else is there? Well a lot of old ones. Papa is having a walk out with one called Lady Muriel something or other who knew uncle Ned. And there is a honeymoon couple very embarrassing. And a clergyman and a lovely pansy with a camera and white suit and lots of families from the industrial north.

So Bertie sends his love to. XXXXXX etc.

Mum bought a shawl and an animal made of lava.

POST-CARD

This is a picture of Taormina. Mum bought a shawl here. V. funny because Miss P. got left as shed made chums only with second officer and he wasn't allowed ashore so when it came to getting into cars Miss P. had to pack in with a family from the industrial north.

S.S. *Glory of Greece*

DARLING,

Hope you got P. C. from Sicily. The moral of that was not to make chums with sailors though who I've made a chum of is the purser who's different on account he leads a very cynical life with a gramophone in his cabin and as many cocktails as he likes and welsh rabbits sometimes and I said but do you pay for all these drinks but he said no that's all right.

So we have three days at sea which the clergyman said is a good thing as it makes us all friendly but it hasn't made me friendly with Miss P. who won't leave poor Bill alone not taking any more chances of being left alone when she goes ashore. The purser says theres always someone like her on board in fact he says that about everyone except me who he says quite rightly is different goodness how decent.

So there are deck games they are hell. And the day before we reach Haifa there is to be a fancy dress dance. Papa is very good at the deck games especially one called shuffle board and eats more than he does in London but I daresay its alright. You have to hire dresses for the ball from the barber I mean we do not you. Miss P. has brought her own. So I've thought of a v. clever thing at least the purser suggested it and that is to wear the clothes of one of the sailors I tried his on and looked a treat. Poor Miss P.

Bertie is madly unpop. he wont play any of the games and being plastered the other night too and tried to climb down a ventilator and the second officer pulled him out and the old ones at the captains table look *askance* at him. New word that. Literary yes? No?

So I think the pansy is writing a book he has a green fountain pen and green ink but I couldn't see what it was. XXXX Pretty good about writing you will say and so I am.

POST-CARD

This is a photograph of the Holyland and the famous sea of Gallillee. It is all v. Eastern with camels. I have a lot to tell you about the ball. *Such* goings on and will write very soon. Papa went off for the day with Lady M. and came back saying enchanting woman Knows the world.

S.S. *Glory of Greece*

DARLING,

Well the Ball we had to come in to dinner in our clothes and everyone clapped as we came downstairs. So I was pretty late on account of not being able to make up my mind whether to wear the hat and in the end did and looked a corker. Well it was rather a faint clap for me considering so when I looked about there were about twenty girls and some women all dressed like me so how cynical the purser turns out to be. Bertie looked horribly dull as an apache. Mum and Papa were sweet. Miss P. had a ballet dress from the Russian ballet which couldnt have been more unsuitable so we had champagne for dinner and were jolly and they threw paper streamers and I threw mine before it was unrolled and hit Miss P. on the nose. Ha ha. So feeling matey I said to the steward isnt this fun and he said yes for them who hasnt got to clear it up goodness how Sad.

Well of course Bertie was plastered and went a bit far particularly in what he said to Lady M. then he sat in the cynical pursers cabin in the dark and cried so bill and 1 found him and Bill gave him some drinks and what do you think he went off with Miss P. and we didn't see either of them again it only shows into what degradation the Demon Drink can drag you him I mean.

Then who should I meet but the young man who had steak and onions on the first morning and is called Robert and said I have been trying to meet you again all the voyage. Then I bitched him a bit goodness how Decent.

Poor Mum got taken up by Bill and he told her all about his wife and how she had disillusioned him with the foreigner so to-morrow we reach Port Said d.v. which is latin in case you didn't know meaning God Willing and all to go up the nile and to Cairo for a week.

Will send P.C. of Sphinx.

XXXXXX

POST-CARD

This is the Sphinx. Goodness how sad.

POST-CARD

This is temple of someone. Darling I cant wait to tell you I'm engaged to Arthur. Arthur is the one I thought was a pansy. Bertie thinks egyptian art is v. inartistic.

POST-CARD

This is Tutankhamens v. famous Tomb. Bertie says it is vulgar and is engaged to Miss P. so hes not one to speak and I call her Mabel now. G how S. Bill wont speak to Bertie Robert wont speak to me Papa and Lady M. seem to have had a row there was a man with a snake in a bag also a little boy who told my fortune which was v. prosperous Mum bought a shawl.

POST-CARD

Saw this Mosque today. Robert is engaged to a new girl called something or other who is lousy.

S.S. *Glory of Greece*

DARLING,

Well so we all came back from Egypt pretty excited and the cynical purser said what news and I said *news* well Im engaged to Arthur and Bertie is engaged to Miss P. and she is called Mabel now which is hardest of all to bear I said and Robert to a lousy girl and Papa has had a row with Lady M. and Bill has had a row with Bertie and Roberts lousy girl was awful to me and Arthur was sweet but the cynical purser wasnt a bit surprised on account he said people always get engaged and have quarrels on the Egyptian trip every cruise so I said I wasn't in the habit of getting engaged lightly thank you and he said I wasnt apparently in the habit of going to Egypt so I wont speak to him again nor will Arthur.

All love.

S.S. *Glory of Greece*

Sweet,

This is Algiers *not* very eastern in fact full of frogs. So it is all off with Arthur I was right about him at the first but who I am engaged to is Robert which is *much* better for all concerned really particularly Arthur on account of what I said originally first impressions always right. Yes? No? Robert and I drove about all day in the Botanic gardens and Goodness he was Decent. Bertie got plastered and had a row with Mabel — Miss P. again — so thats all right too and Robert's lousy girl spent all day on board with second officer. Mum bought shawl. Bill told Lady M. about his disillusionment and she told Robert who said yes we all know so Lady M. said it was very unreticent of Bill and she had very little respect for him and didn't blame his wife or the foreigner.

Love.

POST-CARD

I forget what I said in my last letter but if I mentioned a lousy man called Robert you can take it as unsaid. This is still Algiers and Papa ate *dubious oysters* but is all right. Bertie went to a house full of tarts when he was plastered and is pretty unreticent about it as Lady M. would say.

POST-CARD

So now we are back and sang old lang syne is that how you spell it and I kissed Arthur but wont speak to Robert and he cried not Robert I mean Arthur so then Bertie apologised to most of the people hed insulted but Miss P. walked away pretending not to hear. Goodness what a bitch.

1932

✳ ✳ ✳ ✳ ✳ ✳ ✳ ✳ ✳ ✳ ✳ ✳ ✳ ✳ ✳

BELLA FLEACE
GAVE A PARTY

BALLINGAR IS FOUR AND A HALF HOURS FROM DUBLIN IF YOU
catch the early train from Broadstone Station and five and a
quarter if you wait until the afternoon. It is the market town
of a large and comparatively well-populated district. There
is a pretty Protestant Church in 1820 Gothic on one side of
the square and a vast, unfinished Catholic cathedral opposite
it, conceived in that irresponsible medley of architectural
orders that is so dear to the hearts of transmontane pietists.
Celtic lettering of a sort is beginning to take the place of
the Latin alphabet on the shop fronts that complete the
square. These all deal in identical goods in varying degrees
of dilapidation; Mulligan's Store, Flannigan's Store, Riley's
Store, each sells thick black boots, hanging in bundles, soapy
colonial cheese, hardware and haberdashery, oil and saddlery,
and each is licensed to sell ale and porter for consumption
on or off the premises. The shell of the barracks stands with
empty window frames and blackened interior as a monument
to emancipation. Someone has written *The Pope is a Traitor*
in tar on the green pillar box. A typical Irish town.

Fleacetown is fifteen miles from Ballingar, on a direct uneven road through typical Irish country; vague purple hills in the far distance and towards them, on one side of the road, fitfully visible among drifting patches of white mist, unbroken miles of bog, dotted with occasional stacks of cut peat. On the other side the ground slopes up to the north, divided irregularly into spare fields by banks and stone walls over which the Ballingar hounds have some of their most eventful hunting. Moss lies on everything; in a rough green rug on the walls and banks, soft green velvet on the timber, — blurring the transitions so that there is no knowing where the ground ends and trunk and masonry begin. All the way from Ballingar there is a succession of whitewashed cabins and a dozen or so fair-size farmhouses; but there is no gentleman's house, for all this was Fleace property in the days before the Land Commission. The demesne land is all that belongs to Fleacetown now, and this it let for pasture to neighbouring farmers. Only a few beds are cultivated in the walled kitchen garden; the rest has run to rot, thorned bushes barren of edible fruit spreading everywhere among weedy flowers reverting rankly to type. The hot-houses have been draughty skeletons for ten years. The great gates set in the Georgian arch are permanently padlocked, the lodges are derelict, and the line of the main drive is only just discernible through the meadows. Access to the house is half a mile further up through a farm gate, along a track befouled by cattle.

But the house itself, at the date with which we are dealing, was in a condition of comparatively good repair; compared, that is to say, with Ballingar House or Castle Boycott or Knode Hall. It did not, of course, set up to rival Gordontown, where the American Lady Gordon had installed electric light, central heating and a lift, or Mock House or Newhill, which were leased to sporting Englishmen, or Castle Mockstock, since Lord Mockstock married beneath him. These four houses, with their neatly raked gravel, bathrooms and dynamos, were the wonder and ridicule of the country. But Fleacetown, in fair competition with the essentially Irish houses of the Free State, was unusually habitable.

Its roof was intact; and it is the roof which makes the difference between the second and third grade of Irish country houses. Once that goes you have moss in the bedrooms, ferns on the stairs and cows in the library, and in a very few years you have to move into the dairy or one of the lodges. But so long as he has, literally, a roof over his head, an Irishman's house is still his castle. There were weak bits in Fleacetown, but general opinion held that the leads were good for another twenty years and would certainly survive the present owner.

Miss Annabel Rochfort-Doyle-Fleace, to give her the full name under which she appeared in books of reference, though she was known to the entire countryside as Bella Fleace, was the last of her family. There had been Fleaces and Fleysers living about Ballingar since the days of Strongbow, and farm buildings marked the spot where they had inhabited a stockaded fort two centuries before the immigration of the Boycotts or Gordons or Mockstocks. A family tree emblazed by a nineteenth-century genealogist, showing how the original stock had merged with the equally ancient Rochforts and the respectable though more recent Doyles, hung in the billiard-room. The present home had been built on extravagant lines in the middle of the eighteenth century, when the family, though enervated, was still wealthy and influential. It would be tedious to trace its gradual decline from fortune; enough to say that it was due to no heroic debauchery. The Fleaces just got unobtrusively poorer in the way that families do who make no effort to help themselves. In the last generation, too, there had been marked traces of eccentricity. Bella Fleace's mother — an O'Hara of Newhill — had from the day of her marriage until her death suffered from the delusion that she was a Negress. Her brother, from whom she had inherited, devoted himself to oil painting; his mind ran on the simple subject of assassination, and before his death he had executed pictures of practically every such incident in history from Julius Caesar to General Wilson. He was at work on a painting of his own murder at the time of the troubles, when he was, in fact, ambushed and done to death with a shot-gun on his own drive.

It was under one of her brother's paintings — Abraham Lincoln in his box at the theatre — that Miss Fleace was sitting one colourless morning in November when the idea came to her to give a Christmas party. It would be unnecessary to describe her appearance closely, and somewhat confusing, because it seemed in contradiction to much of her character. She was over eighty, very untidy and very red; streaky grey hair was twisted behind her head into a horsey bun, wisps hung round her cheeks; her nose was prominent and blue-veined; her eyes pale blue, blank and mad; she had a lively smile and spoke with a marked Irish intonation. She walked with the aid of a stick, having been lamed many years back when her horse rolled her among loose stones late in a long day with the Ballingar Hounds; a tipsy sporting doctor had completed the mischief, and she had not been able to ride again. She would appear on foot when hounds drew the Fleacetown coverts and loudly criticize the conduct of the huntsman, but every year fewer of her old friends turned out; strange faces appeared.

They knew Bella, though she did not know them. She had become a by-word in the neighbourhood, a much-valued joke.

"A rotten day," they would report. "We found our fox, but lost again almost at once. But we saw Bella. Wonder how long the old girl will last? She must be nearly ninety. My father remembers when she used to hunt — went like smoke, too."

Indeed, Bella herself was becoming increasingly occupied with the prospect of death. In the winter before the one we are talking of, she had been extremely ill. She emerged in April, rosy cheeked as ever, but slower in her movements and mind. She gave instructions that better attention must be paid to her father's and brother's graves, and in June took the unprecedented step of inviting her heir to visit her. She had always refused to see this young man up till now. He was an Englishman, a very distant cousin, named Banks. He lived in South Kensington and occupied himself in the museum. He arrived in August and wrote long and very amusing letters to all his friends describing his visit, and later translated his experiences into a short story for the *Spectator*. Bella disliked him from the moment he arrived. He had horn-rimmed spectacles and a B.B.C. voice. He spent most of his time photographing the Fleacetown chimney-pieces and the moulding of the doors. One day he came to Bella bearing a pile of calf-bound volumes from the library.

"I say, did you know you had these?" he asked.

"I did," Bella lied.

"All first editions. They must be extremely valuable."

"You put them back where you found them."

Later, when he wrote to thank her for his visit — enclosing prints of some of his photographs — he mentioned the books again. This set Bella thinking. Why should that young puppy go poking round the house putting a price on everything? She wasn't dead yet, Bella thought. And the more she thought of it, the more repugnant it became to think of Archie Banks carrying off her books to South Kensington and removing the chimney-pieces and, as he threatened, writing an essay about the house for the *Architectural Review*. She had often heard that the books were valuable. Well, there were plenty of books in the library and she did not see why Archie Banks should profit by them. So she wrote a letter to a Dublin bookseller. He came to look through the library, and after a while he offered her twelve hundred for the lot, or a thousand for the six books which had attracted Archie Banks's attention. Bella was not sure that she had the right to sell things out of the house; a wholesale clearance would be noticed. So she kept the sermons and military history which made up most of the collection, the Dublin bookseller went off with the first editions, which eventually fetched rather less than he had given, and Bella was left with winter coming on and a thousand pounds in hand.

It was then that it occurred to her to give a party. There were always several parties given round Ballingar at Christmas time, but of late years Bella had not been invited to any, partly because many of her neighbours had never spoken to her, partly because they did not think she would want to come, and partly because they would not have known what to do with her if she had. As a matter of fact she loved parties. She liked sitting down to supper in a noisy room, she liked dance music and gossip about which of the girls was pretty and who was in love with them, and she liked drink and having things brought to her by men in pink evening coats. And though she tried to console herself with contemptuous reflections about the ancestry of the hostesses, it annoyed her very much whenever she heard of a party being given in the neighbourhood to which she was not asked.

And so it came about that, sitting with the *Irish Times* under the picture of Abraham Lincoln and gazing across the bare trees of the park to the hills beyond, Bella took it into her head to give a party. She rose immediately and hobbled across the room to the bell-rope. Presently her butler came into the morning-room; he wore the green baize apron in which he cleaned the silver, and in his hand he carried the plate brush to emphasize the irregularity of the summons.

"Was it yourself ringing?" he asked.

"It was, who else?"

"And I at the silver!"

"Riley," said Bella with some solemnity, "I propose to give a ball at Christmas."

"Indeed!" said her butler. "And for what would you want to be dancing at your age?" But as Bella adumbrated her idea, a sympathetic light began to glitter in Riley's eye.

"There's not been such a ball in the country for twenty-five years. It will cost a fortune."

"It will cost a thousand pounds," said Bella proudly.

The preparations were necessarily stupendous. Seven new

servants were recruited in the village and set to work dusting and cleaning and polishing, clearing out furniture and pulling up carpets. Their industry served only to reveal fresh requirements; plaster mouldings, long rotten, crumbled under the feather brooms, worm-eaten mahogany floorboards came up with the tin tacks; bare brick was disclosed behind the cabinets in the great drawing-room. A second wave of the invasion brought painters, paper-hangers and plumbers, and in a moment of enthusiasm Bella had the cornice and the capitals of the pillars in the hall regilded; windows were reglazed, banisters fitted into gaping sockets, and the stair carpet shifted so that the worn strips were less noticeable.

In all these works Bella was indefatigable. She trotted from drawing-room to hall, down the long gallery, up the staircase, admonishing the hireling servants, lending a hand with the lighter objects of furniture, sliding, when the time came, up and down the mahogany floor of the drawing-room to work in the French chalk. She unloaded chests of silver in the attics, found long-forgotten services of china, went down with Riley into the cellars to count the few remaining and now flat and acid bottles of champagne. And in the evenings, when the manual labourers had retired exhausted to their gross recreations, Bella sat up far into the night turning the pages of cookery books, comparing the estimates of rival caterers, inditing long and detailed letters to the agents for dance bands, and most important of all, drawing up her list of guests and addressing the high double piles of engraved cards that stood in her escritoire.

Distance counts for little in Ireland. People will readily drive three hours to pay an afternoon call, and for a dance

of such importance no journey was too great. Bella had her
list painfully compiled from works of reference, Riley's more
up-to-date social knowledge and her own suddenly animated
memory. Cheerfully, in a steady childish handwriting, she
transferred the names to the cards and addressed the enve-
lopes. It was the work of several late sittings. Many of those
whose names were transcribed were dead or bedridden; some
whom she just remembered seeing as small children were
reaching retiring age in remote corners of the globe; many of
the houses she wrote down were blackened shells, burned
during the troubles and never rebuilt; some had "no one
living in them, only farmers." But at last, none too early, the
last envelope was addressed. A final lap with the stamps and
then later than usual she rose from the desk. Her limbs were
stiff, her eyes dazzled, her tongue cloyed with the gum of the
Free State post office; she felt a little dizzy, but she locked
her desk that evening with the knowledge that the most serious part of the work of the party was over. There had been
several notable and deliberate omissions from that list.

"What's all this I hear about Bella giving a party?" said
Lady Gordon to Lady Mockstock. "I haven't had a card."

"Neither have I yet. I hope the old thing hasn't forgotten
me. I certainly intend to go. I've never been inside the house.
I believe she's got some lovely things."

With true English reserve the lady whose husband had
leased Mock Hall never betrayed the knowledge that any
party was in the air at all at Fleacetown.

As the last days approached Bella concentrated more upon
her own appearance. She had bought few clothes of recent

years, and the Dublin dressmaker with whom she used to deal
had shut up shop. For a delirious instant she played with the
idea of a journey to London and even Paris, and considera-
tions of time alone obliged her to abandon it. In the end she
discovered a shop to suit her, and purchased a very magnificent gown of crimson satin; to this she added long white
gloves and satin shoes. There was no tiara, alas! among her
jewels, but she unearthed large numbers of bright, nondescript Victorian rings, some chains and lockets, pearl brooches,
turquoise earrings, and a collar of garnets. She ordered a
coiffeur down from Dublin to dress her hair.

On the day of the ball she woke early, slightly feverish
with nervous excitement, and wriggled in bed till she was
called, restlessly rehearsing in her mind every detail of the
arrangements. Before noon she had been to supervise the setting of hundreds of candles in the sconces round the ballroom and supper-room, and in the three great chandeliers of
cut Waterford glass; she had seen the supper tables laid out
with silver and glass and stood the massive wine coolers by
the buffet; she had helped bank the staircase and hall with
chrysanthemums. She had no luncheon that day, though Riley
urged her with samples of the delicacies already arrived from
the caterer's. She felt a little faint; lay down for a short time,
but soon rallied to sew with her own hands the crested buttons on to the liveries of the hired servants.

The invitations were timed for eight o'clock. She wondered whether that were too early — she had heard tales of
parties that began very late — but as the afternoon dragged
on unendurably, and rich twilight enveloped the house, Bella
became glad that she had set a short term on this exhausting
wait.

At six she went up to dress. The hairdresser was there with a bag full of tongs and combs. He brushed and coiled her hair and whiffed it up and generally manipulated it until it became orderly and formal and apparently far more copious. She put on all her jewellery, and standing before the cheval glass in her room, could not forbear a gasp of surprise. Then she limped downstairs.

The house looked magnificent in the candlelight. The band was there, the twelve hired footmen, Riley in knee breeches and black silk stockings.

It struck eight. Bella waited. Nobody came.

She sat down on a gilt chair at the head of the stairs, looked steadily before her with her blank, blue eyes. In the hall, in the cloakroom, in the supper-room, the hired footmen looked at one another with knowing winks. "What does the old girl expect? No one'll have finished dinner before ten."

The linkmen on the steps stamped and chafed their hands.

At half-past twelve Bella rose from her chair. Her face gave no indication of what she was thinking.

"Riley, I think I will have some supper. I am not feeling altogether well."

She hobbled slowly to the dining-room.

"Give me a stuffed quail and a glass of wine. Tell the band to start playing."

The *Blue Danube* waltz flooded the house. Bella smiled approval and swayed her head a little to the rhythm.

"Riley, I am really quite hungry. I've had nothing all day. Give me another quail and some more champagne."

Alone among the candles and the hired footmen, Riley

served his mistress with an immense supper. She enjoyed every mouthful.

Presently she rose. "I am afraid there must be some mistake. No one seems to be coming to the ball. It is very disappointing after all our trouble. You may tell the band to go home."

But just as she was leaving the dining-room there was a stir in the hall. Guests were arriving. With wild resolution Bella swung herself up the stairs. She must get to the top before the guests were announced. One hand on the banister, one on her stick, pounding heart, two steps at a time. At last she reached the landing and turned to face the company. There was a mist before her eyes and a singing in her ears. She breathed with effort, but dimly she saw four figures advancing and saw Riley meet them and heard him announce:

"Lord and Lady Mockstock, Sir Samuel and Lady Gordon."

Suddenly the daze in which she had been moving cleared. Here on the stairs were the two women she had not invited — Lady Mockstock the draper's daughter, Lady Gordon the American.

She drew herself up and fixed them with her blank, blue eyes.

"I had not expected this honour," she said. "Please forgive me if I am unable to entertain you."

The Mockstocks and the Gordons stood aghast; saw the mad blue eyes of their hostess, her crimson dress; the ballroom beyond, looking immense in its emptiness; heard the dance music echoing through the empty house. The air was charged with the scent of chrysanthemums. And then the drama and unreality of the scene were dispelled. Miss Fleace suddenly sat down, and holding out her hands to her butler, said, "I don't quite know what's happening."

He and two of the hired footmen carried the old lady to a sofa. She spoke only once more. Her mind was still on the same subject. "They came uninvited, those two . . . and nobody else."

A day later she died.

Mr. Banks arrived for the funeral and spent a week sorting out her effects. Among them he found in her escritoire, stamped, addressed, but unposted, the invitations to the ball.

1934

✵ ✵ ✵ ✵ ✵ ✵ ✵ ✵ ✵ ✵ ✵ ✵ ✵ ✵ ✵

ON GUARD

MILLICENT BLADE HAD A NOTABLE HEAD OF NATURALLY
fair hair; she had a docile and affectionate disposition, and
an expression of face which changed with lightning rapidity
from amiability to laughter and from laughter to respectful
interest. But the feature which, more than any other, endeared her to sentimental Anglo-Saxon manhood was her
nose.

It was not everybody's nose; many prefer one with greater
body; it was not a nose to appeal to painters, for it was far
too small and quite without shape, a mere dab of putty without apparent bone structure; a nose which made it impossible
for its wearer to be haughty or imposing or astute. It would
not have done for a governess or a 'cellist or even for a post-
office clerk, but it suited Miss Blade's book perfectly, for it
was a nose that pierced the thin surface crust of the English
heart to its warm and pulpy core; a nose to take the thoughts
of English manhood back to its schooldays, to the doughy-
faded urchins on whom it had squandered its first affection,
to memories of changing room and chapel and battered straw

boaters. Three Englishmen in five, it is true, grow snobbish about these things in later life and prefer a nose that makes more show in public — but two in five is an average with which any girl of modest fortune may be reasonably content.

Hector kissed her reverently on the tip of this nose. As he did so, his senses reeled and in momentary delirium he saw the fading light of the November afternoon, the raw mist spreading over the playing fields; overheated youth in the scrum; frigid youth at the touchline, shuffling on the duckboards, chafing their fingers and, when their mouths were emptied of biscuit crumbs, cheering their house team to further exertion.

"You will wait for me, won't you?" he said.

"Yes, darling."

"And you will write?"

"Yes, darling," she replied more doubtfully, "sometimes . . . at least I'll try. Writing is not my best thing, you know."

"I shall think of you all the time Out There," said Hector. "It's going to be terrible — miles of impassable waggon track between me and the nearest white man, blinding sun, lions, mosquitoes, hostile natives, work from dawn until sunset singlehanded against the forces of nature, fever, cholera . . . But soon I shall be able to send for you to join me."

"Yes, darling."

"It's bound to be a success. I've discussed it all with Beckthorpe — that's the chap who's selling me the farm. You see, the crop has failed every year so far — first coffee, then sisal, then tobacco, that's all you can grow there, and the year Beckthorpe grew sisal everyone else was making a packet in tobacco, but sisal was no good; then he grew tobacco, but by then it was coffee he ought to have grown, and so on. He stuck it nine years. Well if you work it out mathematically, Beckthorpe says, in three years one's bound to strike the right crop. I can't quite explain why, but it is like roulette and all that sort of thing, you see."

"Yes, darling."

Hector gazed at her little, shapeless, mobile button of a nose and was lost again . . . "Play up, play up," and after the match the smell of crumpets being toasted over a gas-ring in his study . . .

✽ ✽ ✽ 2 ✽ ✽ ✽

Later that evening he dined with Beckthorpe, and, as he dined, he grew more despondent.

"Tomorrow this time I shall be at sea," he said, twiddling his empty port glass.

"Cheer up, old boy," said Beckthorpe.

Hector filled his glass and gazed with growing distaste round the reeking dining-room of Beckthorpe's club. The last awful member had left the room and they were alone with the cold buffet.

"I say, you know, I've been trying to work it out. It *was* in three years you said the crop was bound to be right, wasn't it?"

"That's right, old boy."

"Well, I've been through the sum and it seems to me that it might be eighty-one years before it comes right."

"No, no, old boy, three or nine, or at the most twenty-seven."

"Are you sure?"

"Quite."

"Good . . . you know it's awful leaving Milly behind. Suppose it *is* eighty-one years before the crop succeeds. It's the devil of a time to expect a girl to wait. Some other blighter might turn up, if you see what I mean."

"In the Middle Ages they used to use girdles of chastity."

"Yes, I know. I've been thinking of them. But they sound damned uncomfortable. I doubt if Milly would wear one even if I knew where to find it."

"Tell you what, old boy. You ought to give her something."

"Hell, I'm always giving her things. She either breaks them or loses them or forgets where she got them."

"You must give her something she will always have by her, something that will last."

"Eighty-one years?"

"Well, say twenty-seven. Something to remind her of you."

"I could give her a photograph — but I might change a bit in twenty-seven years."

"No, no, that would be most unsuitable. A photograph wouldn't do at all. I know what I'd give her. I'd give her a dog."

"Dog?"

"A healthy puppy that was over distemper and looked like living a long time. She might even call it Hector."

"Would that be a good thing, Beckthorpe?"

"Best possible, old boy."

So next morning, before catching the boat train, Hector

hurried to one of the mammoth stores of London and was shown the livestock department. "I want a puppy."

"Yes, sir. Any particular sort?"

"One that will live a long time. Eighty-one years, or twenty-seven at the least."

The man looked doubtful. "We have some fine healthy puppies, of course," he admitted, "but none of them carry a guarantee. Now if it was longevity you wanted, might I recommend a tortoise? They live to an extraordinary age and are very safe in traffic."

"No, it must be a pup."

"Or a parrot?"

"No, no, a pup. I would prefer one named Hector."

They walked together past monkeys and kittens and cockatoos to the dog department, which, even at this early hour, had attracted a small congregation of rapt worshippers. There were puppies of all varieties in wire-fronted kennels, ears cocked, tails wagging, noisily soliciting attention. Rather wildly, Hector selected a poodle, and as the salesman disappeared to fetch him his change, he leant down for a moments' intense communion with the beast of his choice. He gazed deep into the sharp little face, avoided a sudden snap and said with profound solemnity:

"You are to look after Milly, Hector. See that she doesn't marry anyone until I get back."

And the pup Hector waved his plume of tail.

✻ ✻ ✻ 3 ✻ ✻ ✻

Millicent came to see him off, but, negligently, went to the wrong station; it could not have mattered, however, for she was twenty minutes late. Hector and the poodle hung about the barrier looking for her, and not until the train was already moving did he bundle the animal into Beckthorpe's arms with instructions to deliver him at Millicent's address. Luggage labelled for Mombasa *Wanted on the voyage* lay in the rack above him. He felt very much neglected.

That evening as the ship pitched and rolled past the Channel lighthouses, he received a radiogram:

MISERABLE TO MISS YOU WENT PADDINGTON LIKE IDIOT, THANK YOU FOR SWEET DOG I LOVE HIM FATHER MINDS DREADFULLY LONGING TO HEAR ABOUT FARM DONT FALL FOR SHIP SIREN ALL LOVE MILLY.

In the Red Sea he received another.

BEWARE SIRENS PUPPY BIT MAN CALLED MIKE.

After that Hector heard nothing of Millicent except for a Christmas card which arrived in the last days of February.

✻ ✻ ✻ 4 ✻ ✻ ✻

Generally speaking, Millicent's fancy for any particular young man was likely to last four months. It depended on how far he had got in that time whether the process of extinction was sudden or protracted. In the case of Hector, her affection had been due to diminish at about the time that she became engaged to him; it had been artificially prolonged during the succeeding three weeks, during which he made strenuous, infectiously earnest efforts to find employment in England; it came to an abrupt end with his departure for Kenya. Accordingly the duties of the puppy Hector began with his first days at home. He was young for the job and wholly inexperienced; it is impossible to blame him for his mistake in the matter of Mike Boswell.

This was a young man who had enjoyed a wholly unromantic friendship with Millicent since she first came out. He had seen her fair hair in all kinds of light, in and out of doors, crowned in hats in succeeding fashions, bound with ribbon, decorated with combs, jauntily stuck with flowers; he had seen her nose uplifted in all kinds of weather, had even, on occasions, playfully tweaked it with his finger and thumb, and had never for one moment felt remotely attracted by her.

But the puppy Hector could hardly be expected to know this. All he knew was that two days after receiving his commission, he observed a tall and personable man of marriageable age who treated his hostess with the sort of familiarity which, among the kennel maids with whom he had been brought up, meant only one thing.

The two young people were having tea together. Hector watched for some time from his place on the sofa, barely stifling his growls. A climax was reached when, in the course of some barely intelligible back-chat, Mike leant forward and patted Millicent on the knee.

It was not a serious bite, a mere snap, in fact; but Hector

had small teeth as sharp as pins. It was the sudden, nervous speed with which Mike withdrew his hand which caused the damage; he swore, wrapped his hand in a handkerchief, and at Millicent's entreaty revealed three or four minute wounds. Millicent spoke harshly to Hector and tenderly to Mike, and hurried to her mother's medicine cupboard for a bottle of iodine.

Now no Englishman, however phlegmatic, can have his hand dabbed with iodine without, momentarily at any rate, falling in love.

Mike had seen the nose countless times before, but that afternoon, as it was bowed over his scratched thumb, and as Millicent said, "Am I hurting terribly?", as it was raised towards him, and as Millicent said, "There. Now it will be all right," Mike suddenly saw it transfigured as its devotees saw it and from that moment, until long after the three months of attention which she accorded him, he was Millicent's besotted suitor.

The pup Hector saw all this and realized his mistake. Never again, he decided, would he give Millicent the excuse to run for the iodine bottle.

❊   ❊   ❊   5   ❊   ❊   ❊

He had on the whole an easy task, for Millicent's naturally capricious nature could, as a rule, be relied upon, unaided, to drive her lovers into extremes of irritation. Moreover, she had come to love the dog. She received very regular letters from Hector, written weekly and arriving in batches of three or four according to the mails. She always opened them; often she read them to the end, but their contents made little impression upon her mind and gradually their writer drifted into oblivion so that when people said to her, "How is darling Hector?" it came naturally to her to reply, "He doesn't like the hot weather much, I'm afraid, and his coat is in a very poor state. I'm thinking of having him plucked," instead of, "He had a go of malaria and there is black worm in his tobacco crop."

Playing upon this affection which had grown up for him, Hector achieved a technique for dealing with Millicent's young men. He no longer growled at them or soiled their trousers; that merely resulted in his being turned from the room; instead, he found it increasingly easy to usurp the conversation.

Tea was the most dangerous time of day, for then Millicent was permitted to entertain friends in her sitting-room; accordingly, though he had a constitutional preference for pungent, meaty dishes, Hector heroically simulated a love of lump sugar. Having made this apparent, at whatever cost to his digestion, it was easy to lead Millicent on to an interest in tricks; he would beg and "trust," lie down as though dead, stand in the corner and raise a fore paw to his ear.

"What does s-u-g-a-r spell?" Millicent would ask, and Hector would walk round the tea table to the sugar-bowl and lay his nose against it, gazing earnestly and clouding the silver with his moist breath.

"He understands everything," Millicent would say in triumph.

When tricks failed, Hector would demand to be let out of the door. The young man would be obliged to interrupt himself to open it. Once on the other side Hector would scratch and whine for re-admission.

In moments of extreme anxiety Hector would affect to be sick — no difficult feat after the unwelcome diet of lump sugar; he would stretch out his neck, retching noisily, till Millicent snatched him up and carried him to the hall, where the floor, paved in marble, was less vulnerable — but by that time a tender atmosphere had been shattered and one wholly prejudicial to romance created to take its place.

This series of devices spaced out through the afternoon and tactfully obtruded whenever the guest showed signs of leading the conversation to a more intimate phase, distracted young man after young man and sent them finally away, baffled and despairing.

Every morning Hector lay on Millicent's bed while she took her breakfast and read the daily paper. This hour from ten to eleven was sacred to the telephone and it was then that the young men with whom she had danced overnight attempted to renew their friendship and make plans for the day. At first Hector sought, not unsuccessfully, to prevent these assignations by entangling himself in the wire, but soon a subtler and more insulting technique suggested itself. He pretended to telephone too. Thus, as soon as the bell rang, he would wag his tail and cock his head on one side in a way that he had learned was engaging. Millicent would begin her conversation and Hector would wriggle up under her arm and nuzzle against the receiver.

"Listen," she would say, "*someone* wants to talk to you.

Isn't he an angel?" Then she would hold the receiver down to him and the young man at the other end would be dazed by a shattering series of yelps. This accomplishment appealed so much to Millicent that often she would not even bother to find out the name of the caller but, instead, would take off the receiver and hold it directly to the black snout, so that some wretched young man half a mile away, feeling, perhaps, none too well in the early morning, found himself barked to silence before he had spoken a word.

At other times young men badly taken with the nose would attempt to waylay Millicent in Hyde Park when she was taking Hector for exercise. Here, at first, Hector would get lost, fight other dogs and bite small children to keep himself constantly in her attention, but soon he adopted a gentler course. He insisted upon carrying Millicent's bag for her. He would trot in front of the couple and whenever he thought an interruption desirable he would drop the bag; the young man was obliged to pick it up and restore it first to Millicent and then, at her request, to the dog. Few young men were sufficiently servile to submit to more than one walk in these degrading conditions.

In this way two years passed. Letters arrived constantly from Kenya, full of devotion, full of minor disasters — blight in the sisal, locusts in the coffee, labour troubles, drought, flood, the local government, the world market. Occasionally Millicent read the letters aloud to the dog, usually she left them unread on her breakfast tray. She and Hector moved together through the leisurely routine of English social life. Wherever she carried her nose, two in five marriageable men fell temporarily in love; wherever Hector followed, their ardour changed to irritation, shame and disgust. Mothers began to remark complacently that it was curious how that fascinating Blade girl never got married.

✻ ✻ ✻ **6** ✻ ✻ ✻

At last in the third year of this régime a new problem presented itself in the person of Major Sir Alexander Dreadnought, Bart., M.P., and Hector immediately realized that he was up against something altogether more formidable than he had hitherto tackled.

Sir Alexander was not a young man; he was forty-five and a widower. He was wealthy, popular and preternaturally patient; he was also mildly distinguished, being joint-master of a Midland pack of hounds and a junior minister; he bore a war record of conspicuous gallantry. Millie's father and mother were delighted when they saw that her nose was having its effect on him. Hector took against him from the first, exerted every art which his two and a half years' practice had perfected, and achieved nothing. Devices that had driven a dozen young men to frenzies of chagrin seemed only to accentuate Sir Alexander's tender solicitude. When he came to the house to fetch Millicent for the evening he was found to have filled the pockets of his evening clothes with lump sugar for Hector; when Hector was sick Sir Alexander was there first, on his knees with a page of *The Times*; Hector resorted to his early, violent manner and bit him frequently and hard, but Sir Alexander merely remarked, "I believe I am making the little fellow jealous. A delightful trait."

For the truth was that Sir Alexander had been persecuted

long and bitterly from his earliest days — his parents, his sisters, his schoolfellows, his company-sergeant and his colonel, his colleagues in politics, his wife, his joint-master, huntsman and hunt secretary, his election agent, his constituents and even his parliamentary private secretary had one and all pitched into Sir Alexander, and he accepted this treatment as a matter of course. For him it was the most natural thing in the world to have his ear-drums outraged by barks when he rang up the young woman of his affections; it was a high privilege to retrieve her handbag when Hector dropped it in the park; the small wounds that Hector was able to inflict on his ankles and wrists were to him knightly scars. In his more ambitious moments he referred to Hector in Millicent's hearing as "my little rival." There could be no doubt whatever of his intentions, and when he asked Millicent and her mamma to visit him in the country, he added at the foot of the letter, *"Of course the invitation includes little Hector."*

The Saturday to Monday visit to Sir Alexander was a nightmare to the poodle. He worked as he had never worked before; every artifice by which he could render his presence odious was attempted and attempted in vain. As far as his host was concerned, that is to say. The rest of the household responded well enough, and he received a vicious kick when, through his own bad management, he found himself alone with the second footman, whom he had succeeded in upsetting with a tray of cups at tea-time.

Conduct that had driven Millicent in shame from half the stately homes of England was meekly accepted here. There were other dogs in the house — elderly, sober, well-behaved animals at whom Hector flew; they turned their heads sadly away from his yaps of defiance, he snapped at their ears. They lolloped sombrely out of reach and Sir Alexander had them shut away for the rest of the visit.

There was an exciting Aubusson carpet in the dining-room to which Hector was able to do irreparable damage; Sir Alexander seemed not to notice.

Hector found a carrion in the park and conscientiously rolled in it — although such a thing was obnoxious to his nature — and, returning, fouled every chair in the drawingroom; Sir Alexander himself helped Millicent wash him and brought some bath salts from his own bathroom for the operation.

Hector howled all night; he hid and had half the household searching for him with lanterns; he killed some young pheasants and made a sporting attempt on a peacock. All to no purpose. He staved off an actual proposal, it is true — once in the Dutch garden, once on the way to the stables, and once while he was being bathed — but when Monday morning arrived and he heard Sir Alexander say, "I hope Hector enjoyed his visit a little. I hope I shall see him here *very, very* often," he knew that he was defeated.

It was now only a matter of waiting. The evenings in London were a time when it was impossible for him to keep Millicent under observation. One of these days he would wake up to hear Millicent telephoning to her girl friends, breaking the good news of her engagement.

Thus it was that after a long conflict of loyalties he came to a desperate resolve. He had grown fond of his young mistress; often and often when her face had been pressed down to his he had felt sympathy with that long line of young men whom it was his duty to persecute. But Hector was no kitchen-haunting mongrel. By the code of all well-born dogs it is money that counts. It is the purchaser, not the mere feeder and fondler, to whom ultimate loyalty is due. The hand which had once fumbled with the fivers in the livestock-department of the mammoth store now tilled the unfertile soil of equatorial Africa, but the sacred words of commission still rang in Hector's memory. All through the Sunday night and the journey of Monday morning, Hector wrestled with his problem; then he came to the decision. *The nose must go.*

✻   ✻ ✻ 7 ✻ ✻   ✻

It was an easy business; one firm snap as she bent over his basket and the work was accomplished. She went to a plastic surgeon and emerged some weeks later without scar or stitch. But it was a different nose; the surgeon in his way was an artist and, as I have said above, Millicent's nose had no sculptural qualities. Now she has a fine aristocratic beak, worthy of the spinster she is about to become. Like all spinsters she watches eagerly for the foreign mails and keeps carefully under lock and key a casket full of depressing agricultural intelligence; like all spinsters she is accompanied everywhere by an ageing lap-dog.

1934

✴ ✴ ✴ ✴ ✴ ✴ ✴ ✴ ✴ ✴ ✴ ✴ ✴ ✴ ✴

PERIOD PIECE

LADY AMELIA HAD BEEN EDUCATED IN THE BELIEF THAT IT was the height of impropriety to read a novel in the morning. Now, in the twilight of her days, when she had singularly little to occupy the two hours between her appearance downstairs at a quarter past eleven, hatted and fragrant with lavender water, and the announcement of luncheon, she adhered rigidly to this principle. As soon as luncheon was over, however, and coffee had been served in the drawing-room; before the hot milk in his saucer had sufficiently cooled for Manchu to drink it; while the sunlight, in summer, streamed through the Venetian blinds of the round-fronted Regency windows; while, in winter, the carefully stacked coal-fire glowed in its round-fronted grate; while Manchu sniffed and sipped at his saucer, and Lady Amelia spread out on her knees the various shades of coarse wool with which her failing eyesight now compelled her to work; while the elegant Regency clock ticked off the two and a half hours to tea-time — it was Miss Myers's duty to read a novel aloud to her employer.

With the passing years Lady Amelia had grown increasingly fond of novels and of novels of a particular type. They were what the assistant in the circulating library termed "strong meat" and kept in a hidden place under her desk. It was Miss Myers's duty to fetch and return them. "Have you anything of the kind Lady Amelia likes?" she would ask sombrely.

"Well, there's this just come in," the assistant would answer, fishing up a volume from somewhere near her feet.

At one time Lady Amelia had enjoyed love stories about the irresponsible rich; then she had had a psychological phase; at the moment her interests were American, in the school of brutal realism and gross slang. "Something else like *Sanctuary* or *Bessie Cotter*," Miss Myers was reluctantly obliged to demand. And as the still afternoon was disturbed by her delicately modulated tones enunciating page by page, in scarcely comprehensible idiom, the narratives of rape and betrayal, Lady Amelia would occasionally chuckle a little over her woolwork.

"Women of my age always devote themselves either to religion or to novels," she said. "I have remarked among my few surviving friends that those who read novels enjoy far better health."

The story they were reading came to an end at half-past four.

"Thank you," said Lady Amelia. "That was *most* entertaining. Make a note of the author's name, please, Miss Myers. You will be able to go to the library after tea and see whether they have another. I hope you enjoyed it."

"Well, it was very sad, wasn't it?"

"Sad?"

"I mean the poor young man who wrote it must come from a terrible home."

"Why do you say that, Miss Myers?"

"Well, it was so far fetched."

"It is odd you should think so. I invariably find modern novels painfully reticent. Of course until lately I never read novels at all. I cannot say what they were like formerly. I was far too busy in the old days living my own life and sharing the lives of my friends — all people who came from anything but terrible homes," she added with a glance at her companion; a glance sharp and smart as a rap on the knuckles with an ivory ruler.

There was half-an-hour before tea; Manchu was asleep on the hearth rug, before the fireless grate; the sun streamed in through the blinds, casting long strips of light on the Aubusson carpet. Lady Amelia fixed her eyes on the embroidered, heraldic firescreen; and proceeded dreamily. "I suppose it would not do. You couldn't write about the things which actually happen. People are so used to novels that they would not believe them. The poor writers are constantly at pains to make the truth seem probable. Dear me, I often think, as you sit, *so kindly*, reading to me, 'If one was just to write down quite simply the events of a few years in *any* household one knows . . . No one would believe it.' I can hear you yourself, dear Miss Myers, saying, 'Perhaps these things *do* happen, very occasionally, once in a century, in terrible homes'; instead of which they are constantly happening, every day, all round us — or at least, they were in my young days.

"Take for example the extremely ironic circumstances of the succession of the present Lord Cornphillip.

"I used to know the Cornphillips very well in the old days,"
said Lady Amelia — "Etty was a cousin of my mother's — and
when we were first married my husband and I used to stay
there every autumn for the pheasant shooting. Billy Cornphillip was a *very* dull man — very dull indeed. He was in
my husband's regiment. I used to know a great many dull
people at the time when I was first married, but Billy Cornphillip was notorious for dullness even among my husband's
friends. Their place is in Wiltshire. I see the boy is trying to
sell it now. I am not surprised. It was very ugly and very un-
healthy. I used to dread our visits there.

"Etty was entirely different, a lively thing with very nice
eyes. People thought her fast. Of course it was a *very* good
match for her; she was one of seven sisters and her father was
a younger son, poor dear. Billy was twelve years older. She
had been after him for years. I remember crying with pleasure
when I received her letter telling me of the engagement . . .
It was at the breakfast table . . . she used a very artistic kind
of writing paper with pale blue edges and bows of blue ribbon at the corner . . .

"Poor Etty was always being artistic; she tried to do something with the house — put up peacocks' feathers and painted
tambourines and some very modern stencil work — but the
result was always depressing. She made a little garden for
herself at some distance from the house, with a high wall
and a padlocked door, where she used to retire to think —
or so she said — for hours at a time. She called it the Garden
of Her Thoughts. I went in with her once, as a great privilege,
after one of her quarrels with Billy. Nothing grew very well
there — because of the high walls, I suppose, and her doing

it all herself. There was a mossy seat in the middle. I suppose she used to sit on it while she thought. The whole place had a nasty dank smell . . .

"Well we were all delighted at Etty's luck and I think she quite liked Billy at first and was prepared to behave well to him, in spite of his dullness. You see it came just when we had all despaired. Billy had been the friend of Lady Instow for a long time and we were all afraid she would never let him marry, but they had a quarrel at Cowes that year and Billy went up to Scotland in a bad temper and little Etty was staying in the house; so everything was arranged and I was one of her bridesmaids.

"The only person who was not pleased was Ralph Bland. You see he was Billy's nearest relative and would inherit if Billy died without children and he had got very hopeful as time went on.

"He came to a very sad end — in fact I don't know *what* became of him — but at the time of which I am speaking he was extremely popular, especially with women . . . Poor Viola Chasm was terribly in love with him. Wanted to run away. She and Lady Anchorage were very jealous of each other about him. It became quite disagreeable, particularly when Viola found that Lady Anchorage was paying her maid five pounds a week to send on all Ralph's letters to her — *before* Viola had read them, that was what she minded. He really had a most agreeable manner and said such ridiculous things . . . The marriage was a great disappointment to Ralph; he was married himself and had two children. She had a little money at one time, but Ralph ran through it. Billy did not get on with Ralph — they had very little in common, of course

— but he treated him quite well and was always getting him out of difficulties. In fact he made him a regular allowance at one time, and what with that and what he got from Viola and Lady Anchorage he was really quite comfortable. But, as he said, he had his children's future to consider, so that Billy's marriage *was* a *great* disappointment to him. He even talked of emigrating and Billy advanced him a large sum of money to purchase a sheep farm in New Zealand, but nothing came of that because Ralph had a Jewish friend in the city who made away with the entire amount. It all happened in a very unfortunate manner because Billy had given him this lump sum on the understanding that he should not expect an allowance. And then Viola and Lady Anchorage were greatly upset at his talk of leaving and made other arrangements so that in one way and another Ralph found himself in very low water, poor thing.

"However he began to recover his spirits when, after two years, there was no sign of an heir. People had babies very much more regularly when I was young. Everybody expected that Etty would have a baby — she was a nice healthy little thing — and when she did not, there was a great deal of ill-natured gossip. Ralph himself behaved very wrongly in the matter. He used to make jokes about it, my husband told me, quite openly at his club in the worst possible taste.

"I well remember the last time that Ralph stayed with the Cornphillips; it was a Christmas party, and he came with his wife and his two children. The eldest boy was about six at the time and there was a very painful scene. I was not there myself, but we were staying nearby with the Lockjaws and of course we heard all about it. Billy seems to have been in his most pompous mood and was showing off the house when Ralph's little boy said solemnly and very loudly, 'Daddy says that when I step into your shoes I can pull the whole place down. The only thing worth worrying about is the money.'

"It was towards the end of a large and rather old-fashioned Christmas party, so no one was feeling in a forgiving mood. There was a final breach between the two cousins. Until then, in spite of the New Zealand venture, Billy had been reluctantly supporting Ralph. Now the allowance ceased once for all and Ralph took it in very bad part.

"You know what it is — or perhaps, dear Miss Myers, you are so fortunate as not to know what it is — when near relatives begin to quarrel. There is no limit to the savagery to which they will resort. I should be ashamed to indicate the behaviour of these two men towards each other during the next two or three years. No one had any sympathy with either.

"For example, Billy, of course, was a Conservative. Ralph came down and stood as a Radical in the General Election in his own country and got in.

"This, you must understand, was in the days before the lower classes began going into politics. It was customary for the candidates on both sides to be men of means and, in the circumstances, there was considerable expenditure involved. Much more in fact than Ralph could well afford, but in those days Members of Parliament had many opportunities for improving their position, so we all thought it a very wise course of Ralph's — the first really sensible thing we had known him to do. What followed was *very* shocking.

"Billy, of course, had refused to lend his interest — that

was only to be expected — but when the election was over, and everybody perfectly satisfied with the result, he did what I always consider a *Very Wrong Thing*. He made an accusation against Ralph of corrupt practices. It was a matter of three pounds which Ralph had given to a gardener whom Billy had discharged for drunkenness. I daresay that all that kind of thing has ceased nowadays, but at the time to which I refer it was universally customary. No one had any sympathy with Billy, but he pressed the charge and poor Ralph was unseated.

"Well, after this time, I really think that poor Ralph became a little unsettled in his mind. It is a very sad thing, Miss Myers, when a middle-aged man becomes obsessed by a grievance. You remember how difficult it was when the Vicar thought that Major Etheridge was persecuting him. He actually informed me that Major Etheridge put water in the petrol tank of his motor-cycle and gave sixpences to the choir boys to sing out of tune — well, it was like that with poor Ralph. He made up his mind that Billy had deliberately ruined him. He took a cottage in the village and used to embarrass Billy terribly by coming to all the village fêtes and staring at Billy fixedly. Poor Billy was always embarrassed when he had to make a speech. Ralph used to laugh ironically at the wrong places, but never so loudly that Billy could have him turned out. And he used to go to public houses and drink far too much. They found him asleep on the terrace twice. And, of course, no one on the place liked to offend him, because at any moment he might become Lord Cornphillip.

"It must have been a very trying time for Billy. He and Etty were not getting on at all well together, poor things, and she spent more and more time in the Garden of Her Thoughts and brought out a very silly little book of sonnets, mostly about Venice and Florence, though she could never induce Billy to take her abroad. He used to think that foreign cooking upset him.

"Billy forbade her to speak to Ralph, which was very awkward, as they were always meeting one another in the village and had been great friends in the old days. In fact Ralph used often to speak very contemptuously of his cousin's manliness and say it was time someone took Etty off his hands. But that was only one of Ralph's jokes, because Etty had been getting terribly thin and dressing in the *most* artistic way, and Ralph *always* liked people who were chic and plump — like poor Viola Chasm. Whatever her faults, — " said Lady Amelia, — "Viola was always chic and plump."

"It was at the time of the Diamond Jubilee that the crisis took place. There was a bonfire and a great deal of merry-making of a rather foolish kind and Ralph got terribly drunk. He began threatening Billy in a very silly way and Billy had him up before the magistrates and they made an order against him to keep the peace and not to reside within ten miles of Cornphillip. 'All right,' Ralph said, in front of the whole Court, 'I'll go away, but I won't go alone.' And will you believe it, Miss Myers, he and Etty went off to Venice together that very afternoon.

"Poor Etty, she had always wanted to go to Venice and had written so many poems about it, but it was a great surprise to us all. Apparently she had been meeting Ralph for some time in the Garden of Her Thoughts.

"I don't think Ralph ever cared about her, because, as I

say, she was not at all his type, but it seemed to him a very good revenge on Billy.

"Well, the elopement was far from successful. They took rooms in a very insanitary palace, and had a gondola and ran up a great many bills. Then Etty got a septic throat as a result of the sanitation and while she was laid up Ralph met an American woman who was *much* more his type. So in less than six weeks poor Etty was back in England. Of course she did not go back to Billy at once. She wanted to stay with us, but, naturally, that wasn't possible. It was very awkward for everyone. There was never, I think, any talk of a divorce. It was long before that became fashionable. But we all felt it would be very inconsiderate to Billy if we had her to stay. And then, this is what will surprise you, Miss Myers, the next thing we heard was that Etty was back at Cornphillip and about to have a baby. It was a son. Billy was very pleased about it and I don't believe that the boy ever knew, until quite lately, at luncheon with Lady Metroland, when my nephew Simon told him, in a rather ill-natured way.

"As for poor Ralph's boy, I am afraid he has come to very little good. He must be middle-aged by now. No one ever seems to hear anything of him. Perhaps he was killed in the war. I cannot remember.

"And here comes Ross with the tray; and I see that Mrs. Samson has made more of those little scones which you always seem to enjoy so much. I am sure, dear Miss Myers, you would suffer much less from your *migraine* if you avoided them. But you take so little care of yourself, dear Miss Myers . . . Give one to Manchu."

1934

✿　✿　✿　✿　✿　✿　✿　✿　✿　✿　✿　✿　✿　✿　✿

EXCURSION IN
REALITY

T HE COMMISSIONAIRE AT ESPINOZA'S RESTAURANT SEEMS TO
maintain under his particular authority all the most decrepit
taxicabs in London. He is a commanding man; across his great
chest the student of military medals may construe a tale of
heroism and experience; Boer farms sink to ashes, fanatical
Fuzzie-wuzzies hurl themselves to paradise, supercilious man-
darins survey the smashing of their porcelain and rending of
fine silk, in that triple row of decorations. He has only to run
from the steps of Espinoza's to call to your service a vehicle
as crazy as all the enemies of the King-Emperor.

Half a crown into the white cotton glove, because Simon
Lent was too tired to ask for change. He and Sylvia huddled
into the darkness on broken springs, between draughty windows. It had been an unsatisfactory evening. They had sat
over their table until two because it was an extension night.
Sylvia would not drink anything because Simon had said he
was broke. So they sat for five or six hours, sometimes silent,
sometimes bickering, sometimes exchanging listless greetings
with the passing couples. Simon dropped Sylvia at her door;

a kiss, clumsily offered, coldly accepted; then back to the attic flat, over a sleepless garage, for which Simon paid six guineas a week.

Outside his door they were sluicing a limousine. He squeezed round it and climbed the narrow stairs that had once echoed to the whistling of ostlers, stamping down to stables before dawn. (Woe to young men in Mewses! Oh woe, to bachelors half in love, living on £800 a year!) There was a small heap of letters on his dessing-table, which had arrived that evening while he was dressing. He lit his gas fire and began to open them. Tailor's bill £56, hosier £43; a reminder that his club subscription for that year had not yet been paid; his account from Espinoza's with a note informing him that the terms were strict, net cash monthly, and that no further credit would be extended to him; "it appeared from the books" of his bank that his last cheque overdrew his account £10 16s. beyond the limit of his guaranteed overdraft; a demand from the income-tax collector for particulars of his employees and their wages (Mrs. Shaw, who came in to make his bed and orange juice for 4s. 6d. a day); small bills for books, spectacles, cigars, hair lotion and Sylvia's last four birthday presents. (Woe to shops that serve young men in Mewses!)

The other part of his mail was in marked contrast to this. There was a box of preserved figs from an admirer in Fresno, California; two letters from young ladies who said they were composing papers about his work for their college literary societies, and would he send a photograph; press cuttings describing him as a "popular," "brilliant," "meteorically successful," and "enviable" young novelist; a request for the loan of two hundred pounds from a paralysed journalist; an invitation to luncheon from Lady Metroland; six pages of closely reasoned abuse from a lunatic asylum in the North of England. For the truth, which no one who saw into Simon Lent's heart could possibly have suspected, was that he was in his way and within his limits quite a famous young man.

There was a last letter with a typewritten address which Simon opened with little expectation of pleasure. The paper was headed with the name of a film studio in one of the suburbs of London. The letter was brief and businesslike.

> *Dear Simon Lent* [a form of address, he had noted before, largely favoured by the theatrical profession],
>
> *I wonder whether you have ever considered writing for the films. We should value your angle on a picture we are now making. Perhaps you would meet me for luncheon to-morrow at the Garrick Club and let me know your reactions to this. Will you leave a message with my night secretary some time before 8 A. M. to-morrow morning or with my day secretary after that hour?*
>
> *Cordially yours,*

Below this were two words written in pen and ink which seemed to be *Jewee Mecceee* with below them the explanatory typescript (*Sir James Macrae*)

Simon read this through twice. Then he rang up Sir James Macrae and informed his night secretary that he would keep the luncheon appointment next day. He had barely put down the telephone before the bell rang.

"This is Sir James Macrae's night secretary speaking. Sir James would be very pleased if Mr. Lent would come round and see him this evening at his house in Hampstead."

Simon looked at his watch. It was nearly three. "Well . . . it's rather late to go so far to-night . . . "

"Sir James is sending a car for you."

Simon was no longer tired. As he waited for the car the telephone rang again. "Simon," said Sylvia's voice, "are you asleep?"

"No; in fact I'm just going out."

"Simon . . . I say, was I beastly to-night?"

"Lousy."

"Well, I thought you were lousy, too."

"Never mind. See you some time."

"Aren't you going to go on talking?"

"Can't, I'm afraid. I've got to do some work."

"*Simon,* what *can* you mean?"

"Can't explain now. There's a car waiting."

"When am I seeing you — to-morrow?"

"Well, I don't really know. Ring me up in the morning. Good night."

A quarter of a mile away, Sylvia put down the telephone, rose from the hearthrug, where she had settled herself in the expectation of twenty minutes' intimate explanation and crept disconsolately into bed.

Simon bowled off to Hampstead through deserted streets. He sat back in the car in a state of pleasant excitement. Presently they began to climb the steep hill and emerged into an open space with a pond and the tops of trees, black and deep as a jungle in the darkness. The night butler admitted him to the low Georgian house and led him to the library, where Sir James Macrae was standing before the fire, dressed in ginger-coloured plus-fours. A table was laid with supper.

"Evening, Lent. Nice of you to come. Have to fit in business when I can. Cocoa or whiskey? Have some rabbit pie; it's rather good. First chance of a meal I've had since breakfast. Ring for some more cocoa, there's a good chap. Now what was it you wanted to see me about?"

"Well, I thought *you* wanted to see *me*."

"Did I? Very likely. Miss Bentham'll know. She arranged the appointment. You might ring the bell on the desk, will you?"

Simon rang and there instantly appeared the neat night secretary.

"Miss Bentham, what did I want to see Mr. Lent about?"

"I'm afraid I couldn't say, Sir James. Miss Harper is responsible for Mr. Lent. When I came on duty this evening I merely found a note from her asking me to fix an appointment as soon as possible."

"Pity," said Sir James. "We'll have to wait until Miss Harper comes on to-morrow."

"I think it was something about writing for films."

"Very likely," said Sir James. "Sure to be something of the kind. I'll let you know without delay. Thanks for dropping in." He put down his cup of cocoa and held out his hand with unaffected cordiality. "Good night, my dear boy." He rang the bell for the night butler. "Sanders, I want Benson to run Mr. Lent back."

"I'm sorry, sir. Benson has just gone down to the studio to fetch Miss Grits."

"Pity," said Sir James. "Still, I expect you'll be able to pick up a taxi or something."

�   ✧   ✧   2   ✧   ✧   ✧

Simon got to bed at half-past four. At ten minutes past eight the telephone by his bed was ringing.

"Mr. Lent? This is Sir James Macrae's secretary speaking. Sir James's car will call for you at half-past eight to take you to the studio."

"I shan't be ready as soon as that, I'm afraid."

There was a shocked pause; then the day secretary said: "Very well, Mr. Lent. I will see if some alternative arrangement is possible and ring you in a few minutes."

In the intervening time Simon fell asleep again. Then the bell woke him once more and the same impersonal voice addressed him.

"Mr. Lent? I have spoken to Sir James. His car will call for you at eight forty-five."

Simon dressed hastily. Mrs. Shaw had not yet arrived, so there was no breakfast for him. He found some stale cake in the kitchen cupboard and was eating it when Sir James's car arrived. He took a slice down with him, still munching.

"You needn't have brought that," said a severe voice from inside the car. "Sir James has sent you some breakfast. Get in quickly; we're late."

In the corner, huddled in rugs, sat a young woman in a jaunty red hat; she had bright eyes and a very firm mouth.

"I expect that you are Miss Harper."

"No. I'm Elfreda Grits. We're working together on this

film, I believe. I've been up all night with Sir James. If you don't mind I'll go to sleep for twenty minutes. You'll find a thermos of cocoa and some rabbit pie in the basket on the floor."

"Does Sir James live on cocoa and rabbit pie?"

"No; those are the remains of his supper. Please don't talk. I want to sleep."

Simon disregarded the pie, but poured some steaming cocoa into the metal cap of the thermos flask. In the corner Miss Grits composed herself for sleep. She took off the jaunty red hat and laid it between them on the seat, veiled her eyes with two blue-pigmented lids and allowed the firm lips to relax and gape a little. Her platinum-blonde wind-swept head bobbed and swayed with the motion of the car as they swept out of London through converging and diverging tram lines. Stucco gave place to brick and the façades of the tube stations changed from tile to concrete; unoccupied building plots appeared and newly planted trees along unnamed avenues. Five minutes exactly before their arrival at the studio Miss Grits opened her eyes, powdered her nose, touched her lips with red, and pulling her hat on to the side of her scalp, sat bolt upright, ready for another day.

Sir James was at work on the lot when they arrived. In a white-hot incandescent hell two young people were carrying on an infinitely tedious conversation at what was presumably the table of a restaurant. A dozen emaciated couples in evening dress danced listlessly behind them. At the other end of the huge shed some carpenters were at work building the façade of a Tudor manor house. Men in eyeshades scuttled in and out. Notices stood everywhere. *Do Not Smoke. Do Not Speak. Keep away from the high-power cable.*

Miss Grits, in defiance of these regulations, lit a cigarette, kicked some electric apparatus out of her path, said, "He's busy. I expect he'll see us when he's through with this scene," and disappeared through a door marked *No admittance.*

Shortly after eleven o'clock Sir James caught sight of Simon. "Nice of you to come. Shan't be long now," he called out to him. "Mr. Briggs, get a chair for Mr. Lent."

At two o'clock he noticed him again. "Had any lunch?"

"No," said Simon.

"No more have I. Just coming."

At half-past three Miss Grits joined him and said: "Well, it's been an easy day so far. You mustn't think we're always as slack as this. There's a canteen across the yard. Come and have something to eat."

An enormous buffet was full of people in a variety of costume and make-up. Disappointed actresses in languorous attitudes served cups of tea and hard-boiled eggs. Simon and Miss Grits ordered sandwiches and were about to eat them when a loud-speaker above their heads suddenly announced with alarming distinctness, "Sir James Macrae calling Mr. Lent and Miss Grits in the Conference Room."

"Come on, quick," said Miss Grits. She bustled him through the swing doors, across the yard, into the office buildings and up a flight of stairs to a solid oak door marked *Conference. Keep Out.*

Too late.

"Sir James has been called away," said the secretary. "Will you meet him at the West End office at five-thirty."

Back to London, this time by tube. At five-thirty they were at the Piccadilly office ready for the next clue in their treasure hunt. This took them to Hampstead. Finally at eight they were back at the studio. Miss Grits showed no sign of exhaustion.

"Decent of the old boy to give us a day off," she remarked. "He's easy to work with in that way — after Hollywood. Let's get some supper."

But as they opened the canteen doors and felt the warm breath of light refreshments, the loud-speaker again announced: "Sir James Macrae calling Mr. Lent and Miss Grits in the Conference Room."

This time they were not too late. Sir James was there at the head of an oval table; round him were grouped the chiefs of his staff. He sat in a greatcoat with his head hung forward, elbows on the table and his hands clasped behind his neck. The staff sat in respectful sympathy. Presently he looked up, shook himself and smiled pleasantly.

"Nice of you to come," he said. "Sorry I couldn't see you before. Lots of small things to see to on a job like this. Had dinner?"

"Not yet."

"Pity. Have to eat, you know. Can't work at full pressure unless you eat plenty."

Then Simon and Miss Grits sat down and Sir James explained his plan. "I want, ladies and gentlemen, to introduce Mr. Lent to you. I'm sure you all know his name already and I daresay some of you know his work. Well, I've called him in to help us and I hope that when he's heard the plan he'll consent to join us. I want to produce a film of *Hamlet*. I daresay you don't think that's a very original idea — but it's *angle* that counts in the film world. I'm going to do it from an entirely new angle. That's why I've called in Mr. Lent. I want him to write dialogue for us."

"But surely," said Simon, "there's quite a lot of dialogue there already?"

"Ah, you don't see my angle. There have been plenty of productions of Shakespeare in modern dress. We are going to produce him in modern speech. How can you expect the public to enjoy Shakespeare when they can't make head or tail of the dialogue. D'you know I began reading a copy the other day and blessed if *I* could understand it. At once I said, 'What the public wants is Shakespeare with all his beauty of thought and character translated into the language of every day life.' Now Mr. Lent here was the man whose name naturally suggested itself. Many of the most high-class critics have commended Mr. Lent's dialogue. Now my idea is that Miss Grits here shall act in an advisory capacity, helping with the continuity and the technical side, and that Mr. Lent shall be given a free hand with the scenario . . . "

The discourse lasted for a quarter of an hour; then the chiefs of staff nodded sagely; Simon was taken into another room and given a contract to sign by which he received £50 a week retaining fee and £250 advance.

"You had better fix up with Miss Grits the times of work most suitable to you. I shall expect your first treatment by the end of the week. I should go and get some dinner if I were you. Must eat."

Slightly dizzy, Simon hurried to the canteen where two languorous blondes were packing up for the night.

"We've been on since four o'clock this morning," they said, "and the supers have eaten everything except the nougat. Sorry."

Sucking a bar of nougat Simon emerged into the now-deserted studio. On three sides of him, to the height of twelve feet, rose in appalling completeness the marble walls of the scene-restaurant; at his elbow a bottle of imitation champagne still stood in its pail of melted ice; above and beyond extended the vast gloom of rafters and ceiling.

"*Fact,*" said Simon to himself, "the world of action . . . the pulse of life . . . Money, hunger . . . *Reality.*"

Next morning he was called with the words, "Two young ladies waiting to see you."

"Two?"

Simon put on his dressing-gown and, orange-juice in hand, entered his sitting-room. Miss Grits nodded pleasantly.

"We arranged to start at ten," she said. "But it doesn't really matter. I shall not require you very much in the early stages. This is Miss Dawkins. She is one of the staff stenographers. Sir James thought you would need one. Miss Dawkins will be attached to you until further notice. He also sent two copies of *Hamlet*. When you've had your bath, I'll read you my notes for our first treatment."

But this was not to be; before Simon was dressed Miss Grits had been recalled to the studio on urgent business.

"I'll ring up and tell you when I am free," she said.

Simon spent the morning dictating letters to everyone he could think of; they began — *Please forgive me for dictating this, but I am so busy just now that I have little time for per-*

sonal correspondence . . ." Miss Dawkins sat deferentially over her pad. He gave her Sylvia's number.

"Will you get on to this number and present my compliments to Miss Lennox and ask her to luncheon at Espinoza's . . . And book a table for two there at one forty-five."

"Darling," said Sylvia, when they met, "why were you out all yesterday, and *who* was that voice this morning?"

"Oh, that was Miss Dawkins, my stenographer."

"Simon, what *can* you mean?"

"You see, I've joined the film industry."

"*Darling.* Do give me a job."

"Well, I'm not paying much attention to casting at the moment — but I'll bear you in mind."

"Goodness. How you've changed in two days!"

"Yes!" said Simon, with great complacency. "Yes, I think I have. You see, for the first time in my life I have come into contact with Real Life. I'm going to give up writing novels. It was a mug's game anyway. The written word is dead — first the papyrus, then the printed book, now the film. The artist must no longer work alone. He is part of the age in which he lives; he must share — only of course, my dear Sylvia, in very different proportions — the weekly wage envelope of the proletarian. Vital art implies a corresponding set of social relationships. Co-operation . . . co-ordination . . . the hive endeavour of the community directed to a single end . . ."

Simon continued in this strain at some length, eating meantime a luncheon of Dickensian dimensions, until, in a small miserable voice, Sylvia said: "It seems to me that you've fallen for some ghastly film star."

"Oh God," said Simon, "only a virgin could be as vulgar as that."

They were about to start one of their old, interminable quarrels when the telephone boy brought a message that Miss Grits wished to resume work instantly.

"So that's her name," said Sylvia.

"If you only knew how funny that was," said Simon scribbling his initials on the bill and leaving the table while Sylvia was still groping with gloves and bag.

As things turned out, however, he became Miss Grits's lover before the week was out. The idea was hers. She suggested it to him one evening at his flat as they corrected the typescript of the final version of their first treatment.

"No, really," Simon said aghast. "No, really. It would be quite impossible. I'm sorry, but . . ."

"Why? Don't you like women?"

"Yes, but . . ."

"Oh, come along," Miss Grits said briskly. "We don't get much time for amusement . . ." And later, as she packed their manuscripts into her attaché case she said, "We must do it again if we have time. Besides I find it's so much easier to work with a man if you're having an *affaire* with him."

✿   ✿   ✿   *3*   ✿   ✿   ✿

For three weeks Simon and Miss Grits — he always thought of her by this name in spite of all subsequent intimacies — worked together in complete harmony. His life was redirected and transfigured. No longer did he lie in bed, glumly preparing himself for the coming day; no longer did he say

every morning, "I *must* get down to the country and finish
that book," and every evening find himself slinking back to
the same urban flat; no longer did he sit over supper tables
with Sylvia, idly bickering; no more listless explanations over
the telephone. Instead he pursued a routine of incalculable
variety, summoned by telephone at all hours to conferences
which rarely assembled; sometimes to Hampstead, sometimes
to the studios, once to Brighton. He spent long periods of
work pacing up and down his sitting-room, with Miss Grits
pacing backwards and forwards along the other wall and
Miss Dawkins obediently perched between them, as the two
dictated, corrected and redrafted their scenario. There were
meals at improbable times and vivid, unsentimental passages
of love with Miss Grits. He ate irregular and improbable
meals, bowling through the suburbs in Sir James's car, pacing
the carpet dictating to Miss Dawkins, perched in deserted
lots upon scenery which seemed made to survive the collapse
of civilization. He lapsed, like Miss Grits, into brief spells of
deathlike unconsciousness, often awakening, startled, to find
that a street or desert or factory had come into being about
him while he slept.

The film meanwhile grew rapidly, daily putting out new
shoots and changing under their eyes in a hundred unexpected ways. Each conference produced some radical change
in the story. Miss Grits in her precise, invariable voice would
read out the fruits of their work. Sir James would sit with his
head in his hand, rocking slightly from side to side and giving
vent to occasional low moans and whimpers; round him sat
the experts — production, direction, casting, continuity, cut-

ting and costing managers, bright eyes, eager to attract the great man's attention with some apt intrusion.

"Well," Sir James would say, "I think we can O.K. that. Any suggestions, gentlemen?"

There would be a pause, until one by one the experts began to deliver their contributions . . . "I've been thinking, sir, that it won't do to have the scene laid in Denmark. The public won't stand for travel stuff. How about setting it in Scotland — then we could have some kilts and clan gathering scenes?"

"Yes, that's a very sensible suggestion. Make a note of that, Lent . . ."

"I was thinking we'd better drop this character of the Queen. She'd much better be dead before the action starts. She hangs up the action. The public won't stand for him abusing his mother."

"Yes, make a note of that, Lent."

"How would it be, sir, to make the ghost the Queen instead of the King . . ."

"Yes, make a note of that, Lent . . ."

"Don't you think, sir, it would be better if Ophelia were Horatio's sister. More poignant, if you see what I mean."

"Yes, make a note of that . . ."

"I think we are losing sight of the essence of the story in the last sequence. After all, it is first and foremost a ghost story, isn't it? . . ."

And so from simple beginnings the story spread majestically. It was in the second week that Sir James, after, it must be admitted, considerable debate, adopted the idea of incorporating with it the story of *Macbeth*. Simon was opposed to the proposition at first, but the appeal of the three witches proved too strong. The title was then changed to *The White Lady of Dunsinane,* and he and Miss Grits settled down to a prodigious week's work in rewriting their entire scenarios.

�֍ �֍ �֍ 4 ✖ ✖ ✖

The end came as suddenly as everything else in this remarkable episode. The third conference was being held at an hotel in the New Forest where Sir James happened to be staying; the experts had assembled by train, car and motorbicycle at a moment's notice and were tired and unresponsive. Miss Grits read the latest scenario; it took some time, for it had now reached the stage when it could be taken as 'white script' ready for shooting. Sir James sat sunk in reflection longer than usual. When he raised his head, it was to utter the single word:

"No."

"No?"

"No, it won't do. We must scrap the whole thing. We've got much too far from the original story. I can't think why you need introduce Julius Caesar and King Arthur at all."

"But, sir, they were your own suggestions at the last conference."

"Were they? Well, I can't help it. I must have been tired and not paying full attention . . . Besides, I don't like the dialogue. It misses all the poetry of the original. What the public wants is Shakespeare, the whole of Shakespeare and nothing but Shakespeare. Now this scenario you've written is all very well in its way — but it's not Shakespeare. I'll tell you what we'll do. We'll use the play exactly as he wrote it and record from that. Make a note of it, Miss Grits."

"Then you'll hardly require my services any more?" said Simon.

"No, I don't think I shall. Still, nice of you to have come."

Next morning Simon woke bright and cheerful as usual and was about to leap from his bed when he suddenly remembered the events of last night. There was nothing for him to do. An empty day lay before him. No Miss Grits, no Miss Dawkins, no scampering off to conferences or dictating of dialogue. He rang up Miss Grits and asked her to lunch with him.

"No, quite impossible, I'm afraid. I have to do the continuity for a scenario of St. John's Gospel before the end of the week. Pretty tough job. We're setting it in Algeria so as to get the atmosphere. Off to Hollywood next month. Don't suppose I shall see you again. Good-bye."

Simon lay in bed with all his energy slowly slipping away. Nothing to do. Well, he supposed, now was the time to go away to the country and get on with his novel. Or should he go abroad? Some quiet café-restaurant in the sun where he could work out those intractable last chapters. That was what he would do . . . sometime . . . the end of the week perhaps.

Meanwhile he leaned over on his elbow, lifted the telephone, and asking for Sylvia's number, prepared himself for twenty-five minutes' acrimonious reconciliation.

1935

❋ ❋ ❋ ❋ ❋ ❋ ❋ ❋ ❋ ❋ ❋ ❋ ❋ ❋ ❋

MR. LOVEDAY'S
LITTLE OUTING

Y<small>OU WILL NOT FIND YOUR FATHER GREATLY CHANGED," RE-</small>marked Lady Moping, as the car turned into the gates of the County Asylum.

"Will he be wearing a uniform?" asked Angela.

"No, dear, of course not. He is receiving the very best attention."

It was Angela's first visit and it was being made at her own suggestion.

Ten years had passed since the showery day in late summer when Lord Moping had been taken away; a day of confused but bitter memories for her; the day of Lady Moping's annual garden party, always bitter, confused that day by the caprice of the weather which, remaining clear and brilliant with promise until the arrival of the first guests, had suddenly blackened into a squall. There had been a scuttle for cover; the marquee had capsized; a frantic carrying of cushions and chairs; a table-cloth lofted to the boughs of the monkey-puzzler, fluttering in the rain; a bright period and the cautious emergence of guests on to the soggy lawns; another squall;

another twenty minutes of sunshine. It had been an abominable afternoon, culminating at about six o'clock in her father's attempted suicide.

Lord Moping habitually threatened suicide on the occasion of the garden party; that year he had been found black in the face, hanging by his braces in the orangery; some neighbours, who were sheltering there from the rain, set him on his feet again, and before dinner a van had called for him. Since then Lady Moping had paid seasonal calls at the asylum and returned in time for tea, rather reticent of her experience.

Many of her neighbours were inclined to be critical of Lord Moping's accommodation. He was not, of course, an ordinary inmate. He lived in a separate wing of the asylum, specially devoted to the segregation of wealthier lunatics. They were given every consideration which their foibles permitted. They might choose their own clothes (many indulged in the liveliest fancies), smoke the most expensive brands of cigars, and, on the anniversaries of their certification, entertain any other inmates for whom they had an attachment to private dinner parties.

The fact remained, however, that it was far from being the most expensive kind of institution; the uncompromising address, COUNTY HOME FOR MENTAL DEFECTIVES, stamped across the notepaper, worked on the uniforms of their attendants, painted, even, upon a prominent hoarding at the main entrance, suggested the lowest associations. From time to time, with less or more tact, her friends attempted to bring to Lady Moping's notice particulars of seaside nursing homes, of "qualified practitioners with large private grounds suitable for the charge of nervous or difficult cases," but she accepted them lightly; when her son came of age he might make any changes that he thought fit; meanwhile she felt no inclination to relax her economical régime; her husband had betrayed her basely on the one day in the year when she looked for loyal support, and was far better off than he deserved.

A few lonely figures in greatcoats were shuffling and loping about the park.

"Those are the lower-class lunatics," observed Lady Moping. "There is a very nice little flower garden for people like your father. I sent them some cuttings last year."

They drove past the blank, yellow brick façade to the doctor's private entrance and were received by him in the Visitors' Room, set aside for interviews of this kind. The window was protected on the inside by bars and wire netting; there was no fireplace; when Angela nervously attempted to move her chair further from the radiator, she found that it was screwed to the floor.

"Lord Moping is quite ready to see you," said the doctor.

"How is he?"

"Oh, very well, very well indeed, I'm glad to say. He had rather a nasty cold some time ago, but apart from that his condition is excellent. He spends a lot of his time in writing."

They heard a shuffling, skipping sound approaching along the flagged passage. Outside the door a high peevish voice, which Angela recognized as her father's, said: "I haven't the time, I tell you. Let them come back later."

A gentler tone, with a slight rural burr, replied, "Now come along. It is a purely formal audience. You need stay no longer than you like."

Then the door was pushed open — it had no lock or fastening — and Lord Moping came into the room. He was attended by an elderly little man with full white hair and an expression of great kindness.

"That is Mr. Loveday who acts as Lord Moping's attendant."

"Secretary," said Lord Moping. He moved with a jogging gait and shook hands with his wife.

"This is Angela. You remember Angela, don't you?"

"No, I can't say that I do. What does she want?"

"We just came to see you."

"Well, you have come at an exceedingly inconvenient time. I am very busy. Have you typed out that letter to the Pope yet, Loveday?"

"No, my lord. If you remember, you asked me to look up the figures about the Newfoundland fisheries first?"

"So I did. Well, it is fortunate, as I think the whole letter will have to be redrafted. A great deal of new information has come to light since luncheon. A great deal . . . You see, my dear, I am fully occupied." He turned his restless, quizzical eyes upon Angela. "I suppose you have come about the Danube. Well, you must come again later. Tell them it will be all right, quite all right, but I have not had time to give my full attention to it. Tell them that."

"Very well, Papa."

"Anyway," said Lord Moping rather petulantly, "it is a matter of secondary importance. There is the Elbe and the Amazon and the Tigris to be dealt with first, eh, Loveday? . . . *Danube* indeed. Nasty little river. I'd only call it a stream myself. Well, can't stop, nice of you to come. I would do more for you if I could, but you see how I'm fixed. Write to me about it. That's it. *Put it in black and white.*"

And with that he left the room.

"You see," said the doctor, "he is in excellent condition. He is putting on weight, eating and sleeping excellently. In fact, the whole tone of his system is above reproach."

The door opened again and Loveday returned.

"Forgive my coming back, sir, but I was afraid that the young lady might be upset at his Lordship's not knowing her. You mustn't mind him, miss. Next time he'll be very pleased to see you. It's only to-day he's put out on account of being behindhand with his work. You see, sir, all this week I've been helping in the library and I haven't been able to get all his Lordship's reports typed out. And he's got muddled with his card index. That's all it is. He doesn't mean any harm."

"What a nice man," said Angela, when Loveday had gone back to his charge.

"Yes, I don't know what we should do without old Loveday. Everybody loves him, staff and patients alike."

"I remember him well. It's a great comfort to know that you are able to get such good warders," said Lady Moping; "people who don't know, say such foolish things about asylums."

"Oh, but Loveday isn't a warder," said the doctor.

"You don't mean he's cuckoo, too?" said Angela.

The doctor corrected her.

"He is an *inmate*. It is rather an interesting case. He has been here for thirty-five years."

"But I've never seen anyone saner," said Angela.

"He certainly has that air," said the doctor, "and in the

last twenty years we have treated him as such. He is the life and soul of the place. Of course he is not one of the private patients, but we allow him to mix freely with them. He plays billiards excellently, does conjuring tricks at the concert, mends their gramophones, valets them, helps them in their crossword puzzles and various — er — hobbies. We allow them to give him small tips for services rendered, and he must by now have amassed quite a little fortune. He has a way with even the most troublesome of them. An invaluable man about the place."

"Yes, but why is he here?"

"Well, it is rather sad. When he was a very young man he killed somebody — a young woman quite unknown to him, whom he knocked off her bicycle and then throttled. He gave himself up immediately afterwards and has been here ever since."

"But surely he is perfectly safe now. Why is he not let out?"

"Well, I suppose if it was to anyone's interest, he would be. He has no relatives except a step-sister who lives in Plymouth. She used to visit him at one time, but she hasn't been for years now. He's perfectly happy here and I can assure you *we* aren't going to take the first steps in turning him out. He's far too useful to us."

"But it doesn't seem fair," said Angela.

"Look at your father," said the doctor. "He'd be quite lost without Loveday to act as his secretary."

"It doesn't seem fair."

✽ ✽ ✽ 2 ✽ ✽ ✽

Angela left the asylum, oppressed by a sense of injustice. Her mother was unsympathetic.

"Think of being locked up in a looney bin all one's life."

"He attempted to hang himself in the orangery," replied Lady Moping, *"in front of the Chester-Martins."*

"I don't mean Papa. I mean Mr. Loveday."

"I don't think I know him."

"Yes, the looney they have put to look after Papa."

"Your father's secretary. A very decent sort of man, I thought, and eminently suited to his work."

Angela left the question for the time, but returned to it again at luncheon on the following day.

"Mums, what does one have to do to get people out of the bin?"

"The bin? Good gracious, child, I hope that you do not anticipate your father's return *here.*"

"No, no. Mr. Loveday."

"Angela, you seem to me to be totally bemused. I see it was a mistake to take you with me on our little visit yester-day."

After luncheon Angela disappeared to the library and was soon immersed in the lunacy laws as represented in the encyclopaedia.

She did not re-open the subject with her mother, but a fortnight later, when there was a question of taking some pheasants over to her father for his eleventh Certification Party she showed an unusual willingness to run over with them. Her mother was occupied with other interests and noticed nothing suspicious.

Angela drove her small car to the asylum, and, after delivering the game, asked for Mr. Loveday. He was busy at the time making a crown for one of his companions who expected hourly to be anointed Emperor of Brazil, but he left his work and enjoyed several minutes' conversation with her. They spoke about her father's health and spirits. After a time Angela remarked, "Don't you ever want to get away?"

Mr. Loveday looked at her with his gentle, blue-grey eyes. "I've got very well used to the life, miss. I'm fond of the poor people here, and I think that several of them are quite fond of me. At least, I think they would miss me if I were to go."

"But don't you ever think of being free again?"

"Oh yes, miss, I think of it — almost all the time I think of it."

"What would you do if you got out? There must be *something* you would sooner do than stay here."

The old man fidgeted uneasily. "Well, miss, it sounds ungrateful, but I can't deny I should welcome a little outing once, before I get too old to enjoy it. I expect we all have our secret ambitions, and there *is* one thing I often wish I could do. You mustn't ask me what . . . It wouldn't take long. But I do feel that if I had done it just for a day, an afternoon even, then I would die quiet. I could settle down again easier, and devote myself to the poor crazed people here with a better heart. Yes, I do feel that."

There were tears in Angela's eyes that afternoon as she drove away. "He *shall* have his little outing, bless him," she said.

✿ ✿ ✿ 3 ✿ ✿ ✿

From that day onwards for many weeks Angela had a new purpose in life. She moved about the ordinary routine of her home with an abstracted air and an unfamiliar, reserved courtesy which greatly disconcerted Lady Moping.

"I believe the child's in love. I only pray that it isn't that uncouth Egbertson boy."

She read a great deal in the library, she cross-examined any guests who had pretensions to legal or medical knowledge, she showed extreme goodwill to old Sir Roderick Lane-Foscote, their Member. The names "alienist," "barrister" or "government official" now had for her the glamour that formerly surrounded film actors and professional wrestlers. She was a woman with a cause, and before the end of the hunting season she had triumphed. Mr. Loveday achieved his liberty.

The doctor at the asylum showed reluctance but no real opposition. Sir Roderick wrote to the Home Office. The necessary papers were signed, and at last the day came when Mr. Loveday took leave of the home where he had spent such long and useful years.

His departure was marked by some ceremony. Angela and Sir Roderick Lane-Foscote sat with the doctors on the stage of the gymnasium. Below them was assembled everyone in

the institution who was thought to be stable enough to en-
dure the excitement.

Lord Moping, with a few suitable expressions of regret, presented Mr. Loveday on behalf of the wealthier lunatics with
a gold cigarette case; those who supposed themselves to be
emperors showered him with decorations and titles of honour.
The warders gave him a silver watch and many of the non-
paying inmates were in tears on the day of the presentation.

The doctor made the main speech of the afternoon. "Remember," he remarked, "that you leave behind you nothing
but our warmest good wishes. You are bound to us by ties
that none will forget. Time will only deepen our sense of
debt to you. If at any time in the future you should grow
tired of your life in the world, there will always be a welcome
for you here. Your post will be open."

A dozen or so variously afflicted lunatics hopped and
skipped after him down the drive until the iron gates opened
and Mr. Loveday stepped into his freedom. His small trunk
had already gone to the station; he elected to walk. He had
been reticent about his plans, but he was well provided with
money, and the general impression was that he would go to
London and enjoy himself a little before visiting his stepsister
in Plymouth.

It was to the surprise of all that he returned within two
hours of his liberation. He was smiling whimsically, a gentle
self-regarding smile of reminiscence.

"I have come back," he informed the doctor. "I think that
now I shall be here for good."

"But, Loveday, what a short holiday. I'm afraid that you
have hardly enjoyed yourself at all."

"Oh yes, sir, thank you, sir, I've enjoyed myself *very much*. I'd been promising myself one little treat, all these years. It was short, sir, but *most* enjoyable. Now I shall be able to settle down again to my work here without any regrets."

Half a mile up the road from the asylum gates, they later discovered an abandoned bicycle. It was a lady's machine of some antiquity. Quite near it in the ditch lay the strangled body of a young woman, who, riding home to her tea, had chanced to overtake Mr. Loveday, as he strode along, musing on his opportunities.

1936

❋ ❋ ❋ ❋ ❋ ❋ ❋ ❋ ❋ ❋ ❋ ❋ ❋ ❋ ❋

WINNER TAKES ALL

WHEN MRS. KENT-CUMBERLAND'S ELDEST SON WAS BORN (in an expensive London nursing home) there was a bonfire on Tomb Beacon; it consumed three barrels of tar, an immense catafalque of timber, and, as things turned out — for the flames spread briskly in the dry gorse and loyal tenantry were too tipsy to extinguish them — the entire vegetation of Tomb Hill.

As soon as mother and child could be moved, they travelled in state to the country, where flags were hung out in the village street and a trellis arch of evergreen boughs obscured the handsome Palladian entrance gates of their home. There were farmers' dinners both at Tomb and on the Kent-Cumberlands' Norfolk estate, and funds for a silver-plated tray were ungrudgingly subscribed.

The christening was celebrated by a garden-party. A princess stood godmother by proxy, and the boy was called Gervase Peregrine Mountjoy St. Eustace — all of them names illustrious in the family's history.

Throughout the service and the subsequent presentations

he maintained an attitude of phlegmatic dignity which confirmed everyone in the high estimate they had already formed
of his capabilities.

After the garden-party there were fireworks and after the
fireworks a very hard week for the gardeners, cleaning up the
mess. The life of the Kent-Cumberlands then resumed its
normal tranquillity until nearly two years later, when, much
to her annoyance, Mrs. Kent-Cumberland discovered that she
was to have another baby.

The second child was born in August in a shoddy modern
house on the East Coast which had been taken for the summer so that Gervase might have the benefit of sea air. Mrs.
Kent-Cumberland was attended by the local doctor, who
antagonized her by his middle-class accent, and proved, when
it came to the point, a great deal more deft than the London
specialist.

Throughout the peevish months of waiting Mrs. Kent-
Cumberland had fortified herself with the hope that she
would have a daughter. It would be a softening influence for
Gervase, who was growing up somewhat unresponsive, to
have a pretty, gentle, sympathetic sister two years younger
than himself. She would come out just when he was going
up to Oxford and would save him from either of the dreadful
extremes of evil company which threatened that stage of development — the bookworm and the hooligan. She would
bring down delightful girls for Eights Week and Commem.
Mrs. Kent-Cumberland had it all planned out. When she was
delivered of another son she named him Thomas, and fretted
through her convalescence with her mind on the coming hunting season.

✿ ✿ ✿ 2 ✿ ✿ ✿

The two brothers developed into sturdy, unremarkable little boys; there was little to choose between them except their two years' difference in age. They were both sandy-haired, courageous, and well-mannered on occasions. Neither was sensitive, artistic, highly strung, or conscious of being misunderstood. Both accepted the fact of Gervase's importance just as they accepted his superiority of knowledge and physique. Mrs. Kent-Cumberland was a fair-minded woman, and in the event of the two being involved in mischief, it was Gervase, as the elder, who was the more severely punished. Tom found that his obscurity was on the whole advantageous, for it excused him from the countless minor performances of ceremony which fell on Gervase.

✿ ✿ ✿ 3 ✿ ✿ ✿

At the age of seven Tom was consumed with desire for a model motor-car, an expensive toy of a size to sit in and pedal about the garden. He prayed for it steadfastly every evening and most mornings for several weeks. Christmas was approaching.

Gervase had a smart pony and was often taken hunting. Tom was alone most of the day and the motor-car occupied a great part of his thoughts. Finally he confided his ambition to an uncle. This uncle was not addicted to expensive present giving, least of all to children (for he was a man of limited means and self-indulgent habits), but something in his nephew's intensity of feeling impressed him.

"Poor little beggar," he reflected, "his brother seems to get all the fun," and when he returned to London he ordered the motor-car for Tom. It arrived some days before Christmas and was put away upstairs with other presents. On Christmas Eve Mrs. Kent-Cumberland came to inspect them. "How very kind," she said, looking at each label in turn, "how very kind."

The motor-car was by far the largest exhibit. It was pillar-box red, complete with electric lights, a hooter and a spare wheel.

"Really," she said. "How *very* kind of Ted."

Then she looked at the label more closely. "But how foolish of him. He's put *Tom's* name on it."

"There was this book for Master Gervase," said the nurse, producing a volume labelled "Gervase with best wishes from Uncle Ted."

"Of course the parcels have been confused at the shop," said Mrs. Kent-Cumberland. "This can't have been meant for Tom. Why, it must have cost six or seven pounds."

She changed the labels and went downstairs to supervise the decoration of the Christmas tree, glad to have rectified an obvious error of justice.

Next morning the presents were revealed. "Oh, Ger. You *are* lucky," said Tom, inspecting the motor-car. "May I ride in it?"

"Yes, only be careful. Nanny says it was awfully expensive."

Tom rode it twice round the room. "May I take it in the garden sometimes?"

"Yes. You can have it when I'm hunting."

Later in the week they wrote to thank their uncle for his presents.

Gervase wrote:

DEAR UNCLE TED,
Thank you for the lovely present. It's lovely. The pony is very well. I am going to hunt again before I go back to school.
                                        Love from Gervase

DEAR UNCLE TED, [wrote Tom],
Thank you ever so much for the lovely present. It is just what I wanted. Again thanking you very much.
                                        With love from Tom

"So that's all the thanks I get. Ungrateful little beggar," said Uncle Ted, resolving to be more economical in future.

But when Gervase went back to school he said, "You can have the motor-car, Tom, to keep."

"What, for *my own*?"

"Yes. It's a kid's toy, anyway."

And by this act of generosity he increased Tom's respect and love for him a hundredfold.

✿　✿　✿　**4**　✿　✿　✿

The war came and profoundly changed the lives of the two boys. It engendered none of the neuroses threatened by pacifists. Air raids remained among Tom's happiest memories, when the school used to be awakened in the middle of the night and hustled downstairs to the basement where, wrapped in eiderdowns, they were regaled with cocoa and cake by the matron, who looked supremely ridiculous in a flannel night-gown. Once a Zeppelin was hit in sight of the school; they all crowded to the dormitory windows to see it sinking slowly in a globe of pink flame. A very young master whose health rendered him unfit for military service danced on the head-master's tennis court crying, "There go the baby killers." Tom made a collection of "War Relics," including a captured German helmet, shell-splinters, *The Times* for August 4, 1914, buttons, cartridge cases, and cap badges, that was voted the best in the school.

The event which radically changed the relationship of the brothers was the death, early in 1915, of their father. Neither knew him well nor particularly liked him. He had represented the division in the House of Commons and spent much of his time in London while the children were at Tomb. They only saw him on three occasions after he joined the army. Gervase and Tom were called out of the class-room and told of his death by the headmaster's wife. They cried, since it was expected of them, and for some days were treated with marked deference by the masters and the rest of the school.

It was in the subsequent holidays that the importance of the change became apparent. Mrs. Kent-Cumberland had suddenly become more emotional and more parsimonious. She was liable to unprecedented outbursts of tears, when she would crush Gervase to her and say, "My poor fatherless boy." At other times she spoke gloomily of "Death Duties."

❋ ❋ ❋ 5 ❋ ❋ ❋

For some years in fact "Death Duties" became the refrain of the household.

When Mrs. Kent-Cumberland let the house in London and closed down a wing at Tomb, when she reduced the servants to four and the gardeners to two, when she "let the flower gardens go," when she stopped asking her brother Ted to stay, when she emptied the stables, and became almost fanatical in her reluctance to use the car, when the bath water was cold and there were no new tennis-balls, when the chimneys were dirty and the lawns covered with sheep, when Gervase's cast-off clothes ceased to fit Tom, when she refused him the "extra" expense at school of carpentry lessons and mid-morning milk — "Death Duties" were responsible.

"It is all for Gervase," Mrs. Kent-Cumberland used to explain. "When he inherits, he must take over free of debt, as his father did."

❋ ❋ ❋ 6 ❋ ❋ ❋

Gervase went to Eton in the year of his father's death. Tom would normally have followed him two years later, but in her new mood of economy Mrs. Kent-Cumberland cancelled his entry and began canvassing her friends' opinions about the less famous, cheaper public schools. "The education is just as good," she said, "and far more suitable for a boy who has his own way to make in the world."

Tom was happy enough at the school to which he was sent. It was very bleak and very new, salubrious, progressive, prosperous in the boom that secondary education enjoyed in the years immediately following the war, and, when all was said and done, "thoroughly suitable for a boy with his own way to make in the world." He had several friends whom he was not allowed to invite to his home during the holidays. He got his House colours for swimming and fives, played once or twice in the second eleven for cricket, and was a platoon commander in the O.T.C.; he was in the sixth form and passed the Higher Certificate in his last year, became a prefect and enjoyed the confidence of his house master, who spoke of him as "a very decent stamp of boy." He left school at the age of eighteen without the smallest desire to re-visit it or see any of its members again.

Gervase was then at Christ Church. Tom went up to visit him, but the magnificent Etonians who romped in and out of his brother's room scared and depressed him. Gervase was in the Bullingdon, spending money freely and enjoying himself. He gave a dinner-party in his rooms, but Tom sat in silence, drinking heavily to hide his embarrassment, and was later sombrely sick in a corner of Peckwater quad. He returned to Tomb next day in the lowest spirits.

"It is not as though Tom were a scholarly boy," said Mrs. Kent-Cumberland to her friends. "I am glad he is not, of course. But if he had been, it might have been right to make the sacrifice and send him to the University. As it is, the sooner he Gets Started the better."

* * * **7** * * *

Getting Tom started, however, proved a matter of some difficulty. During the Death Duty Period, Mrs. Kent-Cumberland had cut herself off from many of her friends. Now she cast round vainly to find someone who would "put Tom into something." Chartered Accountancy, Chinese Customs, estate agencies, "the City," were suggested and abandoned. "The trouble is that he has no particular abilities," she explained. "He is the sort of boy who would be useful in anything — an all-round man — but, of course, he has no capital."

August, September, October passed; Gervase was back at Oxford, in fashionable lodgings in the High Street, but Tom remained at home without employment. Day by day he and his mother sat down together to luncheon and dinner, and his constant presence was a severe strain on Mrs. Kent-Cumberland's equability. She herself was always busy and, as she bustled about her duties, it shocked and distracted her to encounter the large figure of her younger son sprawling on the morning-room sofa or leaning against the stone parapet of the terrace and gazing out apathetically across the familiar landscape.

"Why can't you find something to *do*?" she would complain. "There are *always* things to do about a house. Heaven knows I never have a moment." And when, one afternoon, he was asked out by some neighbours and returned too late to dress

for dinner, she said, "Really, Tom, I should have thought that
you had time for that."

"It is a very serious thing," she remarked on another occasion, "for a young man of your age to get out of the habit of
work. It saps his whole morale."

Accordingly she fell back upon the ancient country house
expedient of Cataloguing the Library. This consisted of an
extensive and dusty collection of books amassed by succeeding generations of a family at no time notable for their
patronage of literature; it had been catalogued before, in the
middle of the nineteenth century, in the spidery, spinsterish
hand of a relative in reduced circumstances; since then the
additions and disturbances had been negligible, but Mrs.
Kent-Cumberland purchased a fumed oak cabinet and several
boxes of cards and instructed Tom how she wanted the
shelves re-numbered and the books twice entered under Subject and Author.

It was a system that should keep a boy employed for some
time, and it was with vexation, therefore, that, a few days
after the task was commenced, she paid a surprise visit to the
scene of his labour and found Tom sitting, almost lying, in an
arm-chair, with his feet on a rung of the library steps, reading.

"I am glad you have found something interesting," she said
in a voice that conveyed very little gladness.

"Well, to tell you the truth, I think I have," said Tom, and
showed her the book.

It was the manuscript journal kept by a Colonel Jasper
Cumberland during the Peninsular War. It had no startling
literary merit, nor did its criticisms of the general staff throw
any new light upon the strategy of the campaign, but it was

a lively, direct, day-to-day narrative, redolent of its period; there was a sprinkling of droll anecdotes, some vigorous descriptions of fox-hunting behind the lines of Torres Vedras, of the Duke of Wellington dining in Mess, of a threatened mutiny that had not yet found its way into history, of the assault on Badajoz; there were some bawdy references to Portuguese women and some pious reflexions about patriotism.

"I was wondering if it might be worth publishing," said Tom.

"I should hardly think so," replied his mother. "But I will certainly show it to Gervase when he comes home."

For the moment the discovery gave a new interest to Tom's life. He read up the history of the period and of his own family. Jasper Cumberland he established as a younger son of the period, who had later emigrated to Canada. There were letters from him among the archives, including the announcement of his marriage to a Papist, which had clearly severed the link with his elder brother. In a case of uncatalogued miniatures in the long drawing-room, he found the portrait of a handsome whiskered soldier, which by a study of contemporary uniforms he was able to identify as the diarist.

Presently, in his round, immature handwriting, Tom began working up his notes into an essay. His mother watched his efforts with unqualified approval. She was glad to see him busy, and glad to see him taking an interest in his family's history. She had begun to fear that by sending him to a school without "tradition" she might have made a socialist of the boy. When, shortly before the Christmas vacation, work was found for Tom, she took charge of his notes. "I am sure Gervase will be extremely interested," she said. "He may even think it worth showing to a publisher."

✿ ✿ ✿ **8** ✿ ✿ ✿

The work that had been found for Tom was not immediately lucrative, but, as his mother said, it was a beginning. It was to go to Wolverhampton and learn the motor business from the bottom. The first two years were to be spent at the works, from where, if he showed talent, he might graduate to the London showrooms. His wages, at first, were thirty-five shillings a week. This was augmented by the allowance of another pound. Lodgings were found for him over a fruit shop in the outskirts of the town, and Gervase gave him his old two-seater car, in which he could travel to and from his work, and for occasional week-ends home.

It was during one of these visits that Gervase told him the good news that a London publisher had read the diary and seen possibilities in it. Six months later it appeared under the title *The Journal of an English Cavalry Officer during the Peninsular War. Edited with notes and a biographical introduction by Gervase Kent-Cumberland*. The miniature portrait was prettily reproduced as a frontispiece, there was a collotype copy of a page of the original manuscript, a contemporary print of Tomb Park; and a map of the campaign. It sold nearly two thousand copies at twelve and sixpence and received two or three respectful reviews in the Saturday and Sunday papers.

The appearance of the *Journal* coincided within a few days with Gervase's twenty-first birthday. The celebrations were extravagant and prolonged, culminating in a ball at which Tom's attendance was required.

He drove over, after the works had shut down, and arrived, just in time for dinner, to find a house-party of thirty and a house entirely transformed.

His own room had been taken for a guest ("as you will only be here for one night," his mother explained). He was sent down to the Cumberland Arms, where he dressed by candle-light in a breathless little bedroom over the bar, and arrived late and slightly dishevelled at dinner, where he sat between two lovely girls who neither knew who he was nor troubled to inquire. The dancing afterwards was in a marquee built on the terrace, which a London catering firm had converted into a fair replica of a Pont Street drawing-room. Tom danced once or twice with the daughters of neighbouring families whom he had known since childhood. They asked him about Wolverhampton and the works. He had to get up early next morning; at midnight he slipped away to his bed at the inn. The evening had bored him; because he was in love.

❋ ❋ ❋ 9 ❋ ❋ ❋

It had occurred to him to ask his mother whether he might bring his fiancée to the ball, but on reflexion, enchanted as he was, he had realized that it would not do. The girl was named Gladys Cruttwell. She was two years older than himself; she had fluffy yellow hair which she washed at home once a week and dried before the gas fire; on the day after the shampoo it was very light and silky; towards the end of the week, darker and slightly greasy. She was a virtuous, affectionate, self-reliant, even-tempered, unintelligent, high-spirited girl, but Tom could not disguise from himself the fact that she would not go down well at Tomb.

She worked for the firm on the clerical side. Tom had noticed her on his second day, as she tripped across the yard, exactly on time, bareheaded (the day after a shampoo) in a woollen coat and skirt which she had knitted herself. He had got into conversation with her in the canteen, by making way for her at the counter with a chivalry that was not much practised at the works. His possession of a car gave him a clear advantage over the other young men about the place.

They discovered that they lived within a few streets of one another, and it presently became Tom's practice to call for her in the mornings and take her home in the evenings. He would sit in the two-seater outside her gate, sound the horn, and she would come running down the path to meet him. As summer approached they went for drives in the evening among leafy Warwickshire lanes. In June they were engaged. Tom was exhilarated, sometimes almost dizzy at the experience, but he hesitated to tell his mother. "After all," he reflected, "it is not as though I were Gervase," but in his own heart he knew that there would be trouble.

Gladys came of a class accustomed to long engagements; marriage seemed a remote prospect; an engagement to her signified the formal recognition that she and Tom spent their spare time in one another's company. Her mother, with whom she lived, accepted him on these terms. In years to come, when Tom had got his place in the London showrooms, it would be time enough to think about marrying. But Tom was born to a less patient tradition. He began to speak about a wedding in the autumn.

"It would be lovely," said Gladys in the tones she would have employed about winning the Irish sweepstake.

He had spoken very little about his family. She understood, vaguely, that they lived in a big house, but it was a part of life that never had been real to her. She knew that there were duchesses and marchionesses in something called "Society"; they were encountered in the papers and the films. She knew there were directors with large salaries; but the fact that there were people like Gervase or Mrs. Kent-Cumberland, and that they would think of themselves as radically different from herself, had not entered her experience. When, eventually, they were brought together Mrs. Kent-Cumberland was extremely gracious and Gladys thought her a very nice old lady. But Tom knew that the meeting was proving disastrous.

"Of course," said Mrs. Kent-Cumberland, "the whole thing is quite impossible. Miss Whatever-her-name-was seemed a thoroughly nice girl, but you are not in a position to think of marriage. Besides," she added with absolute finality, "you must not forget that if anything were to happen to Gervase you would be his heir."

So Tom was removed from the motor business and an opening found for him on a sheep farm in South Australia.

❊   ❊   ❊   **10**   ❊   ❊   ❊

It would not be fair to say that in the ensuing two years Mrs. Kent-Cumberland forgot her younger son. She wrote to him every month and sent him bandana handkerchiefs for Christmas. In the first lonely days he wrote to her frequently, but when, as he grew accustomed to the new life, his letters became less frequent she did not seriously miss them. When they did arrive they were lengthy; she put them aside from her correspondence to read at leisure and, more than once, mislaid them, unopened. But whenever her acquaintances asked after Tom she loyally answered, "Doing splendidly. And enjoying himself *very* much."

She had many other things to occupy and, in some cases, distress her. Gervase was now in authority at Tomb, and the careful régime of his minority wholly reversed. There were six expensive hunters in the stable. The lawns were mown, bedrooms thrown open, additional bathrooms installed; there was even talk of constructing a swimming pool. There was constant Saturday to Monday entertaining. There was the sale, at a poor price, of two Romneys and a Hoppner.

Mrs. Kent-Cumberland watched all this with mingled pride and anxiety. In particular she scrutinized the succession of girls who came to stay, in the irreconcilable, ever-present fears that Gervase would or would not marry. Either conclusion seemed perilous; a wife for Gervase must be well-born, well conducted, rich, of stainless reputation, and affectionately disposed to Mrs. Kent-Cumberland; such a mate seemed difficult to find. The estate was clear of the mortgages necessitated by Death Duties, but dividends were uncertain, and though, as she frequently pointed out, she "never interfered," simple arithmetic and her own close experience of domestic management convinced her that Gervase would not long be able to support the scale of living which he had introduced.

With so much on her mind, it was inevitable that Mrs. Kent-Cumberland should think a great deal about Tomb and very little about South Australia, and should be rudely shocked to read in one of Tom's letters that he was proposing to return to England on a visit, with a fiancée and a future father-in-law; that in fact he had already started, was now on the sea and due to arrive in London in a fortnight. Had she read his earlier letters with attention she might have found hints of such an attachment, but she had not done so, and the announcement came to her as a wholly unpleasant surprise.

"Your brother is coming back."

"Oh, good! When?"

"He is bringing a farmer's daughter to whom he is engaged — and the farmer. They want to come here."

"I say, that's rather a bore. Let's tell them we're having the boilers cleaned."

"You don't seem to realize that this is a serious matter, Gervase."

"Oh, well, you fix things up. I dare say it would be all right if they came next month. We've got to have the Anchorages some time. We might get both over together."

In the end it was decided that Gervase should meet the immigrants in London, vet them and report to his mother whether or no they were suitable fellow-guests for the Anchorages. A week later, on his return to Tomb, his mother greeted him anxiously.

"Well? You never wrote?"

"Wrote? Why should I? I never do. I say, I haven't forgotten a birthday or anything, have I?"

"Don't be absurd, Gervase. I mean, about your brother Tom's unfortunate entanglement. Did you see the girl?"

"Oh, *that*. Yes, I went and had dinner with them. Tom's done himself quite well. Fair, rather fat, saucer-eyed, good-tempered, I should say, by her looks."

"Does she — does she speak with an Australian accent?"

"Didn't notice it."

"And the father?"

"Pompous old boy."

"Would he be all right with the Anchorages?"

"I should think he'd go down like a dinner. But they can't come. They are staying with the Chasms."

"Indeed! What an extraordinary thing. But, of course, Archie Chasm was Governor-General once. Still, it shows they must be fairly respectable. Where are they staying?"

"Claridge's."

"Then they must be quite rich, too. How very interesting. I will write this evening."

�֍   ✣   ✤   **11**   ✤   ✣   ✤

Three weeks later they arrived. Mr. MacDougal, the father, was a tall, lean man, with pince-nez and an interest in statistics. He was a territorial magnate to whom the Tomb estates appeared a cosy small-holding. He did not emphasize this in any boastful fashion, but in his statistical zeal gave Mrs. Kent-Cumberland some staggering figures. "Is Bessie your only child?" asked Mrs. Kent-Cumberland.

"My only child and heir," he replied, coming down to brass tacks at once. "I dare say you have been wondering what sort of settlement I shall be able to make on her. Now that, I regret to say, is a question I cannot answer accurately. We have good years, Mrs. Kent-Cumberland, and we have bad years. It all depends."

"But I dare say that even in bad years the income is quite considerable?"

"In a bad year," said Mr. MacDougal, "in a *very* bad year such as the present, the net profits, after all deductions have been made for running expenses, insurance, taxation, and deterioration, amount to something between" — Mrs. Kent-Cumberland listened breathlessly — "fifty and fifty-two thousand pounds. I know that is a very vague statement, but it is impossible to be more accurate until the last returns are in."

Bessie was bland and creamy. She admired everything. "It's so *antique*," she would remark with relish, whether the object of her attention was the Norman Church of Tomb, the Victorian panelling in the billiard-room, or the central-heating system which Gervase had recently installed. Mrs. Kent-Cumberland took a great liking to the girl.

"Thoroughly Teachable," she pronounced. "But I wonder whether she is *really* suited to Tom . . . I *wonder* . . ."

The MacDougals stayed for four days and, when they left, Mrs. Kent-Cumberland pressed them to return for a longer visit. Bessie had been enchanted with everything she saw.

"I wish we could live here," she had said to Tom on her first evening, "in this dear, quaint old house."

"Yes, darling, so do I. Of course it all belongs to Gervase, but I always look on it as my home."

"Just as we Australians look on England."

"Exactly."

She had insisted on seeing everything; the old gabled manor, once the home of the family, relegated now to the function of dower house since the present mansion was built in the eighteenth century — the house of mean proportions and inconvenient offices where Mrs. Kent-Cumberland, in her moments of depression, pictured her own declining years; the mill and the quarries; the farm, which to the MacDougals seemed minute and formal as a Noah's Ark. On these expeditions it was Gervase who acted as guide. "He, of course, knows so much more about it than Tom," Mrs. Kent-Cumberland explained.

Tom, in fact, found himself very rarely alone with his fiancée. Once, when they were all together after dinner, the question of his marriage was mentioned. He asked Bessie whether, now that she had seen Tomb, she would sooner be married there, at the village church, than in London.

"Oh, there is no need to decide anything hastily," Mrs. Kent-Cumberland had said. "Let Bessie look about a little first."

When the MacDougals left, it was to go to Scotland to see the castle of their ancestors. Mr. MacDougal had traced relationship with various branches of his family, had corresponded with them intermittently, and now wished to make their acquaintance.

Bessie wrote to them all at Tomb; she wrote daily to Tom, but in her thoughts, as she lay sleepless in the appalling bed provided for her by her distant kinsmen, she was conscious for the first time of a light feeling of disappointment and uncertainty. In Australia Tom had seemed so different from everyone else, so gentle and dignified and cultured. Here in England he seemed to recede into obscurity. Everyone in England seemed to be like Tom.

And then there was the house. It was exactly the kind of house which she had always imagined English people to live in, with the dear little park — less than a thousand acres — and the soft grass and the old stone. Tom had fitted into the house. He had fitted too well; had disappeared entirely in it and become part of the background. The central place belonged to Gervase — so like Tom but more handsome; with all Tom's charm but with more personality. Beset with these thoughts, she rolled on the hard and irregular bed until dawn began to show through the lancet window of the Victorian-baronial turret. She loved that turret for all its discomfort. It was so antique.

❉ ❉ ❉ 12 ❉ ❉] ❉

Mrs. Kent-Cumberland was an active woman. It was less than ten days after the MacDougals' visit that she returned triumphantly from a day in London. After dinner, when she sat alone with Tom in the small drawing-room, she said:

"You'll be very much surprised to hear who I saw to-day. *Gladys.*"

"Gladys?"

"Gladys Cruttwell."

"Good heavens. Where on earth did you meet her?"

"It was quite by chance," said his mother vaguely. "She is working there now."

"How was she?"

"Very pretty. Prettier, if anything."

There was a pause. Mrs. Kent-Cumberland stitched away at a gros-point chair seat. "You know, dear boy, that I *never interfere*, but I have often wondered whether you treated Gladys very kindly. I know I was partly to blame, myself. But you were both very young and your prospects so uncertain. I thought a year or two of separation would be a good test of whether you really loved one another."

"Oh, I'm sure she has forgotten about me long ago."

"Indeed, she has not, Tom. I thought she seemed a very unhappy girl."

"But how *can* you know, Mother, just seeing her casually like that?"

"We had luncheon together," said Mrs. Kent-Cumberland. "In an A.B.C. shop."

Another pause.

"But, look here, I've forgotten all about her. I only care about Bessie now."

"You know, dearest boy, I never interfere. I think Bessie is a delightful girl. But are you free? Are you free in your own conscience? You know, and I do not know, on what terms you parted from Gladys."

And there returned, after a long absence, the scene which for the first few months of his Australian venture had been constantly in Tom's memory, of a tearful parting and many intemperate promises. He said nothing. "I did not tell Gladys of your engagement. I thought you had the right to do that — as best you can, in your own way. But I did tell her you were back in England and that you wished to see her. She is coming here to-morrow for a night or two. She looked in need of a holiday, poor child."

When Tom went to meet Gladys at the station they stood for some minutes on the platform not certain of the other's identity. Then their tentative signs of recognition corresponded. Gladys had been engaged twice in the past two years, and was now walking out with a motor salesman. It had been a great surprise when Mrs. Kent-Cumberland sought her out and explained that Tom had returned to England. She had not forgotten him, for she was a loyal and good-hearted girl, but she was embarrassed and touched to learn that his devotion was unshaken.

They were married two weeks later and Mrs. Kent-Cumberland undertook the delicate mission of "explaining everything" to the MacDougals.

They went to Australia, where Mr. MacDougal very magnanimously gave them a post managing one of his more remote estates. He was satisfied with Tom's work. Gladys has a large sunny bungalow and a landscape of grazing-land and wire fences. She does not see very much company nor does she particularly like what she does see. The neighbouring ranches find her very English and aloof.

Bessie and Gervase were married after six weeks' engagement. They live at Tomb. Bessie has two children and Gervase

has six race-horses. Mrs. Kent-Cumberland lives in the house
with them. She and Bessie rarely disagree, and, when they do,
it is Mrs. Kent-Cumberland who gets her way.

The dower house is let on a long lease to a sporting manu-
facturer. Gervase has taken over the hounds and spends money
profusely; everyone in the neighbourhood is content.

1 9 3 9

❊ ❊ ❊ ❊ ❊ ❊ ❊ ❊ ❊ ❊ ❊❊ ❊ ❊ ❊ ❊

AN ENGLISHMAN'S
HOME

M R. BEVERLEY METCALFE TAPPED THE BAROMETER IN THE
back hall and noted with satisfaction that it had fallen several
points during the night. He was by nature a sun-loving man,
but he believed it was one of the marks of a true countryman
to be eternally in need of rain. He had made a study and
noted the points of true countrymen. Had he been of literary
habit and of an earlier generation, his observations might have
formed a little book of aphorisms. The true countryman wore
a dark suit on Sundays unlike the flannelled tripper from the
cities; he loved a bargain and would go to any expense to do
his marketing by private treaty instead of through the normal
channels of retail trade; while ostensibly sceptical and conservative he was readily fascinated by mechanical gadgets; he
was genial but inhospitable, willing to gossip for hours across
a fence with any passing stranger, but reluctant to allow his
closest friends into his house . . . These and a hundred other
characteristics Mr. Metcalfe noted for emulation.

"That's what we need — rain," he said to himself, and
opening the garden door stepped into the balmy morning air.

There was no threat in the cloudless heavens. His gardener passed, pushing the water-barrow.

"Good morning, Boggett. The glass has dropped, I'm glad to say."

"Ur."

"Means rain."

"Noa."

"Down quite low."

"Ah."

"Pity to spend a lot of time watering."

"Them'll burn up else."

"Not if it rains."

"Am't agoin to rain. Don't never rain around heres except you can see clear down-over."

"See clear down-over?"

"Ur. Can always see Pilbury Steeple when rains a-coming."

Mr. Metcalfe accepted this statement gravely. "These old fellows know a thing or two that the scientists don't," he would often remark, simulating an air of patronage which was far from sincere. Boggett, the gardener, was not particularly old and he knew very little; the seeds he planted seldom grew; he wrought stark havoc whenever he was allowed to use the pruning-knife; his ambition in horticulture went no further than the fattening of the largest possible pumpkin; but Mr. Metcalfe regarded him with the simple reverence of peasant for priest. For Mr. Metcalfe was but lately initiated into the cult of the countryside, and any features of it still claimed his devotion — its agricultural processes, its social structure, its vocabulary, its recreations; the aspect of it, glittering now under the cool May sunshine, fruit trees in flower, chestnut in full leaf, the ash budding; the sound and smell of it — Mr. Westmacott calling his cows at dawn, the scent of wet earth and Boggett splashing clumsily among the wallflowers; the heart of it — or what Mr. Metcalfe took to be its heart — pulsing all round him; his own heart beating time, for was he not part of it, a true countryman, a landowner?

He was, it was true, a landowner in rather a small way, but, as he stood on his terrace and surveyed the untroubled valley below him, he congratulated himself that he had not been led away by the house agents into the multitudinous cares of a wider territory. He owned seven acres, more or less, and it seemed to him exactly the right amount; they comprised the policies of the house and a paddock; sixty further acres of farmland had also been available, and for a day or two he had toyed with the rather inebriating idea of acquiring them. He could well have afforded it, of course, but to his habit of mind there was something perverse and downright wrong in an investment which showed a bare two per cent yield on his capital. He wanted a home, not a "seat," and he reflected on the irony of that word; he thought of Lord Brakehurst, with whose property he sometimes like to say that his own "marched" — there was indeed a hundred yards of ha-ha between his paddock and one of Lord Brakehurst's pastures. What could be less sedentary than Lord Brakehurst's life, every day of which was agitated by the cares of his great possessions? No, seven acres, judiciously chosen was the ideal property, and Mr. Metcalfe *had* chosen judiciously. The house-agent had spoken no more than the truth when he described Much Malcock as one of the most unspoilt Cotswold villages. It was exactly such a place as Mr. Metcalfe had dreamed of in the long years in the cotton trade in Alexandria. Mr. Metcalfe's own residence, known for generations by the singular name of Grumps, had been rechristened by a previous owner as Much Malcock Hall. It bore the new name pretty well. It was "a dignified Georgian house of mellowed Cotswold stone; four recep., six principal bed and dressing rooms, replete with period features." The villagers, Mr. Metcalfe observed with regret, could not be induced to speak of it as "the Hall." Boggett always said that he worked "up to Grumps," but the name was not of Mr. Metcalfe's choosing and it looked well on his notepaper. It suggested a primacy in the village that was not undisputed.

Lord Brakehurst, of course, was in a class apart; he was Lord Lieutenant of the County with property in fifty parishes. Lady Brakehurst had not in fact called upon Mrs. Metcalfe, living as she did in a world where card-leaving had lost its importance, but, of the calling class, there were two other households in Much Malcock, and a border-line case — besides the vicar, who had a plebian accent and an inclination to preach against bankers.

The rival gentry were Lady Peabury and Colonel Hodge, both, to the villagers, newcomers, but residents of some twenty years' priority to Mr. Metcalfe.

Lady Peabury lived at Much Malcock House, whose chimneys, soon to be hidden in the full foliage of summer, could still be seen among its budding limes on the opposite slope of the valley. Four acres of meadowland lay between her property and Mr. Metcalfe's, where Westmacott's plump herd enriched the landscape and counterbalanced the slightly suburban splendour of her flower gardens. She was a widow and, like Mr. Metcalfe, had come to Much Malcock from abroad. She was rich and kind and rather greedy, a diligent reader of fiction, mistress of many Cairn terriers and of five steady old maidservants who never broke the Crown Derby.

Colonel Hodge lived at the Manor, a fine gabled house in the village street, whose gardens, too, backed on to Westmacott's meadow. He was impecunious but active in the affairs of the British Legion and the Boy Scouts; he accepted Mr. Metcalfe's invitation to dinner, but spoke of him, in his family circle, as "the cotton wallah."

These neighbours were of unequivocal position; the Hornbeams at the Old Mill were a childless, middle-aged couple who devoted themselves to craftmanship. Mr. Hornbeam senior was a genuine, commercial potter in Staffordshire; he supported them reluctantly and rather exiguously, but this backing of unearned quarterly cheques placed them definitely in the upper strata of local society. Mrs. Hornbeam attended church and Mr. Hornbeam was quite knowledgeable about vegetables. In fact, had they preferred a tennis court to their herb garden, and had Mr. Hornbeam possessed an evening-suit, they might easily have mixed with their neighbours on terms of ostensible equality. At the time of the Peace Ballot, Mrs. Hornbeam had canvassed every cottage in bycycling distance, but she eschewed the Women's Institute, and in Lady Peabury's opinion failed to pull her weight in the village. Mr. Metcalfe thought Mr. Hornbeam Bohemian, and Mr. Hornbeam thought Mr. Metcalfe Philistine. Colonel Hodge had fallen out with them some time back, in a question relating to his Airedale, and cut them year in year out, three or four times a day.

Under their stone-tiled roofs the villagers derived substantial comfort from all these aliens. Foreign visitors impressed by the charge of London restaurants and the splendour of the more accessible ducal palaces often express wonder at the wealth of England. A half has not been told them. It is in remote hamlets like Much Malcock that the great reservoirs of national wealth seep back to the soil. The villagers had their Memorial Hall and their club. In the rafters of their church the death-watch beetle had been expensively exterminated for them; their scouts had a bell tent and silver bugles; the district nurse drove her own car; at Christmas their children were surfeited with trees and parties and the cottagers loaded with hampers; if one of them was indisposed port and soup and grapes and tickets for the seaside arrived in profusion; at evening their menfolk returned from work laden with perquisites, and all the year round they feasted on forced vegetables. The vicar found it impossible to interest them in the Left Book Club.

"God gave all men all earth to love," Mr. Metcalfe quoted, dimly remembering the lines from a calendar which had hung in his office in Alexandria, "but since our hearts are small, Ordained for each one spot should prove, Beloved over all."

He pottered round to the engine-house where his chauffeur was brooding over batteries. He popped his head into another outbuilding and saw no harm had befallen the lawn-mower during the night. He paused in the kitchen garden to nip the blossom off some newly planted black-currant which must not be allowed to fruit that summer. Then, his round finished, he pottered in to breakfast.

His wife was already there.

"I've done my round," he said.

"Yes, dear."

"Everything coming along nicely."

"Yes, dear."

"You can't see Pilbury Steeple, though."

"Good gracious, Beverley, why should you want to do that?"

"It's a sign of rain when you can."

"What a lot of nonsense. You've been listening to Boggett again."

She rose and left him with his papers. She had to see the cook. Servants seem to take up so much time in England; she thought wistfully of the white-gowned Berber boys who had pattered about the cool, tiled floors of her house in Alexandria.

Mr. Metcalfe finished his breakfast and retired to his study with pipe and papers. The *Gazette* came out that morning. A true countryman always reads his "local rag" first, so Mr. Metcalfe patiently toiled through the columns of Women's Institute doings and the reports of a Council meeting on the subject of sewage, before he allowed himself to open the *The Times*.

Serene opening of a day of wrath!

❊   ❊   ❊   **2**   ❊   ❊   ❊

Towards eleven o'clock Mr. Metcalfe put aside the crossword. In the lobby by the garden-door he kept a variety of garden implements specially designed for the use of the elderly. Selecting from among them one which had newly arrived, he sauntered out into the sunshine and addressed himself to the plantains of the lawn. The tool had a handsomely bound leather grip, a spliced cane handle and a head of stainless steel; it worked admirably, and with a minimum of effort Mr. Metcalfe had soon scarred a large area with little pits.

He paused and called towards the house, "Sophie, Sophie, come and see what I've done."

His wife's head emerged from an upper window. "Very pretty, dear," she said.

Encouraged, he set to work again. Boggett passed.

"Useful little tool this, Boggett."

"Ur."

"Think we ought to sow seed in the bare patches?"

"Noa."

"You think the grass will grow over them?"

"Noa. Plantains'll come up again."

"You don't think I've killed the roots?"

"Noa. Makes the roots powerful strong topping 'em off same as you've done."

"Well, what ought I to do?"

"Bain't nothing you can do with plantains. They do always come up again."

Boggett passed. Mr. Metcalfe looked at his gadget with sudden distaste, propped it petulantly against the sundial, and with his hands in his pockets stared out across the valley. Even at this distance Lady Peabury's aubretias struck a discordant note. His eyes dropped and he noticed, casually at first, then with growing curiosity, two unfamiliar figures among Westmacott's cows. They were young men in dark, urban clothes, and they were very busy about something. They had papers in their hands which they constantly consulted; they paced up and down the field as though measuring it; they squatted on their haunches as though roughly taking level; they pointed into the air, to the ground, and to the horizon.

"Boggett," said Mr. Metcalfe sharply, "come here a minute."

"Ur."

"Do you see two men in Mr. Westmacott's field?"

"Noa."

"You don't?"

" 'Er bain't Mr. Westmacott's field. 'E've a sold of 'er."

"Sold it. Good heavens! Who to?"

"Couldn't rightly say who 'e've a sold 'er to. Gentleman from London staying at the Brakehurst. Paid a tidy price for 'er too I've a heard said."

"What on earth for?"

"Couldn't rightly say, but I reckon it be to build hissel a house."

Build. It was a word so hideous that no one in Much Malcock dared use it above a whisper. "Housing scheme," "Development," "Clearance," "Council houses," "Planning" — these obscene words had been expunged from the polite vocabulary of the district, only to be used now and then, with the license allowed to anthropologists, of the fierce tribes beyond the parish boundary. And now the horror was in their midst, the mark of Plague in the court of the Decameron.

After the first moment of shock, Mr. Metcalfe rallied for action, hesitated for a moment whether or no to plunge down the hill and challenge the enemy on his own ground, and decided against it; this was the moment to act with circumspection. He must consult Lady Peabury.

It was three-quarters of a mile to the house; the lane ran

past the gate which gave access to Westmacott's field; a crazily hung elm gate and deep cow-trodden mud, soon in Mr. Metcalfe's imagination to give place to golden privet and red gravel. Mr. Metcalfe could see the heads of the intruders bobbing beyond the hedge; they bore urban, purposeful black hats. He drove on, miserably.

Lady Peabury was in the morning-room reading a novel; early training gave a guilty spice to this reaction, for she had been brought up to believe that to read a novel before luncheon was one of the gravest sins it was possible for a gentlewoman to commit. She slipped the book under a cushion and rose to greet Mr. Metcalfe.

"I was just getting ready to go out," she explained.

Mr. Metcalfe had no time for politenesses.

"Lady Peabury," he began at once, "I have very terrible news."

"Oh dear! Is poor Mr. Cruttwell having trouble with the Wolf Cub account again?"

"No; at least, he is; there's another fourpence gone astray; on the credit side this time, which makes it more worrying. But that isn't what I came about. It is something that threatens our whole lives. They are going to build in Westmacott's field." Briefly, but with emotion, he told Lady Peabury what he had seen.

She listened gravely. When he had finished there was silence in the morning-room; six little clocks ticked among the chintzes and the potted azaleas. At last Lady Peabury spoke:

"Westmacott has behaved very badly," she said.

"I suppose you can't blame him."

"I do blame him, Mr. Metcalfe, very severely. I can't understand it at all. He always seemed a very decent man. . . . I was thinking of making Mrs. Westmacott secretary of the Women's Institute. He had no right to do a thing like that without consulting us. Why, I look right on to that field from my bedroom windows. I could never understand why you didn't buy the field yourself."

It was let for £3 18s.; they had asked £170 for it; there was tithe and property tax on top of that. Lady Peabury knew this.

"Any of us could have bought it at the time of sale," said Mr. Metcalfe rather sharply.

"It always went with your house."

In another minute, Mr. Metcalfe felt, she would be telling him that *he* had behaved very badly; that *he* had always seemed a very decent man.

She was, in fact, thinking on just those lines at the moment. "I daresay it's not too late even now for you to make an offer," she said.

"We are equally threatened," said Mr. Metcalfe. "I think we ought to act together. Hodge won't be any too pleased when he hears the news."

Colonel Hodge had heard, and he was none too pleased. He was waiting at the Hall when Mr. Metcalfe got back.

"Do you know what that scoundrel Westmacott has done?"

"Yes," said Mr. Metcalfe rather wearily, "I know." The interview with Lady Peabury had not gone off quite as he had hoped. She had shown no enthusiasm for common action.

"Sold his field to a lot of jerry builders."

"Yes, I know."

"Funny, I had always thought it was *your* field."

"No," said Mr. Metcalfe, "never."

"It always used to go with this house."

"Yes, I know, but I didn't happen to want it."

"Well, it's put us all in a pretty nasty fix, I must say. D'you suppose they'd sell it back to you now?"

"I don't know that I want to buy it. Why, they'll probably want a building-land price — seventy or eighty pounds an acre."

"More, I daresay. But, good heavens man, you wouldn't let that stop you. Think how it would depreciate your property having a whole town of bungalows right under your windows."

"Come, come, Hodge. We've no reason to suppose that it will be bungalows."

"Well, villas then. You surely aren't sticking up for the fellows?"

"Certainly not. We shall all suffer very much from any development there. My belief is that it can be stopped by law; there's the Society for the Protection of Rural England. We could interest them in it. The County Council could be approached. We could write letters to the papers and petition the Office of Works. The great thing is that we must all stand together over this."

"Fat lot of change we shall get out of that. Think of the building that's gone on over at Metbury."

Mr. Metcalfe thought, and shuddered.

"I should say this was one of the times when money talked loudest. Have you tried Lady Peabury?"

For the first time in their acquaintance Mr. Metcalfe detected a distinctly coarse strain in Colonel Hodge. "I have discussed it with her. She is naturally very much concerned."

"That field has always been known as Lower Grumps," said the Colonel, reverting to his former and doubly offensive line of thought. "It's not really her chicken."

"It is all our chickens," said Mr. Metcalfe, getting confused with the metaphor.

"Well, I don't know what you expect me to do about it," said Colonel Hodge. "You know how I'm placed. It all comes of that parson preaching Bolshevism Sunday after Sunday."

"We ought to get together and discuss it."

"Oh, we'll discuss it all right. I don't suppose we shall discuss anything else for the next three months."

No one in Much Malcock took the crisis harder than the Hornbeams. News of it reached them at midday by means of the village charwoman who dropped in twice a week to despoil their larder. She told them with some pride, innocently assuming that all city gentlemen — as she continued to regard Mr. Hornbeam, in spite of his homespuns and his beard — would welcome an addition to their numbers.

Nervous gloom descended on the Old Mill. There was no explosion of wrath as there had been at the Manor; no moral condemnation as at the House; no call to action as had come from the Hall. Hopeless sorrow reigned unrelieved. Mrs. Hornbeam's pottery went to pieces. Mr. Hornbeam sat listless at the loom. It was their working hour; they sat at opposite ends of the raftered granary. Often, on other afternoons, they sang to one another catches and refrains of folk music as their busy fingers muddled with the clay and the shuttles.

To-day they sat in silence each, according to a Japanese mysti-
cal practice, attempting to drive the new peril into the World
of Unbeing. It had worked well enough with Colonel Hodge
and the Airedale, with the Abyssinian War, and with Mr.
Hornbeam senior's yearly visit, but by sunset the new peril
remained obstinately concrete.

Mrs. Hornbeam set their simple meal of milk, raisins, and
raw turnip; Mr. Hornbeam turned away from his elm platter.
"There is no place for the Artist in the Modern World," he
said. "We ask nothing of their brutish civilization except to
be left alone, to be given one little corner of land, an inch or
two of sky where we can live at peace and occupy ourselves
with making seemly and beautiful things. You wouldn't think
it was too much to ask. We give them the entire globe for their
machines. But it is not enough. They have to hunt us out and
harry us. They knew that as long as there is one spot of loveliness and decency left it is a standing reproach to them."

It was growing dark; Mrs. Hornbeam struck a flint and lit
the rush lights. She wandered to the harp and plucked a few
poignant notes. "Perhaps Mr. Metcalfe will stop it," she said.

"That we should be dependent for the essentials of life upon
a vulgarian like that . . ."

It was in this mood that he received an invitation from Mr.
Metcalfe to confer with his neighbours at Much Malcock
House on the following afternoon.

The choice of meeting place had been a delicate one, for
Lady Peabury was loth to abdicate her position of general
leadership or to appear as leader in this particular matter; on
the other hand, it touched her too closely for her to be able

to ignore it. Accordingly the invitations were issued by Mr. Metcalfe, who thereby accepted responsiblity for the agenda, while the presence of the meeting in her morning-room gave something of the atmosphere of a Cabinet meeting at the Palace.

Opinion had hardened during the day and there was general agreement with Colonel Hodge's judgement: "Metcalfe has got us into this hole by not buying the field in the first place; it's up to him to get us out of it." Though nothing as uncompromising as this was said in front of Mr. Metcalfe, he could feel it in the air. He was the last to arrive. Lady Peabury's welcome to her guests had been lukewarm. "It is very kind of you to come. I really cannot think that it is necessary, but Mr. Metcalfe particularly wished it. I suppose he intends telling us what he is going to do." To Mr. Metcalfe she said, "We are full of curiosity."

"Sorry to be late. I've had a day of it, I can tell you. Been to all the local offiices, got on to all the Societies, and I may as well tell you at once, there's nothing doing from that end. We are not even scheduled as a rural area."

"No," said Colonel Hodge, "I saw to that. Halves the potential value of one's property."

"*Schedules*," moaned Mr. Hornbeam, "that is what we have become. We must be *scheduled* to lead a free life."

" . . . And so," persisted Mr. Metcalfe, in his board-room manner, "we are left to find the solution ourselves. Now this young man has no particular reason, I imagine, for preferring this district above any other in the country. The building has not yet begun; he has no commitments. I cannot help feeling that if he were tactfully approached and offered a reasonable profit on the transaction, he might be induced to re-sell."

"I am sure," said Lady Peabury, "we shall all owe a deep debt of gratitude to Mr. Metcalfe."

"Very public spirited of you," said Colonel Hodge.

"Profits, the cancer of the age . . . "

"I am perfectly willing," said Mr. Metcalfe, "to bear my share of the burden. . . . " At the word "share" his hearers stiffened perceptibly. "My suggestion is that we make a common fund proportionate to our present land holdings. By a rough calculation I work that out as being in the ratio of one to Mr. Hornbeam, two to Colonel Hodge, two to myself, and five to our hostess here. The figures could be adjusted," he added as he noted that his suggestion was falling a little flat.

"You can count me out," said Colonel Hodge. "Couldn't possibly run to it."

"And me," said Mr. Hornbeam.

Lady Peabury was left in, with a difficult hand to stake. Delicacy forbade recognition of the vital fact that Mr. Metcalfe was very much the richer — delicacy tempered with pride. The field must be saved, but there seemed no system of joint purchase by which she could honourably fail to bear the largest part. Duty called, clearly and unmistakably, to Mr. Metcalfe alone. She held her cards and passed the bidding. "Surely," she said, "as a business man you see a great many objections to joint ownership. Do you propose to partition the field, or are we all to share the rent, the tithe and the tax? It would be highly inconvenient. I doubt if it is even legal."

"Certainly, certainly. I merely wished to assure you of my

readiness to co-operate. The field, as such, is of no interest to me, I can assure you. I would willingly stand down."

There was a threat, almost a lack of politeness in his tone. Colonel Hodge scented danger.

"Wouldn't it be best," he said, "to find out first if this fellow is willing to re-sell. Then you can decide which of you keep it."

"I am sure we shall be very interested to hear the results of Mr. Metcalfe's negotiations," said Lady Peabury.

She should not have said that. She would gladly have recalled the words the moment after they were uttered. She had vaguely wanted to say something disagreeable, to punish Mr. Metcalfe for the discomfort in which she found herself. She had not meant to antagonize him, and this she had unmistakably done.

Mr. Metcalfe left the House abruptly, almost precipitately, and all that evening he chafed. For fifteen years Mr. Metcalfe had been president of the British Chamber of Commerce. He had been greatly respected by the whole business community. No one could put anything across him, and he would not touch anything that was not above-board. Egyptian and Levantine merchants who tried to interest Metcalfe in shady business went away with a flea in the ear. It was no good trying to squeeze Metcalfe. That was his repuation in the Union Club, and here, at home, in his own village, an old woman had tried to catch him napping. There was a sudden change. He was no longer the public-spirited countryman; he was cards-on-the-table-brass-tacks-and-twenty-shillings-in-the-pound-treat-him-or-mind-your-step Metcalfe, Metcalfe with his back up, fighting Metcalfe once again, Metcalfe who would

cut off his nose any day to spite his face, sink any ship for a
ha'p'orth of tar that was not legally due, Metcalfe the lion of
the Rotarians.

"She should not have said that," said Colonel Hodge, re-
porting the incident to his wife over their horrible dinner.
"Metcalfe won't do anything now."

"Why don't *you* go and talk to the man who's bought the
field?" said Mrs. Hodge.

"I might . . . I think I will. . . . Tell you what, I'll go now."
He went.

He found the man without difficulty, since there was no
other visitor staying at the Brakehurst Arms. An enquiry from
the landlord elicited his name — Mr. Hargood-Hood. He was
sitting alone in the parlour, sipping whiskey and soda and
working at *The Times* crossword.

The Colonel said, "Evening. My name is Hodge."

"Yes?"

"I daresay you know who I am."

"I'm very sorry, I'm afraid . . . "

"I own the Manor. My garden backs on to Westmacott's
field — the one you've bought."

"Oh," said Mr. Hargood-Hood, "was he called Westmacott?
I didn't know. I leave all these things to my lawyer. I simply
told him to find me a suitable, secluded site for my work. He
told me last week he had found one here. It seems very
suitable. But he didn't tell me anyone's name."

"You didn't pick this village for any particular reason?"

"No, no. But I think it perfectly charming," he added po-
litely.

There was a pause.

"I wanted to talk with you," said Colonel Hodge superfluously. "Have a drink."

"Thank you."

Another pause.

"I'm afraid you won't find it a very healthy site," said the Colonel. "Down in the hollow there."

"I never mind things like that. All I need is seclusion."

"Ah, a writer no doubt."

"No."

"A painter?"

"No, no. I suppose you would call me a scientist."

"I see. And you would be using your house for weekends?"

"No, no, quite the reverse. I and my staff will be working here all the week. And it's not exactly a house I'm building, although, of course, there will be living quarters attached. Perhaps, since we are going to be such close neighbours, you would like to see the plans. . . . "

" . . . You never saw such a thing," said Colonel Hodge next morning to Mr. Metcalfe. "An experimental industrial laboratory he called it. Two great chimneys — have to have those, he said, by law, because of poison fumes, a water tower to get high pressures, six bungalows for his staff . . . ghastly. The odd thing was he seemed quite a decent sort of a fellow. Said it hadn't occurred to him anyone would find it objectionable. Thought we should all be interested. When I brought up the subject of re-selling — tactful, you know — he just said he left all that to his lawyer. . . . "

✿ ✿ ✿ *3* ✿ ✿ ✿

Much Malcock Hall

Dear Lady Peabury,

In pursuance of our conversation of three days ago, I beg to inform you that I have been in communication with Mr. Hargood-Hood, the purchaser of the field which separates our two properties, and his legal representative. As Col. Hodge has already informed you, Mr. Hargood-Hood proposes to erect an experimental industrial laboratory fatal to the amenities of the village. As you are doubtless aware, work has not yet been commenced, and Mr. Hargood-Hood is willing to re-sell the property if duly compensated. The price is to include re-purchase of the field, legal fees and compensation for the architect's work. The young blackguard has us in a cleft stick. He wants £500. It is excessive, but I am prepared to pay half of this if you you will pay the other half. Should you not accede to this generous offer I shall take steps to safeguard my own interests at whatever cost to the neighbourhood.

Yours sincerely
Beverley Metcalfe

P.S. — I mean I shall sell the Hall and develop the property as building lots.

Much Malcock House

Lady Peabury begs to inform Mr. Metcalfe that she has received his note of this morning, the tone of which I am unable to account for. She further begs to inform you that she has no wish to increase my already extensive responsibilities in the district. She cannot accept the principle of equal obligation with Mr. Metcalfe as he has far *less land to look after, and the field in question should rightly form part of your property. She does not think that the scheme for developing his garden as a housing estate is is likely to be a success if Mr. Hargood-Hood's laboratory is as unsightly as is represented which I rather doubt.*

"All right," said Mr. Metcalfe. "That's that and be damned to her."

✿   ✿   ✿ **4** ✿   ✿   ✿

It was ten days later. The lovely valley, so soon to be defiled, lay resplendent in the sunset. Another year, thought Mr. Metcalfe, and this fresh green foliage would be choked with soot, withered with fumes; these mellow roofs and chimneys, which for two hundred years or more had enriched the landscape below the terrace, would be hidden by functional monstrosities in steel and glass and concrete. In the doomed field Mr. Westmacott, almost for the last time, was calling his cattle; next week building was to begin and they must seek other pastures. So, in a manner of speaking, must Mr. Metcalfe. Already his desk was littered with house agents' notices. All for £500 he told himself. There would be redecorations; the cost and loss of moving. The speculative builders to whom he had viciously appealed showed no interest in the site. He was going to lose much more than £500 on the move. But so, he grimly assured himself, was Lady Peabury. She would learn that no one could put a fast one over on Beverley Metcalfe.

And she, on the opposing slope, surveyed the scene with

corresponding melancholy. The great shadows of the cedars lay across the lawn; they had scarcely altered during her long tenancy, but the box hedge had been her planting; it was she who had planned the lily pond and glorified it with lead flamingoes; she had reared the irregular heap of stones under the west wall and stocked it with Alpines; the flowering shrubs were hers; she could not take them with her where she was going. Where? She was too old now to begin another garden, to make other friends. She would move, like so many of her contemporaries, from hotel to hotel, at home and abroad, cruise a little, settle for prolonged rather unwelcome visits on her relatives. All this for £250, for £12 10s. a year, for less than she gave to charity. It was not the money; it was Principle. She would not compromise with Wrong; with that ill-bred fellow on the hill opposite.

Despite the splendour of the evening, an unhappy spirit obsessed Much Malcock. The Hornbeams moped and drooped; Colonel Hodge fretted. He paced the threadbare carpet of his smoking-room. "It's enough to make a fellow turn Bolshie, like that parson," he said. "What does Metcalfe care? He's rich. He can move anywhere. What does Lady Peabury care? It's the small man, trying to make ends meet who suffers."

Even Mr. Hargood-Hood seemed affected by the general gloom. His lawyer was visiting him at the Brakehurst. All day they had been in intermittent, rather anxious, consultation. "I think I might go and talk to that Colonel again," he said, and set off up the village street, under the deepening shadows, for the Manor House. And from this dramatic last minute move for conciliation sprang the great Hodge Plan for appeasement and peace-in-our-time.

❁ ❁ ❁ 5 ❁ ❁ ❁

" . . . the Scouts are badly in need of a new hut," said Colonel Hodge.

"No use coming to me," said Mr. Metcalfe. "I'm leaving the neighbourhood."

"I was thinking," said Colonel Hodge," that Westmacott's field would be just the place for it. . . . "

And so it was arranged. Mr. Hornbeam gave a pound, Colonel Hodge a guinea, Lady Peabury £250. A jumble sale, a white-elephant tea, a raffle, a pageant and a house-to-house collection, produced a further 30s. Mr. Metcalfe found the rest. It cost him, all told, a little over £500. He gave with a good heart. There was no question of jockeying him into a raw deal. In the rôle of public benefactor he gave with positive relish, and when Lady Peabury suggested that the field should be reserved for a camping site and the building of the hut postponed, it was Mr. Metcalfe who pressed on with the building and secured the old stone tiles from the roof of a dismantled barn. In the circumstances, Lady Peabury could not protest when the building was named the Metcalfe-Peabury Hall. Mr. Metcalfe found the title invigorating and was soon in negotiation with the brewery for a change of name at the Brakehurst Arms. It is true that Boggett still speaks of it as "the Brakehurst," but the new name is plainly lettered for all to read: THE METCALFE ARMS.

And so Mr. Hargood-Hood passed out of the history of Much

Malcock. He and his lawyer drove away to their home beyond the hills. The lawyer was Mr. Hargood-Hood's brother.

"We cut that pretty fine, Jock. I thought, for once, we were going to be left with the baby."

They drove to Mr. Hargood-Hood's home, a double quadrangle of mellow brick that was famous far beyond the county. On the days when the gardens were open to the public, record crowds came to admire the topiary work, yews and boxes of prodigious size and fantastic shape which gave perpetual employment to three gardeners. Mr. Hargood-Hood's ancestors had built the house and planted the gardens in a happier time, before the days of property tax and imported grain. A sterner age demanded more strenuous efforts for their preservation.

"Well, that has settled Schedule A for another year and left something over for cleaning the fish-ponds. But it was an anxious month. I shouldn't care to go through it again. We must be more careful next time, Jock. How about moving east?"

Together the two brothers unfolded the inch ordnance map of Norfolk, spread it on the table of the Great Hall and began their preliminary, expert search for a likely, unspoilt, well-loved village.

1941

❋ ❋ ❋ ❋ ❋ ❋ ❋ ❋ ❋ ❋ ❋ ❋ ❋ ❋ ❋

WORK SUSPENDED

PART I

A Death

At the time of my father's death I was in Morocco, at a small French hotel outside the fortifications of Fez. I had been there for six weeks, doing little else but write, and my book, *Murder at Mountrichard Castle*, was within twenty thousand words of its end. In three weeks I should pack it up for the typist; perhaps sooner, for I had nearly passed that heavy middle period where less conscientious writers introduce their second corpse. I was thirty-four years of age at the time, and a serious writer. I had always been a one-corpse man. I took pains with my work and I found it excellent. Each of my seven books sold better than its predecessor. Moreover, the sale was in their first three months, at seven and sixpence. I did not have to relabel the library edition for the bookstalls. People bought my books and kept them — not in the spare bedrooms but in the library, all seven of them together on a shelf. In six weeks' time, when my manuscript had been typed, revised and delivered, I should receive a cheque for something over nine hundred pounds. Had I wished it, I could have earned considerably more. I never tried to sell my stories as serials; the delicate fibres of a story suffer when it is chopped up into weekly or monthly parts and never completely heal. Often, when I have been reading the work of a competitor, I have said, "She was writing with an eye on the magazines. She had to close this episode prematurely; she had to introduce that extraneous bit of melodrama, so as to make each instalment a readable unit. Well," I would reflect, "she has a husband to support and two sons at school. She must not expect to do two jobs well, to be a good mother and a good novelist." I chose to live modestly on the royalties of my books.

I have never found economy the least irksome; on the contrary, I take pleasure in it. My friends, I know, considered me parsimonious; it was a joke among them, which I found quite inoffensive. My ambition was to eradicate money as much as I could from my life. I acquired as few possessions as possible. I preferred to pay interest to my bank rather than be bothered by tradesmen's bills. I decided what I wanted to do and then devised ways of doing it cheaply and tidily; money wasted meant more money to be earned. I disliked profusion.

I chose my career deliberately at the age of twenty-one. I had a naturally ingenious and constructive mind and the taste of writing. I was youthfully zealous of good fame. There seemed few ways of which a writer need not be ashamed by which he could make a decent living. To produce something, saleable in large quantities to the public, which had absolutely nothing of myself in it; to sell something for which the kind of people I liked and respected would have a use; that was what I sought, and detective stories fulfilled the purpose. They were an art which admitted of classical canons of tech-

nique and taste. It was immune, too, from the obnoxious comment to which lighter work is exposed: "How you must revel
in writing your delicious books, Mr. So-and-so." My friend,
Roger Simmonds, who was with me at the University and set
up as a professional humorist at the same time as I wrote
Vengeance at the Vatican, was constantly plagued by that
kind of remark. Instead, women said to me, "How difficult it
must be to think of all those complicated clues, Mr. Plant."
I agreed. "It *is,* intolerably difficult." "And do you do your
writing here in London?" "No, I find I have to go away to
work." "Away from telephones and parties and things?"
"Exactly."

I had tried a dozen or more retreats in England and abroad
— country inns, furnished cottages, seaside hotels out of the
season — Fez was by far the best of them. It is a splendid,
compact city, and in early March, with flowers springing
everywhere in the surrounding hills and in the untidy patios of
the Arab houses, one of the most beautiful in the world. I
liked the little hotel. It was cheap and rather chilly — an indispensable austerity. The food was digestible with, again,
that element of sparseness which I find agreeable. I had an
intermediate place between the semi-Egyptian splendours of
the tourists' palace on the hill, and the bustling commercial
hotels of the new town, half an hour's walk away. The clien-
tele was exclusively French; the wives of civil servants and
elderly couples of small means wintering in the sun. In the
evening Spahi officers came to the bar to play bagatelle. I used
to work on the verandah of my room, overlooking a ravine
where Senegalese infantrymen were constantly washing their
linen. My recreations were few and simple. Once a week after

dinner I took the bus to the Moulay Abdullah; once a week I dined at the Consulate. The consul allowed me to come to him for a bath. I used to walk up, under the walls, swinging my sponge-bag through the dusk. He, his wife and their governess were the only English people I met; the only people, indeed, with whom I did more than exchange bare civilities. Sometimes I visited the native cinema where old, silent films were shown in a babel of catcalls. On other evenings I took a dose of Dial and was asleep by half-past nine. In these circumstances the book progressed well. I have since, on occasions, looked back at them with envy.

As an odd survival of the age of capitulations there was at that time a British Post Office at the Consulate, used mainly, the French believed, for treasonable purposes by disaffected Arabs. When there was anything for me the postman used to come down the hill on his bicycle to my hotel. He had a badge in his cap and on his arm a brassard with the royal escutcheon; he invariably honoured me with a stiff, military salute which increased my importance in the hotel at the expense of my reputation as an innocent and unofficial man of letters. It was this postman who brought the news of my father's death in a letter from my Uncle Andrew, his brother.

My father, it appeared, had been knocked down by a motor car more than a week ago and had died without regaining consciousness. I was his only child and, with the exception of my uncle, his only near relative. "All arrangements" had been made. The funeral was taking place that day. "In spite of your father's opinions, in the absence of any formal instructions to the contrary," my Uncle Andrew wrote, "your Aunt and I thought it best to have a religious ceremony of an unostentatious kind."

"He might have telegraphed," I thought; and then, later, "Why should he have?" There was no question of my having been able to see my father before he died; participation in a "religious ceremony of an unostentatious kind" was neither in my line nor my father's; nor — to do him justice — in my Uncle Andrew's. It would satisfy the Jellabies.

With regard to the Jellabies my father always avowed a ruthlessness which he was far from practising; he would in fact put himself to considerable inconvenience to accommodate them, but in principle he abhorred any suggestion of discretion or solicitude. It was his belief that no one but himself dealt properly with servants. Two contrasted attitudes drove him to equal fury; what he called the "*pas-devant* tomfoolery" of his childhood — the precept that scandal and the mention of exact sums of money should be hushed in their presence — and the more recent idea that their quarters should be prettily decorated and themselves given opportunity for cultural development. "Jellaby has been with me twenty years," he would say, "and is fully cognisant of the facts of life. He and Mrs. Jellaby know my income to the nearest shilling, and they know the full history of everyone who comes to this house. I pay them abominably and they supplement their wages by cooking the books. Servants prefer it that way. It preserves their independence and self-respect. The Jellabies eat continually, sleep with the windows shut, go to church every Sunday morning and to chapel in the evening, and entertain surreptitiously at my expense whenever I am out of the house. Jellaby's a teetotaler; Mrs. Jellaby takes the port." He rang the bell whenever he wanted anything fetched and sat as long as he wanted over his wine. "Poor old Armstrong," he used to say of a fellow academician, "lives like a Hottentot. He keeps a lot of twittering women like waitresses in a railway station buffet. After the first glass of port they open the dining-room door and stick their heads in. After the second glass they do it again. Then instead of throwing something at them, Armstrong says, 'I think they want to clear, and we have to move out.'"

But he had a warm affection for the Jellabies, and I believe it was largely on Mrs. Jellaby's account that he allowed himself to be put up for the Academy. They, in their turn, served him faithfully. It would have been a cruel betrayal to deny them a funeral service, and I am sure my father had them in mind when he omitted any provision against it in his will. He was an exact man who would not have forgotten a point of that kind. On the other hand, he was a dogmatic atheist of the old-fashioned cast and would not have set anything down which might be construed as apostasy. He had left it to my Uncle Andrew's tact. No doubt, too, it was part of my uncle's tact to save me the embarrassment of being present.

✿ ✿ ✿ 2 ✿ ✿ ✿

I sat on my verandah for some time, smoking and considering the situation in its various aspects. There seemed no good reason for a change of plan. My Uncle Andrew would see to everything. The Jellabies would be provided for. Apart from them my father had no obligations. His affairs were always simple and in good order. The counterfoils of his cheques and his own excellent memory were his only account books; he had never owned any investments except the freehold of the house in St. John's Wood, which he had bought with the small capital sum left him by his mother. He lived up to his income and saved nothing. In him the parsimony which I had inherited took the form of a Gallic repugnance to paying direct taxes or, as he preferred it, to subscribing to "the support of the politicians." He had, moreover, the conviction that anything he put by would be filched by the Radicals. Lloyd George's ascent to power was the last contemporary event to impress him. Since then he believed, or professed to believe, that public life had become an open conspiracy for the destruction of himself and his class. This class, of which he considered himself the sole survivor, was for him the object of romantic loyalty; he spoke of it as a Jacobite clan proscribed and dispersed after Culloden, in a way which sometimes embarrassed those who did not know him well. "We have been uprooted and harried," he would say. "There are only three classes in England now — politicians, tradesmen and slaves." Then he would particularize. "Seventy years ago the politicians and the tradesmen were in alliance; they destroyed the gentry by destroying the value of land; some of the gentry became politicians themselves, others tradesmen; out of what was left they created the new class into which I was born, the moneyless, landless, educated gentry who managed the country for them. My grandfather was a Canon of Christ Church, my father was in the Bengal Civil Service. All the capital they left their sons was education and moral principle. Now the politicians are in alliance with the slaves to destroy the tradesmen. They don't need to bother about us. We are extinct already. I am a Dodo," he used to say, defiantly staring at his audience.

"You, my poor son, are a petrified egg." There is a caricature of him by Max Beerbohm, in this posture, saying these words.

My choice of profession confirmed his view. "Marjorie Steyle's boy works below the streets in a basement, selling haberdashery at four pounds a week. Dick Anderson has married his daughter to a grocer. My son John took a second in Mods and a first in Greats. He writes penny dreadfuls for a living," he would say.

I always sent him my books, and I think he read them. "At least your grammar is all right," he once said. "Your books will translate, and that's more than can be said for most of these fellows who set up to write Literature." He had a naturally hierarchic mind, and in his scheme of things, detective stories stood slightly above the librettos of musical comedy and well below political journalism. I once showed him a reference to *Death in the Dukeries* by the Professor of Poetry, in which it was described as "a work of art." "Anyone can buy a don," was his only comment.

But he was gratified by my prosperity. "Family love and financial dependence don't go together," he said. "My father made me an allowance of thirty shillings a week for the first three years I was in London, and he never forgave it me, *never*. He hadn't cost his father a penny after he took his degree. Nor had *his* father before him. You ran into debt at the University. That was a thing I never did. It was two years before you were keeping yourself, and you went about as a dandy those two years, which I never did while I was learning to draw. But you've done very well. No nonsense about Literature. You've cut out quite a line for yourself. I saw old Etheridge at the club the other evening. He reads all your books, he told me, and likes 'em. Poor old Etheridge; he brought his boy up to be a barrister and he still has to keep him at the age of thirty-seven."

My father seldom referred to his contemporaries without the epithet "old" — usually as "poor old so-and-so," unless they had prospered conspicuously when they were "that old humbug." On the other hand, he spoke of men a few years his juniors as "whipper-snappers" and "young puppies." The truth was that he could not bear to think of anyone as being the same age as himself. It was all part of the aloofness that was his dominant concern in life. It was enough for him to learn that an opinion of his had popular support for him to question and abandon it. His atheism was his response to the simple piety and confused agnosticism of his family circle. He never came to hear much about Marxism; had he done so he would, I am sure, have discovered a number of proofs of the existence of God. In his later years I observed two reversions of opinion in reaction to contemporary fashion. In my boyhood, in the time of their Edwardian popularity, he denounced the Jews roundly on all occasions, and later attributed to them the vogue of post-impressionist painting: "There was a poor booby called Cézanne, a kind of village idiot who was given a box of paints to keep him quiet. He very properly left his horrible canvases behind him in the hedges. The Jews discovered him and crept round behind him picking them up — just to get something for nothing. Then when he was safely dead and couldn't share in the profits they hired a lot of mercenary lunatics to write him up. They've made thousands out of it." To the last he maintained that Dreyfus had been guilty, but when, in the early thirties, anti-Semitism showed signs of becoming a popular force, he supported the Jewish cause in many unpublished letters to *The Times*.

Similarly he was used once to profess an esteem for Roman Catholics. "Their religious opinions are preposterous," he said. "But so were those of the ancient Greeks. Think of Socrates spending half his last evening babbling about the topography of the nether world. Grant them their first absurdities and you will find Roman Catholics a reasonable people — and they have civilized habits." Later, however, when he saw signs of this view gaining acceptance, he became convinced of the existence of a Jesuit conspiracy to embroil the world in war, and wrote several letters to *The Times* on the subject; they, too, were unpublished. But in neither of these periods did his opinions greatly affect his personal relations; Jews and Catholics were among his closest friends all his life.

My father dressed as he thought a painter should, in a distinct and recognizable garb which made him a familiar and, in his later years, a venerable figure as he took his exercise in the streets round his house. There was no element of ostentation in his poncho capes, check suits, sombrero hats and stock ties. It was rather that he thought it fitting for a man to proclaim unequivocally his station in life, and despised those of his colleagues who seemed to be passing themselves off as guardsmen and stockbrokers. In general he liked his fellow academicians, though I never heard him express anything but contempt for their work. He regarded the Academy as a club; he enjoyed the dinners and frequently attended the schools, where he was able to state his views on art in Johnsonian terms. He never doubted that the function of painting was representational. He criticized his colleagues for such faults as innocent anatomy, "triviality" and "insincerity." For this he was loosely spoken of as a conservative, but that he never was where his art was concerned. He abominated the standards of his youth. He must have been an intransigently old-fashioned young man, for he was brought up in the hey-day of Whistlerian decorative painting, and his first exhibited work was of a balloon ascent in Manchester — a large canvas crowded with human drama, in the manner of Frith. His practice was chiefly in portraits — many of them posthumous — for presentation to colleges and guildhalls. He seldom succeeded with women, whom he endowed with a statuesque absurdity which was half deliberate, but given the robes of a Doctor of Music or a Knight of Malta he would do something fit to hang with the best panelling in the country; given some whiskers he was a master. "As a young man I specialized in hair," he would say, rather as a doctor might say he specialized in noses and throats. "I paint it incomparably. Nowadays nobody has any to paint," and it was this aptitude of his which led him to the long, increasingly unsaleable series of historical and scriptural groups, and the scenes of domestic melodrama by which he is known — subjects which had already become slightly ludicrous when he was in his cradle, but which he continued to produce year after year while experimental painters came and went until, right at the end of his life, he suddenly, without realizing it, found himself in the fashion. The first sign of this was in 1935, when his "Agag before Samuel" was bought at a provincial exhibition for 750 guineas. It was a large canvas at which he had been at work intermittently since 1908. Even he spoke of it, with conscious understatement, as "something of a white elephant." White elephants indeed were almost the sole species of four-footed animal that was not somewhere worked into this elaborate composition. When asked why he had intro-duced such a variety of fauna, he replied, "I'm sick of Samuel. I've lived with him for twenty years. Every time it comes back from an exhibition I paint out an Israelite and put in an animal. If I live long enough I'll have a Noah's ark in its back-ground."

The purchaser of this work was Sir Lionel Sterne.

"Honest Sir Lionel," said my father, as he saw the great canvas packed off to Kensington Palace Gardens, "I should dearly have liked to shake his hairy paw. I can see him well — a fine, meaty fellow with a great gold watch-chain across his belly, who's been decently employed boiling soap or smelting copper all his life, with no time to read Clive Bell. In every age it has been men like him who kept painting alive."

I tried to explain that Lionel Sterne was the youthful and elegant millionaire who for ten years had been a leader of aesthetic fashion. "Nonsense!" said my father. "Fellows like that collect disjointed Negresses by Gauguin. Only Philistines like my work and, by God, I like only Philistines."

There was also another, rather less reputable side to my father's business. He received a regular yearly retaining fee from Goodchild and Godley, the Duke Street dealers, for what was called "restoration." This sum was a very important part of his income; without it the comfortable little dinners, the trips abroad, the cabs to and fro, between St. John's Wood and the Athenaeum, the faithful, predatory Jellabies, the orchid in his buttonhole — all the substantial comforts and refinements which endeared the world and provided him with his air of gentlemanly ease — would have been impossible to him. The truth was that, while excelling at Lely, my father could paint, very passably, in the manner of almost any of the masters of English portraiture, and the private and public collections of the New World were richly representative of his versatility. Very few of his friends knew this traffic; to those who did, he defended it with complete candour. "Goodchild and Godley buy these pictures for what they are — my own work. They pay me no more than my dexterity merits. What they do with them afterwards is their own business. It would ill become me to go officiously about the markets identifying my own handicraft and upsetting a number of perfectly contented people. It is a great deal better for them to look at beautiful pictures and enjoy them under a misconception about the date, than to make themselves dizzy by goggling at genuine Picassos."

It was largely on account of his work for Goodchild and Godley that his studio was strictly reserved as a workshop. It was a separate building approached through the garden, and it was excluded from general use. Once a year, when he went abroad, it was "done out"; once a year, on the Sunday before sending-in day at the Royal Academy, it was open to his friends.

He took a peculiar relish in the gloom of these annual tea-parties, and was at the same pains to make them dismal as he was to enliven his other entertainments. There was a species of dry bright-yellow caraway cake which was known to my childhood as "Academy cake," and appeared then and only then, from a grocer in Praed Street; there was an enormous Worcester tea service — a wedding present — which was known as "Academy cups"; there were "Academy sandwiches" — tiny, triangular and quite tasteless. All these things were part of my earliest memories. I do not know at what date these parties changed from a rather tedious convention to what they certainly were to my father at the end of his life, a huge, grim and solitary jest. If I was in England I was required to attend and to bring a friend or two. It was difficult, until the last two years when, as I have said, my father became the object of fashionable interest, to collect guests. "When I was a young man," my father said, sardonically surveying the company, "there were twenty or more of these parties in St. John's Wood alone. People of culture drove round from three in the afternoon to six, from Campden Hill to Hampstead. To-day I believe our little gathering is the sole survivor of that deleterious tradition."

On these occasions his year's work — Goodchild and Godley's items excepted — would be ranged round the studio on mahogany easels; the most important work had a wall to itself against a background of scarlet rep. I had been present at the last of the parties the year before. Lionel Sterne was there with Lady Metroland and a dozen fashionable connoisseurs. My father was at first rather suspicious of his new clients and suspected an impertinent intrusion into his own private joke, a calling of his bluff of seed-cake and cress-sandwiches; but their commissions reassured him. People did not carry a joke to such extravagant lengths. Mrs. Algernon Stitch paid 500 guineas for his picture of the year — a tableau of contemporary life conceived and painted with elaborate mastery. My father attached great importance to suitable titles for his work, and after toying with "The People's Idol," "Feet of Clay," "Not on the First Night," "Their Night of Triumph," "Success and Failure," "Not Invited," "Also Present," he finally called this picture rather enigmatically "The Neglected Cue." It represented the dressing room of a leading actress at the close of a triumphant first night. She sat at the dressing-table, her back turned on the company, and her face visible in the mirror, momentarily relaxed in fatigue. Her protector with proprietary swagger was filling the glasses for a circle of admirers. In the background the dresser was in colloquy at the half-open door with an elderly couple of provincial appearance; it is evident from their costume that they have seen the piece from the cheaper seats, and a commissionaire stands behind them uncertain whether he did right in admitting them. He did not do right; they are her old parents arriving most inopportunely. There was no questioning Mrs. Stitch's rapturous enjoyment of her acquisition.

I was never to know how my father would react to his vogue. He could paint in any way he chose; perhaps he would have embarked on those vague assemblages of picnic litter which used to cover the walls of the Mansard Gallery in the early twenties; he might have retreated to the standards of the Grosvenor Gallery in the nineties. He might, perhaps, have found popularity less inacceptable than he supposed and allowed himself a luxurious and cosseted old age. He died with his 1939 picture still unfinished. I saw its early stage on my last visit to him; it was to have been called "Again?" and represented a one-armed veteran of the First World War meditating over a German helmet. My father had given the man a grizzled beard and was revelling in it. That was the last time I saw him.

I had given up living in St. John's Wood for four or five years. There was never a definite moment when I "left home."

For all official purposes the house remained my domicile.
There was a bedroom that was known as mine; I kept several
trunks full of clothes there and a shelf or two of books. I never
set up for myself anywhere else, but during the last five years
of my father's life I do not suppose I slept ten nights under
his roof. This was not due to any estrangement. I enjoyed his
company, and he seemed to enjoy mine, but I was never in
London for more than a week or two at a time, and I found
that as an occasional visitor I strained and upset my father's
household. He and they tried to do too much, and he liked to
have his plans clear for some way ahead. "My dear boy," he
would say on my first evening. "Please do not misunderstand
me. I hope you will stay as long as you possibly can, but I do
wish to know whether you will still be here on Thursday the
fourteenth, and if so, whether you will be in to dinner." So I
took to staying at my club or with more casual hosts, and to
visiting St. John's Wood as often as I could, but with formal
prearrangements.

Nevertheless, I realized, the house had been an important
part of my life. It had remained unaltered for as long as I
could remember. It was a decent house, built in 1840 or there-
abouts, in the contemporary Swiss mode of stucco and orna-
mental weather boards, one of a street of similar, detached
houses when I first saw it. By the time of my father's death the
transformation of the district, though not complete, was painfully evident. The skyline of the garden was broken on three
sides by blocks of flats. The first of them drove my father into
a frenzy of indignation. He wrote to *The Times* about it,
addressed a meeting of ratepayers, and for six weeks sported
a board advertising the house for sale. At the end of that time

he received a liberal offer from the syndicate, who wished to extend their block over the site, and he immediately withdrew it from the market.

This was the period of his lowest professional fortunes, when his subject-pictures remained unsold, the market for dubious old masters was dropping, and public bodies were beginning to look for something "modern" in their memorial portraits; the period, moreover, when I had finished with the University and was still dependent on my father for pocket money. It was a very unsatisfactory time in his life. I had not then learned to appreciate the massive defences of what people call the "border-line of sanity," and I was at moments genuinely afraid that my father was going out of his mind; there had always seemed an element of persecution-mania about his foibles which might, at a time of great strain, go beyond his control. He used to stand on the opposite pavement watching the new building rise, a conspicuous figure muttering objurgations. I used to imagine scenes in which a policeman would ask him to move on and be met with a wild outburst. I imagined these scenes vividly — my father in swirling cape being hustled off, waving his umbrella. Nothing of the kind occurred. My father, for all his oddity, was a man of indestructible sanity, and in his later years he found a keen pleasure in contemplating the rapid deterioration of the hated buildings. "Very good news of Hill Crest Court," he announced one day. "Typhoid and rats." And on another occasion, "Jellaby reports the presence of prostitutes at St. Eustace's. They'll have a suicide there soon, you'll see." There was a suicide, and for two rapturous days my father watched the coming and going of police and journalists. After that fewer chintz curtains were visible in the windows, rents began to fall and the lift-man smoked on duty. My father observed and gleefully noted all these signs. Hill Crest Court changed hands; decorators', plumbers' and electricians' boards appeared all round it; a commissionaire with a new uniform stood at the doors. On the last evening I dined with my father he told me about a visit he had made there, posing as a potential tenant. "The place is a deserted slum," he said. "A miserable, down-at-heel kind of secretary took me round flat after flat — all empty. There were great cracks in the concrete stuffed up with putty. The hot pipes were cold. The doors jammed. He started asking three hundred pounds a year for the best of them, and dropped to one hundred and seventy-five pounds before I saw the kitchen. Then he made it one hundred and fifty pounds. In the end he proposed what he called a 'special form of tenancy for people of good social position' — offered to let me live there for a pound a week on condition I turned out if he found someone who was willing to pay the real rent. 'Strictly between ourselves,' he said, 'I can promise you will not be disturbed.' Poor beast, I nearly took his flat, he was so paintable."

Now, I supposed, the house would be sold; another speculator would pull it to pieces; another great, uninhabitable barrack would appear, like a refugee ship in harbour; it would be filled, sold, emptied, resold, refilled, re-emptied while the concrete got discoloured and the green wood shrank, and the rats crept up in their thousands out of the Metropolitan Railway tunnel; and the trees and gardens all round it disappeared one by one until the place became a working-class district and at last took on a gaiety and life of some sort; until it was condemned by government inspectors and its inhabitants driven

further into the country and the process began all over again.
I thought of all this, sadly, as I looked out at the fine masonry
of Fez, cut four hundred years back by Portuguese prisoners.
. . . I must go back to England soon to arrange for the destruction of my father's house. Meanwhile there seemed no reason
for an immediate change of plan.

It was the evening when I usually visited the Moulay Abdullah — the walled *quartier toléré* between the old city and
the ghetto. I had gone there first with a sense of adventure;
now it had become part of my routine, a regular resort, like
the cinema and the Consulate, one of the recreations which
gave incident to my week and helped clear my mind of the
elaborate villainies of Lady Mountrichard.

I dined at seven and soon afterwards caught my bus at the
new gate. Before starting I removed my watch and emptied
my pockets of all except the few francs which I proposed to
spend — a superstitious precaution which still survived from
the first evening, when memories of Marseilles and Naples had
even moved me to carry a life-preserver. The Moulay Abdullah was an orderly place, particularly in the early evening
when I frequented it. I had formed an attachment for this sole
place of its kind which endowed its trade with something
approaching glamour. There really was a memory of "the
East," as adolescents imagine it, in that silent courtyard with
its single light, the Negro sentries on either side of the lofty

Moorish arch, the black lane beyond, between the walls and
the water-wheel, full of the thump and stumble of French
military boots and the soft pad and rustle of the natives, the
second arch into the lighted bazaar, the bright open doors and
the tiled patios, the little one-roomed huts where the women
stood against the lamplight — shadows without race or age —
the larger houses with their bars and gramophones.

I always visited the same house and the same girl — a
chubby little Berber with the scarred cheeks of her people and
tattooed ornaments, blue on brown, at her forehead and throat.
She spoke the peculiar French which she had picked up from
the soldiers, and she went by the unassuming, professional
name of Fatima. Other girls of the place called themselves
"Lola" and "Fifi"; there was even an arrogant, coal-black
Sudanese named "Whiskey-soda." But Fatima had none of
these airs; she was a cheerful, affectionate girl working hard
to collect her marriage dot; she professed to like everyone in
the house, even the proprietress, a forbidding Levantine from
Tetuan, and the proprietress's Algerian husband, who wore a
Euopean suit, carried round the mint tea, put records on the
gramophone and collected the money. (The Moors are a strict
people and take no share in the profits of the Moulay Abdullah.)

To regular and serious customers it was an inexpensive place
— fifteen francs to the house, ten to Fatima, five for the mint
tea, a few sous to the old fellow who tidied Fatima's alcove
and blew up the brazier of sweet gum. Soldiers paid less, but
they had to make way for more important customers; often
they were penniless men from the Foreign Legion who
dropped in merely to hear the music and left nothing behind

them but cigarette ends. Now and then tourists appeared with a guide from the big hotel, and the girls were made to line up and give a performance of shuffling and hand clapping which was called a native dance. Women tourists particularly seemed to like these expeditions and paid heavily for them — a hundred francs or more. But they were unpopular with everyone, particularly with the girls, who regarded it as an unseemly proceeding. Once I came in when Fatima was taking part in one of these dances and saw her genuinely and deeply abashed.

On my visit I told Fatima that I had a wife and six children in England; this greatly enhanced my importance in her eyes and she always asked after them.

"You have had a letter from England? The littles ones are well?"

"They are very well."

"And your father and mother?"

"They, too."

We sat in a tiled hall, two steps below street level, drinking our mint tea — or, rather, Fatima drank hers while I let mine cool in the glass. It was a noisome beverage.

"Whiskey-soda lent me some cigarettes yesterday. Will you give her them?"

I ordered a packet from the bar.

"Yesterday I had a stomach-ache and stayed in my room. That is why Whiskey-soda gave me her cigarettes."

She asked about my business.

I had told her I exported dates.

The date market was steady, I assured her.

When I was in the Moulay Abdullah I almost believed in

this aspect of myself as a philoprogenitive fruiterer; St. John's Wood and Mountrichard Castle seemed equally remote. That was the charm of the quarter for me — not its simple pleasures but its privacy and anonymity, the hide-and-seek with one's own personality which redeems vice of its tedium.

That night there was a rude interruption. The gramophone suddenly stopped playing; there was a scuttling among the alcoves; two seedy figures in raincoats strode across the room and began questioning the proprietress; a guard of military police stood at the street door.

Raids of this kind, to round up bad characters, are common enough in French Protectorates. It was the first time I had been caught in one. The girls were made to stand along one wall while the detectives checked their medical certificates. Then two or three soldiers stood to attention and gave a satisfactory account of themselves. Then I was asked for my *carte d'identité*. By the capitulations the French police had little authority over British subjects, and since the criminal class of Morocco mostly possessed Maltese papers, this immunity was good ground for vexation. The detectives were surly fellows, African born. Even the sacred word "tourist" failed to soften them. Where was my guide? Tourists did not visit the Moulay Adbullah alone. Where was my passport? At my hotel. The Jamai Palace? No? Tourists did not stay at the hotel I mentioned. Was I registered at the police headquarters? Yes. Very well, I must come with them. In the morning I should have the opportunity to identify myself. A hundred francs, no doubt, would have established my respectability, but my money lay with my passport in the hotel. I did not relish a night in gaol in company with the paperless characters of the Moulay Abdullah. I told them I was a friend of the British Consul. He would vouch for me. They grumbled that they had no time for special enquiries of that kind. The Chief would see about it next morning. Then when I had despaired, they despaired too. There was clearly no money coming for them. They had been in the profession long enough to know that no lasting satisfaction results from vexing British subjects. There was a police post in the quarter and they consented to telephone from it. A few minutes later I was set at liberty with a curt reminder that it was advisable to keep my passport accessible if I wanted to wander about the town at night.

I did not return to Fatima. Instead I set off for the bus stop, but the annoyances of the night were not yet over. I was halted again at the gates and the interrogation was repeated. I explained that I had already satisfied their colleagues and had been discharged. We re-enacted the scene, with the fading hope of a tip as the recurring motive. Finally they, too, telephoned to the Consulate, and I was free to take my bus home.

They were still serving dinner at the hotel; the same game of billiards was in progress in the bar; it was less than an hour since I went out. But that hour had been decisive; I was finished with Fez; its privacy had been violated. My weekly visit to the Consulate could never be repeated on the same terms. Twice in twenty minutes the Consul had been called to the telephone to learn that I was in the hands of the police in the Moulay Abdullah; he would not, I thought, be censorious or resentful; the vexation had been mild and the situation slightly absurd — nothing more; but when we next met our relations would be changed. Till then they had been serenely remote; we had talked of the news from England and the Moorish antiquities. We had exposed the bare minimum of ourselves; now a sudden, mutually unwelcome confidence had been forced. The bitterness lay, not in the Consul's knowing the fact of my private recreations, but in his knowing that I knew he knew. It was a salient in the defensive line between us that could only be made safe by a wide rectification of frontier or by a complete evacuation. I had no friendly territory into which to withdraw. I was deployed on the dunes between the sea and the foothills. The transports riding at anchor were my sole lines of support.

In the matter of Good Conscience, I was a man of few possessions, and held them at a corresponding value. As a spinster in mean lodgings fusses over her fragments of gentility — a rosewood work-box, a Spode plate, a crested tea-kettle — which in a house of abundance would be risked in the rough and tumble of general use, I set a price on Modesty which those of ampler virtues might justly regard as fanciful.

Next day I set off for London with my book unfinished.

❊ ❊ ❊ 4 ❊ ❊ ❊

I travelled from spring into winter; sunlit spray in the Straits of Gibralter changed to dark, heavy seas in the Bay of Biscay; fog off Finisterre, fog in the Channel, clear grey weather in the Thames estuary and a horizon of factories and naked trees. We berthed in London and I drove through cold and dirty streets to meet my Uncle Andrew.

He told me the full circumstances of my father's death; the commercial traveller, against whom a case was being brought for reckless driving, had outraged my uncle by sending a wreath of flowers to the funeral; apart from this everything had been satisfactory. My uncle passed over to me the undertaker's receipted account; he had questioned one or two of the items and obtained an inconsiderable reduction. "I am convinced," my uncle said, "that there is a great deal of sharp practice among these people. They trade upon the popular conception of delicacy. In fact they are the only profession who literally rob the widow and the orphan." I thanked my uncle for having saved me £3 18s. It was a matter of principle, he said.

As I expected, I was my father's sole heir. Besides the house and its contents I inherited £2000 in an insurance policy which my father had taken out at the time of his marriage and, without my knowledge, kept up ever since. An injunction, in the brief will, to "provide suitably" for the servants in my father's employment, had already been obeyed. The Jellabies had been given £250. It was clear from my father's words that he had no conception of what a suitable provision should be. Neither had I, and I was grateful to my uncle for taking responsibility in the matter. For their part the Jellabies had expected nothing. My father, as long ago as I could remember him, was accustomed to talk with relish of his approaching death. I had heard him often admonish Jellaby: "You have joined fortune with a poor man. Make what you can while I still have my faculties. My death will be an occasion for unrelieved lamentation," and the Jellabies, in the manner of their kind, took his words literally, kept a keen watch on all sources of perquisite, and expected nothing. Jellaby took his cheque, my uncle said, without any demonstration of gratitude or disappointment, murmuring ungraciously that it would come in quite useful. No doubt he thought no thanks were due to my uncle, for it was not his money; nor to my father, for it was no intention of his to give it. It was a last, substantial perquisite.

The Jellabies had been much in my mind, off and on, during the journey from Fez. I had fretted, in a way I have, imagining our meeting and a scene of embarrassing condolence and reminiscence, questioning the propriety of removing them immediately, if ever, from the place where they had spent so much of their lives; I even saw myself, on the Jellabies' account, assuming my father's way of life, settling in St. John's Wood, entertaining small dinner parties, lunching regularly at my club and taking three weeks' holiday abroad in the early summer. As things turned out, however, I never saw the Jellabies again. They had done their packing before the funeral, and went straight to the railway station in their black clothes. Their plans had been laid years in advance. They had put away a fair sum and invested it in Portsmouth, not, as would have been conventional, in a lodging-house, but in a shop in a poor quarter of the town which enjoyed a trade in second-hand wireless apparatus. Mrs. Jellaby's step-brother had been keeping the business warm for them, and there they retired with an alacrity which was slightly shocking but highly convenient. I wrote to them some time later when I was going through my father's possessions, to ask if they would like to have some small personal memento of him; they might value one of his sketches, I suggested, for the walls of their new home. The answer took some time in coming. When it came it was on a sheet of trade-paper with a printed heading: "*T. Jellaby. Every Radio want promptly supplied for cash.*" Mrs. Jellaby wrote the letter. They had not much room for pictures, she said, but would greatly appreciate some blankets, as it was chilly at nights in Portsmouth; she specified a particular pair which my father had bought shortly before his death; they were lying, folded, in the hot cupboard. . . .

Uncle Andrew gave me the keys of my father's house. I went straight there from lunching with him. The shutters were up and the curtains drawn; the water and electric light were already cut off; all this my uncle had accomplished in a few days. I stumbled among sheeted furniture to the windows and let in the daylight. I went from room to room in this way. The place still retained its own smell — an agreeable, rather stuffy atmosphere of cigar smoke and cantaloup; a masculine smell — women had always seemed a little out of place, as in a London club on Coronation Day.

The house was sombre, but never positively shabby, so that, I suppose, various imperceptible renovations and replacements must have occurred from time to time. It looked what it was, the house of an unfashionable artist of the 1880s. The curtains and chair-covers were of indestructible Morris tapestry; there were Dutch tiles round the fire-places; Levantine rugs on the floors; on the walls Arundel prints, photographs from the old masters, and majolica dishes. The furniture, now shrouded, had the inimitable air of having been in the same place for a generation; it was a harmonious, unobstructive jumble of inherited rosewood and mahogany, and of inexpensive collected pieces of carved German oak, Spanish walnut, English chests and dressers, copper ewers and brass candlesticks. Every object was familiar and yet so much a part of its surroundings that later, when they came to be moved, I found a number of things which I barely recognized. Books of an antiquated sort were all over the house in a variety of hanging, standing and revolving shelves.

I opened the French windows in my father's study and stepped down into the garden. There was little of spring to be seen here. The two plane trees were bare; under the sooty laurels last year's leaves lay rotting. It was never a garden of any character. Once, before the flats came, we used to dine there sometimes, in extreme discomfort, under the catalpa tree; for years now it had been a no-man's land, isolating the studio at the further end; on one side, behind a trellis, were some neglected frames and beds where my father had once tried to raise French vegetables. The mottled concrete of the flats, with its soil-pipes and fire-escapes and its rash of iron-framed casement windows, shut out half the sky. The tenants of these flats were forbidden, in their leases, to do their laundry, but the owners had long since despaired of a genteel appearance, and you could tell which of the rooms were occupied by the stockings hanging to dry along the window-sills.

In his death my father's privacy was still respected, and no one had laid dust-sheets in the studio. "Again?" stood as he had left it on the easel. More than half was finished. My father made copious and elaborate studies for his pictures and worked quickly when he came to their final stage, painting over a monochrome sketch, methodically, in fine detail, left to right across the canvas as though he were lifting the backing of a child's "transfer." "Do your thinking *first*," he used to tell the Academy students. "Don't muddle it out on the canvas. Have the whole composition clear in your head before you start," and if anyone objected that this was seldom the method of the greatest masters, he would say, "You're here to become Royal Academicians, not great masters. If you want to write books on Art, trot around Europe studying the Rubenses. If you want to learn to paint, watch me." The four or five square feet of finished painting were a monument of my father's art. There had been a time when I had scant respect for it. Lately I had come to see that it was more than a mere matter of dexterity and resolution. He had an historic position, for he completed a period of English painting that through other circumstances had never, until him, come to maturity. Phrases, as though for an obituary article, came to my mind: ". . . fulfilling the broken promise of the young Millais. . . . Winterhalter suffused with the spirit of Dickens. . . . English painting as it might have been, had there not been any Aesthetic Movement . . . " and with the phrases my esteem for my father took form and my sense of loss became tangible and permanent.

No good comes of this dependence on verbal forms. It saves nothing in the end. Suffering is none the less acute and much more lasting when it is put into words. In the house my memories had been all of myself — of the countless home-comings and departures of thirty-three years, of adolescence like a stained tablecloth — but in the studio my thoughts were of my father and grief, nearly a week delayed, overtook and overwhelmed me. It had been delayed somewhat by the strangeness of my surroundings and the business of travel, but most by this literary habit; it had lacked words. Now the words came; I began, in my mind, to lament my father, addressing, as it were, funeral orations to my own literary memories, and sorrow, dammed and canalized, flowed fast.

For the civilized man there are none of those swift transitions of joy and pain which possess the savage; words form slowly like pus about his hurts; there are no clean wounds for him; first a numbness, then a long festering, then a scar ever ready to re-open. Not until they have assumed the livery of the defence can his emotions pass through the lines; sometimes they come massed in a wooden horse, sometimes as single spies, but there is always a Fifth Column among the garrison ready to receive them. Sabotage behind the lines, a blind raised and lowered at a lighted window, a wire cut, a bolt loosened, a file disordered — that is how the civilized man is undone.

I returned to the house and darkened the rooms once more, relaid the dust sheets I had lifted, and left everything as it had been.

✿ ✿ ✿ 5 ✿ ✿ ✿

The manuscript of *Murder at Mountrichard Castle* lay on the chest of drawers in my club bedroom, reproaching me morning, evening and night. It was promised for publication in June, and I had never before disappointed my publishers. This year, however, I should have to ask grace for a postponement. I made two attempts at it, bearing the pile of foolscap to an upper room of the club which was known as the library and used by the elder members for sleeping between luncheon and tea. But I found it impossible to take up the story with any interest; so I went to my publishers and tried to explain. "I have been writing for over eight years," I said, "and am nearing a climacteric."

"I don't quite follow," said Mr. Benwell anxiously.

"I mean a turning point in my career."

"Oh, dear, I hope you're not thinking of making a contract elsewhere?"

"No, no. I mean that I feel in danger of turning into a stock best-seller."

"If I may say so, in very imminent danger," said Benwell, and he made a kind of little bow from the seat of his swivel chair and smirked in the wry fashion people sometimes assume when they feel they have said something elaborately polite; a smile normally kept for his women writers; the word "climacteric" had clearly upset him.

"I mean, I am in danger of becoming purely a technical expert. Take my father . . . "

Mr. Benwell gave a deferential grunt and quickly changed his expression to one of gravity suitable to the mention of someone recently dead.

"He spent his whole life perfecting his technique. It seems to me I am in danger of becoming mechanical, turning out year after year the kind of book I know I can write well. I feel I have got as good as I ever can be at this particular sort of writing. I need new worlds to conquer." I added this last remark in compassion for Mr. Benwell, whose gravity had deepened to genuine concern. I believed he would feel the easier for a little facetiousness — erroneously, for Mr. Benwell had suffered similar, too serious conversations with other writers than me.

"You've not been writing *poetry* in Morocco?"

"No, no."

"Sooner or later almost all my novelists come to me and say

they have written poetry. I can't think why. It does them infinite harm. Only last week Roger Simmonds was here with a kind of play. You never saw such a thing. All the characters were parts of a motor-car — not in the least funny."

"Oh, it won't be anything like that," I said. "Just some new technical experiments. I don't suppose the average reader will notice them at all."

"I hope not," said Mr. Benwell. "I mean, now you've found your public . . . well, look at Simmonds."

I knew what he was thinking: "The trouble about Plant is, he's come in to money."

In a way he was right. The money my father had left me, and the proceeds which I expected from the sale of the house, relieved me of the need to work for two or three years; it was a matter of pure athletics to go on doing something merely because one did it well. The heap of foolscap began to disgust me. Twice I hid it under my shirts, twice the club valet unearthed it and laid it in the open. I had nowhere to keep things, except in this little hired room above the traffic.

This sense of homelessness was new to me. Before I had moved constantly from one place to another; every few weeks I would descend upon St. John's Wood with a trunk, leave some books, collect others, put away summer clothes for the winter; seldom as I slept there, the house in St. John's Wood had been my headquarters and my home; that earth had now been stopped, and I thought, not far away, I could hear the hounds.

My worries at this period became symbolized in a single problem; what to do with my hats. I owned what now seemed a multitude of them, of one sort and another; two of them of silk — the tall hat I took to weddings and a second I had bought some years earlier when I thought for a time that I was going to take to fox-hunting; there were a bowler, a panama, a black, a brown and a grey soft hat, a green hat from Salzburg, a sombrero, some tweed caps for use on board ship and in trains — all these had accumulated from time to time and all, with the possible exception of the sombrero, were more or less indispensable. Was I doomed for the rest of my life to travel everywhere with this preposterous collection? At the moment they were, most of them, in St. John's Wood, but, any day now, the negotiations for the sale might be finished and the furniture removed, sold or sent to store.

Somewhere to hang up my hat, that was what I needed.

I consulted Roger Simmonds, who was lunching with me. I felt as though I had known Roger all my life; actually I had first met him in our second year at Oxford; we edited an undergraduate weekly together, and had been close associates ever since. He was one of the very few people I corresponded with when I was away; we met often when I was in London. Sometimes I even stayed with him, for he and half a dozen others constituted a kind of set. We had all known each other intimately over a number of years, had from time to time passed on girls from one to the other, borrowed and lent freely. When we were together we drank more and talked more boastfully than we normally did. We had grown rather to dislike one another; certainly when any two or three of us were alone we blackguarded the rest, and if asked about them on neutral ground I denied their friendship. About Roger I used to say, "I don't think he's interested in anything except politics now."

This was more or less true. In the late twenties he set up as a writer and published some genuinely funny novels on the strength of which he filled a succession of jobs with newspapers and film companies, but lately he had married an unknown heiress, joined the Socialist party, and become generally conventional.

"I never wear a hat now I am married," said Roger virtuously. "Lucy says they're *kulak*. Besides, I was beginning to lose my hair."

"My dear Roger, you've been bald as a coot for ten years. But it isn't only a question of hats. There are overcoats."

"Only in front. It's as thick as anything at the back. How many overcoats have you got?"

"Four, I think."

"Too many."

We discussed at length and decided it was possible to manage with three.

"Workers pawn their overcoats in June and take them out again in October," Roger said. He wanted to talk about his play, *Internal Combustion*. "The usual trouble with ideological drama," he said, "is that it's too mechanical. I mean the characters are economic types, not individuals, and as long as they look and speak like individuals it's bad art. D'you see what I mean?"

"I do, indeed."

"Human beings without human interest."

"Very true. I . . ."

"Well, I've cut human beings out altogether."

"Sounds rather like an old-fashioned ballet."

"*Exactly*," Roger said with great pleasure. "It *is* an old-fashioned ballet. I knew you'd understand. Poor old Benwell couldn't. The Finsbury International Theatre are sitting on it now, and if it's orthodox — and I *think* it is — they may put it on this summer if Lucy finds the money."

"Is she keen, too?"

"Well, not very, as a matter of fact. You see, she's having a baby, and that seems to keep her interested at the moment."

"But to return to the question of my hats . . ."

"Tell you what. Why don't you buy a nice quiet house in the country? I shall want somewhere to stay while this baby is born."

There was the rub. It was precisely this fear that had been working in my mind for days, the fear of making myself a sitting shot to the world. It lay at the root of the problem of privacy; the choice which torments to the verge of mania, between perpetual flight and perpetual siege; and the unresolved universal paradox of losing things in order to find them.

"Surely that is odd advice from a Socialist?"

Roger became suddenly wary; he had been caught and challenged in loose talk. "Ideally, of course, it would be," he said. "But I daresay that in practice, for the first generation, we shall allow a certain amount of private property where its value is purely sentimental. Anyway, any investment you make now is bound to be temporary. That's why I feel no repugnance about living on Lucy's money . . ." Marxist ethics kept him talking until we had finished luncheon. Over the coffee he referred to Ingres as a "bourgeois" painter. When he left me I sat for some time in the leather arm-chair finishing my cigar. The club was emptying as the younger members went back to their work and their elders padded off to the library for the afternoon nap. I belonged to neither world. I had nothing whatever to do. At three in the afternoon my friends would all be busy and, in any case, I did not want to see them. I was ready for a new deal. I climbed to my room, began re-reading the early chapters of *Murder at Mountrichard Castle*, put it from me and faced the boredom of an afternoon in London. Then the telephone rang and the porter said, "Mr. Thurston is downstairs to see you."

"Who?"

"Mr. Thurston. He says he has an appointment."

"I don't know anything about him. Will you ask what he wants?"

A pause: "Mr. Thurston says will you see him very particular."

"Very well, I'll come down."

A tall young man in a raincoat was standing in the hall. He had reddish hair and an unusually low, concave forehead. He looked as though he had come to sell some hopelessly unsuitable commodity and had already despaired of success.

"Mr. Thurston?" He took my hand in a savage grip. "You say you have an appointment with me. I am afraid I don't remember it."

"No, well, you see, I thought we ought to have a yarn, and you know how suspicious these porter fellows are at clubs. I knew you wouldn't mind my stretching a point." He spoke with a kind of fierce jauntiness. "I had to give up my club. Couldn't run it."

"Perhaps you will tell me what I can do for you."

"I used to belong to the Wimpole. I expect you know it?"

"I'm not sure that I do."

"No. You would have liked it. I could have taken you there and introduced you to some of the chaps."

"That, I gather, is now impossible."

"Yes. It's a pity. There are some good scouts there. I daresay you know the Bachelors?"

"Yes. Were you a member there, too?"

"Yes — at least, not exactly, but a great pal of mine was — Jimmie Grainger. I expect you've often run across Jimmie?"

"No, I don't think I have."

"Funny. Jimmie knows almost everyone. You'd like him. I must bring you together." Having failed to establish contact, Thurston seemed now to think that responsibility for the conversation devolved on me.

"Mr. Thurston," I said, "is there anything particular you wished to say to me? Because otherwise . . ."

"I was coming to that," said Thurston. "Isn't there somewhere more private where we could go and talk?"

It was a reasonable suggestion. Two page boys sat on a bench beside us, the hall porter watched us curiously from behind his glass screen, two or three members passing through paused by the tape machine to take a closer look at my odd visitor. I was tolerably certain that he was not one of the enthusiasts for my work who occasionally beset me, but was either a beggar or a madman or both; at another time I should have sent him away, but that afternoon, with no prospect of other interest, I hesitated. "Be a good scout," he urged.

There is at my club a nondescript little room of depressing aspect where members give interviews to the press, go through figures with their accountants, and in general transact business which they think would be conspicuous in the more public rooms. I took Thurston there.

"Snug little place," he said. "O.K. if I smoke?"

"Perfectly."

"Have one?"

"No, thank you."

He lit a cigarette, drew a deep breath of smoke, gazed at the ceiling and, as though coming to the point, said, "Quite like the old Wimpole."

My heart sank. "Mr. Thurston," I said, "you have surely not troubled to come here simply to talk to me about the Wimpole Club?"

"No. But, you see, it's rather awkward. Don't exactly know how to begin. I thought I might lead up to it naturally. But I realize that your time's valuable, Mr. Plant, so I may as well admit right out that I owe you an apology."

"Yes?"

"Yes. I'm here under false pretences. My name isn't Thurston."

"No?"

"No. I'd better tell you who I am, hadn't I?"

"If you wish to."

"Well, here goes. I'm Arthur Atwater." The name was spoken with such an air of bravado, with such confidence of its making a stir, that I felt bewildered. It meant absolutely nothing to me. Where and how should I have heard it? Was this a fellow-writer, a distant cousin, a popular athlete? Atwater? Atwater? I repeated it to myself. No association came. My visitor meanwhile seemed unconscious of how flat his revelation had fallen, and was talking away vehemently:

"Now you see why I couldn't give my name. It's awfully decent of you to take it like this. I might have known you were a good scout. I've been through hell, I can tell you, ever since it happened. I haven't slept a wink. It's been terrible. You know how it is when one's nerve's gone. I shouldn't be fit for work now even if they'd kept me on in the job. Not that I care about that. Let them keep their lousy job. I told the manager that to his face. I wasn't brought up and educated to sell stockings. I ought to have gone abroad long ago. There's no opportunity in England now, unless you've got influence or are willing to suck up to a lot of snobs. You get a fair chance out there in the colonies where one man's as good as another and no questions asked."

I can seldom bear to let a misstatement pass uncorrected. "Believe me, Mr. Atwater," I said, "you have a totally mistaken view of colonial life. You will find people just as discriminating and inquisitive there as they are here."

"Not where I'm going," he said. "I'm clearing right out. I'm fed up. This case hanging over me and nothing to do all day except think about the accident. It *was* an accident, too. No one can try and hang the blame on me and get away with it. I was on my proper side of the road and hooted twice. It wasn't a Belisha crossing. It was my road. The old man just wouldn't budge. He saw me coming, looked straight at me, as if he was daring me to drive into him. Well, I thought I'd give him a fright. You know how it is when you're driving all day. You get fed to the teeth with people making one get out of their way all the time. I like to wake them up now and then when there's no copper near, and make them jump for it. It seems like an hour now, but it all happened in two seconds. I kept on, waiting for him to skip, and he kept on, strolling across the road as if he'd bought it. It wasn't till I was right on top of him I realized he didn't intend to move. Then it was too late to stop. I put on my brakes and tried to swerve. Even then I might have missed him if he'd stopped, but he just kept on walking right into me and the mudguard got him. That's how it was. No one can blame it on me."

It was just as my uncle Andrew had described it.

"Mr. Atwater," I said, "do I understand that you are the man who killed my father?"

"Don't put it that way, Mr. Plant. I feel sore enough about it. He was a great artist. I read about him in the papers. It makes it worse, his having been a great artist. There's too little beauty in the world as it is. I should have liked to be an artist myself, only the family went broke. Father took me away from school young, just when I might have got into the eleven. Since then I've had nothing but odd jobs. I've never had a real chance. I want to start again, somewhere else."

I interrupted him, frigidly I thought. "And why, precisely, have you come to me?"

But nothing could disabuse him of the idea that I was well disposed. "I knew I could rely on you," he said. "And I'll never forget it, not as long as I live. I've thought everything out. I've a pal who went out to Rhodesia; I think it was Rhodesia. Somewhere in Africa, anyway. He'll give me a shakedown till I get on my feet. He's a great fellow. Won't he be surprised when I walk in on him! All I need is my passage money — third class, I don't care. I'm used to roughing it these days — and something to make a start with. I could do it on fifty pounds."

"Mr. Atwater," I said, "have I misunderstood you, or are you asking me to break the law by helping you to evade your trial and also give you a large sum of money?"

"You'll get it back, every penny of it."

"And our sole connexion is the fact that, through pure insolence, you killed my father."

"Oh, well, if you feel like that about it . . ."

"I am afraid you greatly overrate my good nature."

"Tell you what. I'll make you a sporting offer. You give me fifty pounds now and I'll pay it back in a year plus another fifty pounds to any charity you care to name. How's that?"

"Will you please go?"

"Certainly I'll go. If that's how you take it. I'm sorry I ever came. It's typical of the world," he said rising huffily. "Everyone's all over you till you get into a spot of trouble. It's 'good old Arthur' while you're in funds. Then, when you need a pal it's 'you overrate my good nature. Mr. Atwater.'"

I followed him across the room, but before we reached the door his mood had changed. "You don't understand," he said. "They may send me to prison for this. That's what happens in this country to a man earning his living. If I'd been driving my own Rolls Royce they'd all be touching their caps. 'Very regrettable accident,' they'd be saying. 'Hope your nerves have not been shocked, Mr. Atwater' — but to a poor man driving a two-seater . . . Mr. Plant, your father wouldn't have wanted me sent to prison."

"He often expressed the view that all motorists of all classes should be kept permanently in prison."

Atwater received this with disconcerting enthusiasm. "And he was quite right," he cried in louder tones than can ever have been used in that room except perhaps during spring cleaning. "I'm fed to the teeth with motor-cars. I'm fed to the teeth with civilization. I want to farm. That's a man's life."

"Mr. Atwater, will nothing I say persuade you that your aspirations are no concern of mine?"

"There's no call to be sarcastic. If I'm not wanted, you've only to say so straight."

"You are not wanted."

"Thank you," he said. "That's all I wanted to know."

I got him through the door, but half-way across the front hall he paused again. "I spent my last ten bob on a wreath."

"I'm sorry you did that. I'll refund it."

He turned on me with a look of scorn. "Plant," he said, "I didn't think it was in you to say a thing like that. Those flowers were a sacred thing. You wouldn't understand that, would you? I'd have starved to send them. I may have sunk pretty low, but I have some decency left, and that's more than some people can say even if they belong to posh clubs and look down on fellows who earn a decent living. Good-bye, Plant. We shall not meet again. D'you mind if I don't shake hands?"

That was how he left me, but it was not the last of him. That evening I was called to the telephone to speak to a Mr. Long. Familiar tones, jaunty once more, greeted me. "That you, Plant? Atwater here. Excuse the alias, won't you? I say, I hope you didn't take offence at the way I went off to-day. I've been thinking, and I see you were perfectly right. May I come round for another yarn?"

"No."

"To-morrow, then?"

"No."

"Well, when shall I come?"

"Never."

"No, I quite understand, old man. I'd feel the same myself. It's only this. In the circumstances I'd like to accept your very sporting offer to pay for those flowers. I'll call round for the money if you like, or will you send it?"

"I'll send it."

"Care of the Holborn Post Office finds me. Fifteen bob they cost."

"You said ten this afternoon."

"Did I? I meant fifteen."

"I will send you ten shillings. Good-bye."

"Good scout," said Atwater.

So I put a note in an envelope and sent it to the man who killed my father.

✳ ✳ ✳ 6 ✳ ✳ ✳

Time dragged.

The sale of the house in St. John's Wood proved more irksome than I had expected. Ten years before the St. John's Wood Residential Amenities Company, who built the neighbouring flats, had offered my father £6000 for his freehold; he had preserved the letter, which was signed "Alfred Hardcastle, Chairman." Their successors, the Hill Crest Court Exploitation Co., now offered me £2500; their letter was also signed Mr. Hardcastle. I refused, and put the house into an agent's hands; after two months they reported one offer — of £2500 from a Mr. Hardcastle, the managing director of St. John's Wood Residential Estates Ltd. "In the circumstances," they wrote, "we consider this a satisfactory price." The circumstances were that no one who liked that kind of house would tolerate its surroundings; having dominated the district, the flats could make their own price. I accepted it and went to sign the final papers at Mr. Hardcastle's office, expecting an atmosphere of opulence and bluster; instead, I found a modest pair of rooms, one of the unlet flats at the top of the building. On the door were painted the names of half a dozen real-estate companies, and the woodwork bore traces of other names which had stood there and been obliterated; the chairman opened the door himself and let me in. He was a large, neat, middle-aged, melancholy, likeable fellow, who before coming to business praised my father's painting with what I believe was complete sincerity.

There was no other visible staff; just Mr. Hardcastle sitting among his folders and filing cabinets, telling me how he had felt when he lost his own father. Throughout all the vicissitudes of the flats this man had controlled them and lived for them; little companies had gone into liquidation; little, allied companies had been floated; the names of nephews and brothers-in-law had come and gone at the head of the notepaper; stocks had been written down and up, new shares had been issued, bonuses and dividends declared, mortgages transferred and foreclosed, little blocks of figures moved from one balance sheet to another, all in this single room. For the last ten years a few thousand pounds capital had been borrowed and lent backwards and forwards from one account to another and somehow, working sixteen hours a day, doing his own typing and accountancy, Mr. Hardcastle had sustained life, kept his shoes polished and his trousers creased, had his hair cut regularly and often, bought occasional concert tickets on family anniversaries and educated, he told me, a son in the United States and a daughter in Belgium. The company to which I finally conveyed my freehold was a brand new one, registered for the occasion and soon, no doubt, doomed to lose its identity in the kaleidoscopic changes of small finance. The cheque, signed by Mr. Hardcastle, was duly honoured, and when the sum, largely depleted by my solicitor, was paid into my account, I found that with the insurance money added and my overdraft taken away, I had a credit balance for the first time in my life, of rather more than £3500. With this I set about planning a new life.

Mr. Hardcastle had been willing to wait a long time to make his purchase; once it was done, however, his plans developed with surprising speed. Workmen were cutting the trees and erecting a screen of hoarding while the vans were removing the furniture to store; a week later I came to visit the house; it was a ruin; it might have been mined. Presumably there is some method in the business of demolition; none was apparent to a layman: the roof was off, the front was down, and on one side the basement lay open; on the other the walls still stood their full height, and the rooms, three-sided like stage settings, exposed their Morris papers, flapping loose in the wind where the fireplaces and window-frames had been torn out. The studio had disappeared, leaving a square of rubble to mark its site; new shoots appeared here and there in the trampled mess of the garden. A dozen or more workmen were there, two or three of them delving away in a leisurely fashion, the rest leaning on their tools and talking; it seemed inconceivable that in this fashion they could have done so much in such little time. The air was full of flying grit. It was no place to linger. When next I passed that way, a great concrete wing covered the site; it was cleaner than the rest of the block and, by a miscalculation of the architects, the windows were each a foot or two below the general line; but, like them, were devoid of curtains.

PART II

A Birth

My project of settling in the country was well received by my friends.

Each saw in it a likely convenience for himself. I understood their attitude well. Country houses meant something particular and important in their lives, a system of permanent bolt-holes. They had, most of them, gradually dropped out of the round of formal entertaining; country life for them meant not a series of invitations, but of successful, predatory raids. Their lives were liable to sharp reverses; their quarters in London were camps which could be struck at an hour's notice, as soon as the telephone was cut off. Country houses were permanent; even when the owner was abroad, the house was there, with a couple of servants or, at the worst, someone at a cottage who came in to light fires and open windows, someone who, at a pinch, could be persuaded also to make the bed and wash up. They were places where wives and children could be left for long periods, where one retired to write a book, where one could be ill, where, in the course of a love affair, one could take a girl and, by being her guide and sponsor in strange surroundings, establish a degree of proprietorship impossible on the neutral ground of London. The owners of these places were, by their nature, a patient race, but repeated abuse was apt to sour them; new blood in their ranks was highly welcome. I detected this greeting in every eye.

There was also another, more amiable, reason for their interest. Nearly all of them — and, for that matter, myself as well — professed a specialized enthusiasm for domestic architecture. It was one of the pecularities of my generation, and there is no accounting for it. In youth we had pruned our aesthetic emotions hard back so that in many cases they had reverted to briar stock; we none of us wrote or read poetry, or, if we did, it was of a kind which left unsatisfied those wistful, half-romantic, half-aesthetic, peculiarly British longings which, in the past, used to find expression in so many slim lambskin volumes. When the poetic mood was on us, we turned to buildings, and gave them the place which our fathers accorded to Nature — to almost any buildings, but particularly those in the classical tradition, and, more particularly, in its decay. It was a kind of nostalgia for the style of living which we emphatically rejected in practical affairs. The nobilities of Whig society became, for us, what the Arthurian paladins were in the time of Tennyson. There was never a time when so many landless men could talk at length about landscape gardening. Even Roger compromised with his Marxist austerities so far as to keep up his collection of the works of Batty Langley and William Halfpenny. "The nucleus of my museum," he explained. "When the revolution comes, I've no ambitions to be a commissar or a secret policeman. I want to be director of the Museum of Bourgeois Art."

He was overworking the Marxist vocabulary. That was

always Roger's way, to become obsessed with a new set of words and to extend them, deliberately, beyond the limits of sense; it corresponded to some sombre, interior need of his to parody whatever, for the moment, he found venerable; when he indulged it I was reminded of the ecclesiastical jokes of those on the verge of religious melancholy. Roger had been in that phase himself when I first met him.

One evening, at his house, the talk was all about the kind of house I should buy. It was clear that my friends had very much more elaborate plans for me than I had for myself. After dinner Roger produced a copper engraving of 1767 of *A Composed Hermitage in the Chinese Taste*. It was a preposterous design. "He actually built it," Roger said, "and it's still standing a mile or two out of Bath. We went to see it the other day. It only wants putting into repair. Just the house for you."

Everyone seemed to agree.

I knew exactly what he meant. It *was* just the house one would want someone else to have. I was graduating from the exploiting to the exploited class.

But Lucy said: "I can't think why John should want to have a house like that."

When she said that I had a sudden sense of keen pleasure. She and I were on the same side.

Roger and Lucy had become my main interest during the months while I was waiting to settle up in St. John's Wood. They lived in Victoria Square, where they had taken a three years' lease of a furnished house. "Bourgeois furniture," Roger complained, rather more accurately than usual. They shut away the model ships and fire-bucket wastepaper baskets in a store cupboard and introduced a prodigious radio-gramophone; they hung their own pictures in place of the Bartolozzi prints, but in the house retained its character, and Roger and Lucy, each in a different way, looked out of place there. It was here that Roger had written his ideological play.

They had been married in November. I had spent all the previous autumn abroad on a leisurely, aimless trip before settling at Fez for the winter's work. My mail at Malta, in September, told me that Roger had taken up with a rich girl and was having difficulty with her family; at Tetuan I learned that he was married. Apparently he had been in pursuit of her all the summer, unknown to us. It was not until I reached London that I heard the full story. Basil Seal told me, rather resentfully, because for many years now he had himself been in search of an heiress and had evolved theories on the subject of how and where they might be taken. "You must go to the provinces," he used to say. "The competition in London is far too hot for chaps like us. Americans and Colonials want value for money. The trouble is that the very rich have a natural affinity for one another. You can see it happening all the time — stinking rich people getting fixed up. And what happens? They simply double their supertax and no one is the better off. But they respect brains in the provinces. They like a man to be ambitious there, with his way to make in the world, and there are plenty of solid, mercantile families who can settle a hundred thousand on a daughter without turning a hair, who don't care a hoot about polo, but think a Member of Parliament very fine. That's the way to get in with them. Stand for Parliament."

In accordance with this plan Basil had stood three times

—or rather had three times been adopted as candidate; on two occasions he fell out with his committee before the election. At least that was his excuse to his friends for not standing; in fact he, too, thought it a fine thing to be a Member of Parliament. He never got in, and he was still unmarried. A kind of truculent honesty which he could never dissemble for long always stood in his way. It was bitter for him to be still living at home, dependent on his mother for pocket money, liable to be impelled by her into unwelcome jobs two or three times a year while Roger had established himself almost effortlessly and was sitting back in comfort to await the World Revolution.

Not that Lucy was really rich, Basil hastened to assure me, but she had been left an orphan at an early age, and her originally modest fortune had doubled itself. "Fifty-eight thousand in trustee stock, old boy. I wanted Lucy to take it out and let me handle it for her. I could have fixed her up very nicely. But Roger wasn't playing. He's always groaning about things being bourgeois. I can't think of anything more bourgeois than three and a half per cent."

"Is she hideous?" I asked.

"No, that's the worst part about it. She's a grand girl. She's all right for a chap."

"What like?"

"Remember Trixie?"

"Vaguely."

"Well, not at all like her."

Trixie had been Roger's last girl. Basil had passed her on to him, resumed the use of her for a week or two, then passed her back. None of us had liked Trixie. She always gave the impression that she was not being treated with the respect she was used to.

"How did he come by her?"

Basil told me at length, unable to hide his admiration for Roger's duplicity in the matter. All the previous summer, during the second Trixie period, Roger had been at work, without a word to any of us. I remembered, now, that he had suddenly become rather conspicuous in his clothes, affecting dark shirts and light ties, and a generally artistic appearance which, had he not been so bald, would have gone with long, untidy hair. It had embarrassed Trixie, she said, when at a bar they saw cousins of hers who were in the Air Force. "They'll tell everyone I'm going about with a pansy." So that was the explanation. It was greatly to Roger's credit, we agreed.

Improbable as it sounded, the truth was that they had met at a ball in Pont Street, given by a relative of Roger's. He had gone, under protest, to make up the table at dinner in answer to an S.O.S. half an hour before the time. Someone had fallen out. It was five or six years since he had been in a London ballroom and, he explained afterwards, the spectacle of his pimply and inept juniors had inflated him with a self-esteem which must, he said, have been infectious. He had sat next to Lucy at dinner. She was, for our world, very young but, for her own, of a hoary age; that is to say, she was twenty-four. For six years she had been sent to dances by her aunt, keeping in an unfashionable, middle stratum of life in which her contemporaries had either married or taken to other occupations. This aunt occupied a peculiar position with regard to Lucy; she had brought her up and now did what she described as "making a home" for her, which meant that she subsisted largely upon Lucy's income. She had two other nieces younger than Lucy, and it was greatly to their interest that they should move to London annually for the season. The aunt was a lady of delicate conscience where the issues of Lucy's marriage were involved. Once or twice before she had been apprehensive — without cause as it happened — that Lucy was preparing to "throw herself away." Roger, however, was a case that admitted of no doubt. Everything she learned about him was reprehensible; she fought him in the full confidence of a just cause, but she had no serviceable weapon. In six years of social life Lucy had never met anyone the least like Roger.

"And he took care she wouldn't meet us," said Basil. "What's more, she thinks him a great writer."

This was true. I did not believe Basil, but after I had seen her and Roger together I was forced to accept it. It was one of the most disconcerting features of the marriage for all of us. It is hard to explain exactly why I found it so shocking. Roger was a very good novelist — every bit as good in his own way as I in mine; when one came to think of it, it was impossible to name anyone else, alive, who could do what he did, there was no good reason why his books should not be compared with those of prominent writers of the past, nor why we should not speculate about their ultimate fame. But to do so struck us all as the worst of taste. Whatever, secretly, we thought about our own work, we professed, in public, to regard it as drudgery and our triumphs as successful impostures on the world at large. To speak otherwise would be to suggest that we were concerned with anyone else's interest but our own; it would be a denial of the *sauve qui peut* principle which we had all adopted. But Lucy, I soon realized, found this attitude unintelligible. She was a serious girl. When we talked cynically about our own work she simply thought less of it and of us; if we treated Roger in the same way, she resented it as bad manners. It was greatly to Roger's credit that he had spotted this idiosyncrasy of hers at once and played his game accordingly. Hence the undergraduate costume and the talk about the Art of the Transition. Lucy had not abandoned her young cousins without grave thought. She perfectly understood that, for them, happiness of a particular kind depended on her continued support; but she also thought it a great wrong that a man of Roger's genius should waste his talents on film scenarios and advertisements. Roger convinced her that a succession of London seasons and marriage to a well-born chartered accountant were not really the highest possible good. Moreover, she was in love with Roger.

"So the poor fellow has had to become a highbrow again," said Basil. "Back exactly where he started in the New College Essay Society."

"She doesn't sound too keen on this play of his."

"She isn't. She's a critical girl. That's going to be Roger's headache."

This was Basil's version of the marriage and it was substanially accurate. It omits, however, as any narrative of Basil's was bound to, the consideration that Roger was, in his way, in love with Lucy. Her fortune was a secondary attraction; he lacked the Mediterranean mentality that can regard marriage as an honourable profession, perhaps because he lacked Mediterranean respect for the permanence of the arrangement. At the time when he met Lucy he was earning an ample income without undue exertion; money alone would not have been worth the pains he had taken for her; the artistic clothes and the intellectual talk were measures of the respect in which he held Lucy. Her fifty-eight thousand in trustee stock was, no doubt, what made him push his suit to the extreme of marriage, but the prime motive and zest of the campaign was Lucy herself.

To write of someone loved, of oneself loving, above all of oneself being loved — how can these things be done with propriety? How can they be done at all? I have treated of love in my published work; I have used it — with avarice, envy, revenge — as one of the compelling motives of conduct. I have written it up as something prolonged and passionate and tragic; I have written it down as a modest but sufficient annuity with which to reward the just; I have spoken of it continually as a game of profit and loss. How does any of this avail for the simple task of describing, so that others may see her, the woman one loves? How can others see her except through one's own eyes, and how, so seeing her, can they turn the pages and close the book and live on as they have lived before, without becoming themselves the author and themselves the lover? The catalogues of excellencies of the Renaissance poets, those competitive advertisements, each man outdoing the next in metaphor, that great blurb — like a publisher's list in the Sunday newspapers — the Song of Solomon, how do these accord with the voice of love — love that delights in weakness, seeks out and fills the empty places and completes itself in its work of completion; how can one transcribe those accents? Love, which has its own life, its hours of sleep and waking, its health and sickness, growth, death and immortality, its ignorance and knowledge, experiment and mastery — how can one relate this hooded stranger to the men and women with whom he keeps pace? It is a problem beyond the proper scope of letters.

I first met Lucy after I had been some weeks in London; I had seen Roger several times; he always said, "You must come and meet Lucy," but nothing came of these vague proposals until finally, full of curiosity, I went with Basil uninvited.

I met him in the London Library, late one afternoon.

"Are you going to the young Simmondses?" he said.

"Not so far as I know."

"They've a party to-day."

"Roger never said anything to me about it."

"He told me to tell everyone. I'm just on my way there now. Why don't you come along?"

So we took a taxi to Victoria Square, for which I paid.

As it turned out, Roger and Lucy were not expecting anyone. He went to work now, in the afternoons, with a committee for the relief of Spanish refugees; he had only just come in and was in his bath. Lucy was listening to the six o'clock news on the wireless. She said, "D'you mind if I keep it on for a minute? There may be something about the dock strike in Madras. Roger will be down in a minute."

She did not say anything about a drink, so Basil said, "May I go and look for the whisky?"

"Yes, of course. How stupid of me. I always forget. There's probably some in the dining room."

He went out and I stayed with Lucy in her hired drawing-room. She sat quite still listening to the announcer's voice. She was five months gone with child — "Even Roger has to admit that it's proletarian action," she said later — but as yet scarcely showed it in body; but she was pale, paler, I guessed, than normal, and she wore that incurious, self-regarding expression which sometimes goes with a first pregnancy. Above the sound of the wireless I heard Basil outside, calling upstairs, "Roger. Where do you keep the corkscrew?" When they got back to the stock prices, Lucy switched off. "Nothing from Madras," she said. "But perhaps you aren't interested in politics."

"Not much," I said.

"Very few of Roger's friends seem to be."

"It's rather a new thing with him," I said.

"I expect he doesn't talk about it unless he thinks people are interested."

That was outrageous, first because it amounted to the claim to know Roger better than I did and, secondly, because I was still smarting with the ruthless boredom of my last two or three meetings with him.

"You'd be doing us all a great service if you could keep him to that," I said.

It is a most painful experience to find, when one has been rude, that one has caused no surprise. That is how Lucy received my remark. She merely said, "We've got to go out almost at once. We're going to the theatre in Finsbury and it starts at seven."

"Very inconvenient."

"It suits the workers," she said. "They have to get up earlier than we do, you see."

Then Roger and Basil came in with the drinks. Roger said, "We're just going out. They're doing the Tractor Trilogy at Finsbury. Why don't you come, too? We could probably get another seat, couldn't we, Lucy?"

"I doubt it," said Lucy. "They're tremendously booked up."

"I don't think I will," I said.

"Anyway, join us afterwards at the Café Royal."

"I might," I said.

"What have you and Lucy been talking about?"

"We listened to the news," said Lucy. "Nothing from Madras."

"They've probably got orders to shut down on it. I.D.C. have got the B.B.C. in their pocket."

"I.D.C.?" I asked.

"Imperial Defence College. They're the new hush-hush crypto-fascist department. They're in up to the neck with I.C.I. and the oil companies."

"I.C.I.?"

"Imperial Chemicals."

"Roger," said Lucy, "we really must go if we're to get anything to eat."

"All right," he said. "See you later at the Café."

I waited for Lucy to say something encouraging. She said, "We shall be there by eleven," and began looking for her bag among the chintz cushions.

I said, "I doubt if I can manage it."

"Are we taking the car?" Roger asked.

"No, I sent it away. I've had him out all day."

"I'll order some taxis."

"We could drop Basil and John somewhere," said Lucy.

"No," I said, "get two."

"We're going by way of Appenrodts," said Lucy.

"No good for me," I said, although, in fact, they would pass the corner of St. James's, where I was bound.

"I'll come and watch you eat your sandwiches," said Basil.

That was the end of our first meeting. I came away feeling badly about it, particularly the way in which she had used my Christian name and acquiesced in my joining them later. A commonplace girl who wanted to be snubbing would have been conspicuously aloof and have said, "Mr.. Plant," and I should have recovered some of the lost ground. But Lucy was faultless.

I have seen so many young wives go wrong on this point. They have either tried to force an intimacy with their husband's friends, claiming, as it were, continuity and identity with the powers of the invaded territory, or they have cancelled the passports of the old régime and proclaimed that fresh application must be made to the new authorities and applicants be treated strictly on their merits. Lucy seemed serenely unaware of either danger. I had come inopportunely and been rather rude, but I was one of Roger's friends; they were like his family to her, or hers to him; we had manifest defects which it was none of her business to reform; we had the right to come to her house unexpectedly, to shout upstairs for the corkscrew, to join her table at supper. The question of intrusion did not arise. It was simply that as far as she was concerned we had no separate or individual existence. It was, as I say, a faultless and highly provocative attitude. I found that in the next few days a surprising amount of my time, which, anyway, was lying heavy on me, was occupied in considering how this attitude, with regard to myself, could be altered.

My first move was to ask her and Roger to luncheon. I was confident that none of their other friends — none of those, that is to say, from whom I wished to dissociate myself — would have done such a thing. I did it formally, some days ahead, by letter to Lucy. All this, I knew, would come as a surprise to Roger. He telephoned me to ask, "What's all this Lucy tells me about you asking us to luncheon?"

"Can you come?"

"Yes, I suppose so. But what's it all about?"

"It's not 'about' anything. I just want you to lunch with me."

"Why?"

"It's quite usual, you know, when one's friends marry. Just politeness."

"You haven't got some ghastly foreigners you stayed with abroad?"

"No, nothing like that."

"Well, it all seems very odd to me. Writing a letter, I mean, and everything. . . . "

I rang off.

Lucy answered with a formal acceptance. I studied her writing; she wrote like a man.

DEAR JOHN,

Roger and I shall be delighted to lunch with you at the Ritz on Thursday week at 1.30.

Yours sincerely,

LUCY SIMMONDS

Should it not have been "Yours ever" after the "Dear John"?
I wondered whether she had wondered what to put. Another
girl might have written "Yours" with a non-committal squig-
gle, but her writing did not lend itself to that kind of evasion.
I had ended my note, "Love to Roger."

Was she not a little over-formal in repeating the place and
time? Had she written straight off, without thinking, or had
she sucked the top of her pen a little?

The paper was presumably the choice of their landlord, in
unobtrusive good taste. I smelled it and thought I detected a
whiff of soap.

At this point I lost patience with myself; it was ludicrous to
sit brooding over a note of this kind. I began, instead, to wonder whom I should ask to meet her — certainly none of the
gang she had learned to look on as "Roger's friends." On the
other hand, it must be clear that the party was for her. Roger
would be the first to impute that they were being made use of.
In the end, after due thought and one or two failures, I secured a middle-aged, highly reputable woman-novelist and
Andrew Desert and his wife — an eminently sociable couple.
When Roger saw his fellow guests he was more puzzled than
ever. I could see him all through luncheon trying to work it
out, why I should have spent five pounds in this peculiar
fashion.

I enjoyed my party. Lucy began by talking about my father's
painting.

"Yes," I said, "it's very fashionable at the moment."

"Oh, I don't mean that," she said in frank surprise, and went
on to tell me how she had stopped before a shop window in
Duke Street where a battle picture of my father's was on

view; there had been two private soldiers construing it together, point by point. "I think that's worth a dozen columns
of praise in the weekly papers," she said.

"Just like Kipling's *Light That Failed*," said the woman-
novelist.

"Is it? I didn't know." She told us she had never read any
Kipling.

"That shows the ten years between us," I said, and so the
conversation became a little more personal as we discussed
the differences between those who were born before the First
World War and those born after it; in fact, so far as it could
be worked, the differences between Lucy and myself.

Roger always showed signs of persecution-mania in the Ritz.
He did not like it when we knew people at other tables whom
he didn't know and, when the waiter brought him the wrong
dish, he began on a set-piece which I had heard him use
before in this same place. "Fashionable restaurants are the
same all over the world," he said. "There are always exactly
twenty per cent more tables than the waiters can manage.
It's a very good thing for the workers' cause that no one except
the rich know the deficiencies of the luxury world. Think of
the idea Hollywood gives of a place like this," he said, warm-
ing to his subject. "A *maître d'hôtel* like an ambassador, bow-
ing famous beauties across acres of unencumbered carpet —
and look at poor Lorenzo there, sweating under his collar,
jostling a way through for dowdy Middle West Americans.
. . . " But it was not a success. Lucy, I could see, thought it
odd of him to complain when he was a guest. I pointed out
that the couple Roger condemned as Middle West Americans
were in fact called Lord and Lady Settringham, and Andrew

led the conversation, where Roger could not follow it, to the topic of which ambassadors looked like *maîtres d'hôtel.* The woman-novelist began a eulogy of the Middle West which she knew and Roger did not. So he was left with his theme undeveloped. All this was worth five pounds to me, and more.

I thought it typical of the way Lucy had been brought up that she returned my invitation in a day or two.

Roger got in first on the telephone. "I say, are you free on Wednesday evening?"

"I'm not sure. Why?"

"I wondered if you'd dine with us."

"Not at half-past six for the Finsbury Theatre?"

"No. I work late these days at the Relief Committee."

"What time then?"

"Oh, any time after eight. Dress or not, just as you feel like it."

"What will you and Lucy be doing?"

"Well, I suppose we shall dress. In case anyone wants to go on anywhere."

"In fact, it's a dinner party?"

"Well, yes, in a kind of way."

It was plain that poor Roger was dismayed at this social mushroom which had sprung up under his nose, As a face-saver the telephone call was misconceived, for a little note from Lucy was already in the post for me. It was not for me to mock these little notes; I had begun it. But an end had to be made to them, so I decided to answer this by telephone, choosing the early afternoon when I assumed Roger would be out. He was in, and answered me. "I wanted to speak to Lucy."

"Yes?"

"Just to accept her invitation to dinner."

"But you've already accepted."

"Yes, but I thought I'd better just tell her."

"I told her. What d'you think?"

"Ah, good, I was afraid you might have forgotten."

I had come badly out of that.

From first to last the whole episode of the dinner was calamitous. It was a party of ten, and one glance round the room showed me that this was an occasion of what Lucy had been brought up to call "duty." That is to say, we were all people whom for one reason or another she had felt obliged to ask. She was offering us all up together in a single propitiatory holocaust to the gods of the schoolroom. Even Mr. Benwell was there. He did not realize that Lucy had taken the house furnished, and was congratulating her upon the decorations; "I like a London house to look like a London house," he was saying.

Roger was carrying things off rather splendidly with a kind of sardonic gusto which he could often assume in times of stress. I knew him in that mood and respected it. I knew, too, that my presence added a particular zest to his performance. Throughout the evening I caught him in constant inquiry of me: was I attending to this parody of himself? I was his audience, not Lucy.

The fate in store for myself was manifest as soon as I came into the room. It was Lucy's cousin Julia, the younger of the two girls Basil had told me of, the one whose début had been so disturbed by Lucy's marriage. It would not, I felt, be a grave setback. Julia had that particular kind of succulent

charm — bright, dotty, soft, eager, acquiescent, flattering, im-
pudent — that is specially, it seems, produced for the delight
of Anglo-Saxon manhood. She had no need of a London season
to find a happy future. "Julia is staying with us. She is a great
fan of yours," said Lucy in her Pont Street manner; a manner
which, like Roger's but much more subtly, had an element of
dumb crambo in it. What she said turned out to be true.

"My word, this *is* exciting," said Julia, and settled down to
enjoy me as though I were a box of chocolates open on her
knees.

"What a lot of people Lucy's got here to-night."

"Yes, it's her first real dinner party, and she says it will be
her last. She says she doesn't like parties any more."

"Did she ever?" I was ready to talk about Lucy at length,
but this was not Julia's plan.

"Everyone does at first," she said briefly, and then began
the conversation as she had rehearsed it, I am sure, in her
bath. "I knew you the moment you came into the room. Guess
how."

"You heard my name announced."

"Oh, no. Guess again."

An American hero would have said, "For Christ's sake," but
I said, "Really, I've no idea, unless perhaps you knew everyone
else already."

"Oh, no. Shall I tell you? I saw you in the Ritz the day Lucy
lunched with you."

"Why didn't you come and talk to us?"

"Lucy wouldn't let me. She said she'd ask you to dinner
instead."

"Ah."

"You see, for years and years the one thing in the world I've wanted most — or nearly most — was to meet you, and when Lucy calmly said she was going to lunch with you I cried with envy — literally, so I had to put a cold sponge on my eyes before going out."

Talking to this delicious girl about Lucy, I thought, was like sitting in the dentist's chair with one's mouth full of instruments and the certainty that, all in good time, he would begin to hurt.

"Did she talk about it much before she came to lunch?"

"Oh no, she just said 'I'm afraid I've got to leave you today as Roger wants me to lunch with one of his old friends.' So I said, 'How rotten, who?' and she said, 'John Plant,' just like that, and I said, '*John Plant,*' and she said, 'Oh, I forgot you were keen on thrillers.' *Thrillers,* as though you were just anybody. And I said, 'Couldn't I possibly come?' and she said, 'Not possibly,' and then when I was crying she said I might come with her to the lounge and sit behind a pillar and see you come in."

"How did she describe me?"

"She just said you'd be the one who paid for the cocktails. Isn't that just like Lucy, or don't you know her well enough to tell?"

"What did she say about the lunch afterwards?"

"She said everyone talked about Kipling."

"Was that all?"

"And she thought Roger had behaved badly because he doesn't like smart restaurants, and she said neither did she, but it had cost you a lot of money, so it was nasty to complain. Of course, I wanted to hear all about *you* and what *you* said, and she couldn't remember anything. She just said you seemed very clever."

"Oh, she said that."

"She says that about all Roger's friends. But, anyway, it's my turn now. I've got you to myself for the evening."

She had. We were sitting at dinner now. Lucy was still talking to Mr. Benwell. On my other side there was some kind of relative of Roger's. She talked to me for a bit about how Roger had settled down since marriage. "I don't take those political opinions of his seriously," she said, "and, anyway, it's all right to be a Communist nowadays. Everyone is."

"I'm not," I said.

"Well, I mean all the clever young people."

So I turned back to Julia. She was waiting for me.

"D'you know you once wrote me a letter?"

"Good gracious. Why?"

"Dear Madam, — Thank you for your letter. If you will read the passage in question more attentively you will note that the down train was four minutes late at Frasham. There was thus ample time for the disposal of the bicycle bell. Yours faithfully, John Plant," she quoted.

"Did I write that?"

"Don't you remember?"

"Vaguely. It was about *The Frightened Footman*, wasn't it?"

"Mm. Of course I knew perfectly well about the train. I just wrote in the hope of getting an answer, and it worked. I liked you for being so severe. There was another girl at school was literary, too, and she had a crush on Gilbert Warwick. *He* wrote *her* three pages beginning, My Dear Anthea, all about his house and the tithe barn he's turned into his work-room,

and ending, Write to me again; I hope you like Sylvia as much
as Heather — those were two of his heroines — and she
thought it showed what a better writer he was than you, but
I knew just the opposite. And later Anthea did write again,
and she had another long letter just like the first all about his
tithe barn, and that made her very cynical. So I wrote to you
again to show how different you were."

"Did I answer?"

"No. So then all the Literary Club took to admiring you
instead of Gilbert Warwick."

"Because I didn't answer letters?"

"Yes. You see, it showed you were a real artist and didn't
care a bit for your public, and just lived for your work."

"I see."

After dinner Roger said, "Has little Julia been boring you
frightfully?"

"Yes."

"I thought she was. She's very pretty. It's a great evening
for her."

Eventually we returned to the drawing-room and sat about.
Roger did not know how to manage this stage of his party. He
talked vaguely of going on somewhere to dance and of playing
a new parlour game that had lately arrived from New York.
No one encouraged him. I did not speak to Lucy until I came
to say good-bye, which was very early, as soon as the first
guest moved and everyone, on the instant, rose too. When I
said good-bye to her, Julia said, "Please, I must tell you. You're
a thousand times grander than I ever imagined. It was half a
game before — now it's serious."

I could imagine the relief in the house as the last of us left,

Roger and Lucy emerging into one another's arms as though from shelter after a storm. . . . "So that's over. Was it as bad as you expected?" "Worse, worse. You were splendid" . . . perhaps they — and Julia, too? — were cutting a caper on the drawing-room carpet in an ecstasy of liberation.

"That," I said to myself, "is what you have bought with your five pounds."

That evening, next day and for several days, I disliked Lucy. I made a story for all who knew him, of Roger's dinner party, leaving the impression that this was the kind of life Lucy enjoyed and that she was driving Roger into it. But for all that I did not abate my resolve to force my friendship upon her. I sought recognition. I wanted to assert the simple fact of my separate and individual existence. I could not by any effort of will regard her as being, like Trixie, "one of Roger's girls," and I demanded reciprocation; I would not be regarded as, like Basil, "one of Roger's friends"; still less, like Mr. Benwell, as someone who had to be asked to dinner every now and then. I had little else to think about at the time, and the thing became an itch with me. I felt about her, I suppose, as old men feel who are impelled by habit to touch every third lamp-post on their walks; occasionally something happens to distract them, they see a friend or a street accident and they pass a lamp-post by; then all day they fret and fidget until, after tea, they set out shamefacedly to put the matter right. That was how I felt about Lucy; our relationship constituted a tiny disorder in my life that had to be adjusted.

That at least is how, in those earliest days, I explained my obsession to myself, but looking at it now, down the mirrored corridor of cumulative emotion, I see no beginning to the perspective. There is in the apprehension of woman's beauty an exquisite, early intimation of loveliness when, seeing some face, strange or familiar, one gains, suddenly, a further glimpse and foresees, out of a thousand possible futures, how it might be transfigured by love. With Lucy — her grace daily more encumbered by her pregnancy; deprived of sex, as women are, by its fulfilment — the vision was extended and clarified until, with no perceptible transition, it became the reality. But I cannot say when it first appeared. Perhaps, that evening when she said, about the *Composed Hermitage in the Chinese Taste*, "I can't think why John should want to have a house like that," but it came without surprise; I had sensed it on its way, as an animal, still in profound darkness and sur-rounded by all the sounds of night, will lift its head, sniff, and know, inwardly, that dawn is near. Meanwhile, I moved for advantage as in a parlour game.

Julia brought me success. Our meeting, so far from dis-illusioning her, made her cult of me keener and more direct. It was no fault of mine, I assured Roger, when he came to grumble about it; I had not been in the least agreeable to her; indeed, towards the end of the evening I had been openly savage.

"The girl's a masochist," he said, adding with deeper gloom, "and Lucy says she's a virgin."

"There's plenty of time for her. The two troubles are often cured simultaneously."

"That's all very well, but she's staying another ten days. She never stops talking about you."

"Does Lucy mind?"

"Of course she minds. It's driving us both nuts. Does she write you a lot of letters?"

"Yes."

"What does she say?"

"I don't read them. I feel as though they were meant for somebody else. Besides, they're in pencil."

"I expect she writes them in bed. No one's ever gone for me like that."

"Nor for me," I said. "It's not really at all disagreeable."

"I daresay not," said Roger. "I thought only actors and sex-novelists and clergymen came in for it."

"No, no, anybody may — scientists, politicians, professional cyclists — anyone whose name gets into the papers. It's just that young girls are naturally religious."

"Julia's eighteen."

"She'll get over it soon. She's been stirred up by suddenly meeting me in the flesh after two or three years' distant devotion. She's a nice child."

"That's all very well," said Roger, returning sulkily to his original point. "It isn't Julia I'm worried about, it's ourselves, Lucy and me — she's staying another ten days. Lucy says you've got to be nice about it, and come out this evening, the four of us. I'm sorry, but there it is."

So for a week I went often to Victoria Square, and there was the beginning of a half-secret joke between Lucy and me in Julia's devotion. While I was there Julia sat smug and gay; she was a child of enchanting prettiness. When I was absent, Roger told me, she moped a good deal and spent much time in her bedroom writing and destroying letters to me. She talked about herself, mostly, and her sister and family. Her father was a major and they lived at Aldershot; they would have to stay there all the year round now that Lucy no longer needed their company in London. She did not like Roger. "He's not very nice about you," she said.

"Roger and I are like that," I explained. "We're always foul about each other. It's our fun. Is Lucy nice about me?"

"Lucy's an angel," said Julia, "that's why we hate Roger so."

Finally there was the evening of Julia's last party. Eight of us went to dance at a restaurant. Julia was at first very gay, but her spirits dropped towards the end of the evening. I was living in Ebury Street; it was easy for me to walk home from Victoria Square, so I went back with them and had a last drink. "Lucy's promised to leave us alone, just for a minute, to say good-bye," Julia whispered.

When we were alone, she said, "It's been absolutely wonderful the last two weeks. I didn't know it was possible to be so happy. I wish you'd give me something as a kind of souvenir."

"Of course. I'll send you one of my books, shall I?"

"No," she said, "I'm not interested in your books any more. At least, of course, I am, terribly, but I mean it's *you* I love."

"Nonsense," I said.

"Will you kiss me, once, just to say good-bye."

I kissed her paternally on the cheek.

Then she said suddenly, "You're in love with Lucy, aren't you?"

"Good heavens, no. What on earth put that into your head?"

"I can tell. Through loving you so much, I expect. You may not know it, but you are. And it's no good. She loves that horrid Roger. Oh, dear, they're coming back. I'll come and say good-bye to you to-morrow, may I?"

"No."

"Please. This hasn't been how I planned it at all."

Then Roger and Lucy came into the room with a sly look as though they had been discussing what was going on and how long they should give us. So I shook hands with Julia and went home.

She came to my rooms at ten next morning. Mrs. Legge, the landlady, showed her up. She stood in the door, swinging a small parcel. "I've got five minutes," she said, "the taxi's waiting. I told Lucy I had some last-minute shopping."

"You know you oughtn't to do this sort of thing."

"I've been here before. When I knew you were out. I pretended I was your sister and had come to fetch something for you."

"Mrs. Legge never said anything to me about it."

"No. I asked her not to. In fact, I gave her ten shillings. You see, she caught me at it."

"At what?"

"Well, it sounds rather silly. I was in your bedroom, kissing things — you know, pillows, pyjamas, hair brushes. I'd just got to the washstand and was kissing your razor when I looked up and found Mrs. Whatever-she's-called standing in the door."

"Good God, I shall never be able to look her in the face again."

"Oh, she was quite sympathetic. I suppose I must have looked funny, like a goose grazing." She gave a little, rather hysterical giggle, and added, "Oh, John, I do love you so."

"Nonsense. I shall turn you out if you talk like that."

"Well, I do. And I've got you a present." She gave me the square parcel. "Open it."

"I shan't accept it," I said, unwrapping a box of cigars.

"But you must. You see, they'd be no good to me, would they? Are they good ones?"

"Yes," I said, looking at the box. "Very good ones indeed."

"The best."

"Quite the best, but . . ."

"That's what the man in the shop said. Smoke one now."

"Julia, dear, I couldn't. I've only just finished breakfast."

She saw the point of that. "When will you smoke the first one? After luncheon? I'd like to think of you smoking the first one."

"Julia, dear, it's perfectly sweet of you, but I can't honestly . . ."

"I know what you're thinking, that I can't afford it. Well, that's all right. You see, Lucy gave me five pounds yesterday to buy a hat. I thought she would — she often does. But I had to wait and be sure. I'd got them ready, hidden yesterday evening. I meant to give you them then. But I never got a proper chance. So here they are." And then, as I hesitated, with rising voice, "Don't you see I'd much rather give you cigars than have a new hat? Don't you see I shall go back to Aldershot absolutely miserable, the whole time in London quite spoilt, if you won't take them?"

She had clearly been crying that morning and was near tears again.

"Of course I'll take them," I said. "I think it's perfectly sweet of you."

Her face cleared in sudden, infectious joy.

"There. Now we can say good-bye."

She stood waiting for me, not petitioning this time, but

claiming her right. I put my hands on her shoulders and gave her a single, warm kiss on the lips. She shut her eyes and sighed. "Thank you," she said in a small voice, and hurried out to her waiting taxi, leaving the box of cigars on my table.

Sweet Julia! I thought. It was a supremely unselfish present; something quite impersonal and unsentimental — no keepsake — something which would be gone, literally in smoke, in less than six weeks; a thing she had not even the fun of choosing for herself; she had gone to the counter and left it to the shopman — "I want a box of the best cigars you keep, please — as many as I can get for five pounds." She just wanted something which she could be sure would give pleasure.

And chiefly because she thought I had been kind to her cousin, Lucy took me into her friendship.

Roger's engraving showed a pavilion, still rigidly orthodox in plan, but, in elevation decked with ornament conceived in a wild ignorance of oriental forms; there were balconies and balustrades of geometric patterns; the cornices swerved upwards at the corners in the lines of a pagoda; the roof was crowned with an onion cupola which might have been Russian, bells hung from the capitals of barley-sugar columns; the windows were freely derived from the Alhambra; there was a minaret. To complete the atmosphere the engraver had added a little group of Turkish military performing the bastinado upon a curiously complacent malefactor, an Arabian camel and a mandarin carrying a bird in a cage.

"My word, what a gem," they said. "It is really all there?"

"The minaret's down and it's all rather overgrown."

"What a chance. John must get it."

"It will be fun to furnish. I know just the chairs for it."

This was the first time I had been to Victoria Square since Julia left.

And Lucy said, "I can't think why John should want to have a house like that."

❋ ❋ ❋ 2 ❋ ❋ ❋

Lucy was a girl of few friends; she had, in fact, at the time I was admitted to their number, only two: a man named Peter Baverstock, in the Malay States, whom I never saw, and a Miss Muriel Meikeljohn, whom I saw all too often. Peter Baverstock had wanted to marry Lucy since she was seven, and proposed to her whenever he came home on leave, every eighteen months, until she married Roger, when he sent her a very elaborate wedding present, an immense thing in carved wood, ivory and gilt which caused much speculation with regard to its purpose; later he wrote and explained. I forget the explanation. I think it was the gift which, by local usage, men of high birth gave to their granddaughters when they were delivered of male twins; it was, anyway, connected with twins and grandparents, of great rarity, and a token of high esteem in the parts it came from. Lucy wrote long letters to Baverstock every fortnight. I often watched her at work on those letters, sitting square to her table, head bowed, hand travelling evenly across the page, as, I remembered reading in some book of memoirs, Sir Walter Scott's had been seen at a lighted window, writing the Waverley novels. It was a tradition of her upbringing that letters for the East must always be written on very thin, lined paper. "I'm just telling Peter about your house," she would say.

"How can that possibly interest him?"

"Oh, he's interested in everything. He's so far away."

It seemed an odd reason.

Miss Meikeljohn was a pale, possessive girl, who had been a fellow boarder with Lucy in the house of a distressed gentlewoman in Vienna where they had both been sent to learn singing. They had shared a passion for a leading tenor, and had once got into his dressing-room at the Opera House by wearing mackintoshes and pretending to be reporters sent to interview him. Lucy still kept a photograph of this tenor, in costume, on her dressing-table, but she had shed her musical aspirations with the rest of her Pont Street life. Miss Meikeljohn still sang, once a week, to a tutor. It was after these lessons that she came to luncheon with Lucy, and the afternoon was hers by prescriptive right for shopping, or for a cinema, or for what she liked best, a "good talk." These Tuesdays were "Muriel's days," and no one might interfere with them.

"They are the only times she comes into London. Her parents are separated and terribly poor," Lucy said, as though in complete explanation.

When they went to the cinema or play together they went in the cheap seats because Miss Meikeljohn insisted on paying her share. Lucy thought this evidence of Miss Meikeljohn's integrity of character; she often came back from these entertainments with a headache from having had to sit so close to the screen.

The friendship was odd in many ways, notably because Miss Meikeljohn luxuriated in heart-to-heart confidences — in what my father's generation coarsely called "taking down her back hair," an exhibition that was abhorrent to Lucy, who in friendship had all the modesty of the naked savage.

I must accept the modesty of the naked savage on trust, on the authority of numerous travel books. The savages I have met on my travels have all been formidably overdressed. But if there existed nowhere else on the globe that lithe, chaste and unstudied nudity of which I have so often read, it was there, dazzlingly, in the mind of Lucy. There were no reservations in her friendship, and it was an experience for which I was little qualified, to be admitted, as it were, through a door in the wall to wander at will over that rich estate. The idea of an occasional opening to the public in aid of the cottage hospital, of extra gardeners working a week beforehand to tidy the walks, of an upper housemaid to act as guide, of red cord looped across the arms of the chairs, of special objects of value to be noted, of "that door leads to the family's private apartments. They are never shown," of vigilance at the hot-house for fear of a nectarine being pocketed, of "now you have seen *everything*: please make way for the next party," and of the open palm — of all, in fact, which constituted Miss Meikeljohn's, and most people's, habit of intimacy, was inconceivable to Lucy.

When I began to realize the spaces and treasures of which I had been made free, I was like a slum child alternately afraid to touch or impudently curious. Or, rather, I felt too old. Years earlier when Lucy was in her cradle, I had known this kind of friendship. There was a boy at my private school with whom I enjoyed a week of unrestrained confidence; one afternoon, sitting with him in a kind of nest, itself a secret, which we had devised for ourselves from a gym mat and piled benches in a corner of the place where we played on wet afternoons, I revealed my greatest secret, that my father was an artist and not, as I had given it out, an officer in the Navy; by tea-time the story was all over the school, that Plant's pater had long hair and did not wash. (Revenge came sooner than I could have hoped, for this was the summer term, 1914, and my betrayer had an aunt married to an Austrian nobleman; he had boasted at length of staying in their castle; when school reassembled in September I was at the head of the mob which hounded him in tears to the matron's room with cries of "German spy.") It was the first and, to my mind, most dramatic of the normal betrayals of adolescence. With the years I had grown cautious. There was little love and no trust at all between any of my friends. Moreover, we were bored; each knew the other so well that it was only by making our relationship into a kind of competitive parlour game that we kept it alive at all. We had all from time to time cut out divergent trails and camped in new ground, but we always, as it were, returned to the same base for supplies, and swapped yarns of our exploration. That was what I meant by friendship at the age of thirty-four, and Lucy, finding herself without preparation among people like myself, had been disconcerted. That was the origin of what, at first, I took for priggishness in her. Her lack of shyness cut her off from us. She could not cope with the attack and defence, deception and exposure, which was our habitual intercourse. Anything less than absolute intimacy embarrassed her, so she fell back upon her good upbringing, that armoury of schoolroom virtues and graces with which she had been equipped, and lived, as best she could, independently, rather as, it is said, Chinese gentlemen of the old school can pursue interminable, courteous, traditionally prescribed conversations with their minds abstracted in realms of distant beauty.

But it was not enough. She was lonely. In particular she was cut off by her pregnancy from Roger. For a term of months she was unsexed, the roots of her love for Roger wintering, out of sight in the ground, without leaf. So she looked for a friend and, because she thought I had been kind to Julia, and because, in a way, I had responded to her in her schoolroom mood, she chose me. I had not misinterpreted her change of manner. She had made up her mind that I was to be a friend. I began, almost at once, to spend the greater part of the day in her company, and as my preoccupation at the time was in finding a house that quest became the structure of our friendship. Together we went over the sheaves of house agents' notices, and several times we went on long expeditions together to look at houses in the country. We talked of everything except the single topic of politics. The attraction of Socialism for Lucy was double. It was a part of the break she had made with Aldershot and Pont Street, and it relieved her of the responsibility she felt for her own private fortune. Money, her money, was of great importance to her. If she had lived among the rich it would have been different; she would then have thought it normal to be assured, for life, of the possessions for which others toiled; she would, indeed, have thought herself rather meagrely provided. But she had been brought up among people poorer than herself to regard herself as somebody quite singular. When the age came of her going to dances, her aunt had impressed on her the danger she ran of fortune-hunters and, indeed, nearly all the young men with whom she consorted, and their mothers, re-garded £58,000 as a notable prize. "Sometimes by the way that girl talks," Basil had said, "you'd think she was the Wool-worth heiress." It was quite true. She did think herself ex-tremely rich and responsible. One of the advantages to her of marrying Roger was the belief that her money was being put to good use in rescuing a literary genius from wage-slavery. She was much more afraid of misusing her money than of los-ing it. Thus when she was convinced that all private fortunes like her own were very shortly to be abolished and all un-deserved prominence levelled, she was delighted. Moreover, her conversion had coincided with her falling in love. She and Roger had been to meetings together, and together read epitomes of Marxist philosophy. Her faith, like a Christian's, was essential to her marriage, so, knowing that I was hostile, she sequestered it from me.

It was convenient for Roger to have me in attendance. He was not domestic by nature. He did not, as some husbands do, resent his wife's pregnancy. It was as though he had bought a hunter at the end of the season and turned him out; discerning friends, he knew, would appreciate the fine lines under the rough coat, but he would sooner have shown some-thing glossy in the stable. He had summer business to do, moreover; the horse must wait till the late autumn. That, at least, was one way in which he saw the situation, but the analogy was incomplete. It was rather *he* that had been ac-quired and put to grass, and he was conscious of that aspect, too. Roger was hobbled and prevented from taking the full stride required of him, by the habit, long settled, of regarding sex relationships in terms of ownership and use. Confronted with the new fact of pregnancy, of joint ownership, his terms failed him. As a result he was restless and no longer master of the situation; the practical business of getting through the day was becoming onerous, so that my adhesion was agreeable to him. Grossly, it confirmed his opinion of Lucy's value and at the same time took her off his hands. Then one morning, when I made my now habitual call at Victoria Square, Lucy, not yet up but lying in bed in a chaos of newspapers, letters and manicure tools, greeted me by saying, "Roger's writing."

Couched as she was, amid quilted bed-jacket and tumbled sheets — one arm bare to the elbow where the wide sleeve fell back and showed the tender places of wrist and forearm, the other lost in the warm depths of the bed, with her pale skin taking colour against the dead white linen, and her smile of confident, morning welcome; as I had greeted her countless times and always with a keener joy, until that morning I seemed to have come to the end of an investigation and held as a certainty what before I had roughly surmised — her beauty rang through the room like a peal of bells; thus I have stood, stunned, in a Somerset garden, with the close turf wet and glittering underfoot in the dew, when, from beyond the walls of box, the grey church tower had suddenly scattered the heavens in tumult.

"Poor fellow," I said. "What about?"

"It's my fault," she said, "a detective story," and she went on to explain that since I had talked to her about my books, she had read them — "You were perfectly right. They *are* works of art. I had no idea" — and talked of them to Roger until he had suddenly said, "Oh, God, another Julia." Then he had told her that for many years he had kept a plot in his mind, waiting for a suitable time to put it into writing.

"He'll do it very well," I said. "Roger can write anything."

"Yes."

But while she was telling me this and I was answering, I thought only of Lucy's new beauty. I knew that beauty of that kind did not come from a suitable light or a lucky way with the hair or a sound eight hours' sleep, but from an inner secret; and I knew this morning that the secret was the fact of Roger's jealousy. So another stage was reached in my falling in love with Lucy, while each week she grew heavier and slower and less apt for love, so that I accepted the joy of her companionship without reasoning. Lucy and I were like characters in the stock intrigue of Renaissance comedy, where the heroine follows the hero in male attire and is wooed by him, unknowing, in the terms of rough friendship.

In these weeks Lucy and I grew adept in construing the jargon of the estate agents. I had a clear idea of what I required. In the first place, it must not cost, all told, when the decorators and plumbers had moved out and the lawyers been paid for the conveyance, more than £3000; it must be in agricultural country, preferably within five miles of an antiquated market town, it must be at least a hundred years old, and it must be a *house*, no matter how dingy, rather than a cottage, however luxurious; there must be a cellar, two staircases, high ceilings, a marble chimneypiece in the drawing-room, room to turn a car at the front door, a coach-house and stable yard, a walled kitchen garden, a paddock and one or two substantial trees — these seemed to me the minimum requisites of the standard of gentility at which I aimed, something between the squire's and the retired admiral's. Lucy had a womanly love of sunlight and a Marxist faith in the superior beauties of concrete and steel. She had, moreover, a horror, born of long association, of the rural bourgeois with whom I was determined to enroll myself. I was able to excuse my predilection to others by describing it as Gallic; French writers, I explained, owed their great strength, as had the writers of nineteenth-century England, to their middle-class status; the best of them all owned square white houses, saved their money, dined with the mayor and had their eyes closed for them at death by faithful, repellent housekeepers; English and American writers squandered their energy in being fashionable or Bohemian or, worst of all, in an unhappy alternation between the two. This theme went down well with Mr. Benwell, who, in the week or two after I expounded it to him, gave deathless offence to several of his authors by exhorting them to be middle-class, too, but it left Lucy unimpressed. She thought the object of my search grotesque, but followed in a cheerful and purely sporting spirit as one may hunt a fox which one has no taste to eat.

The last occasion of her leaving London before her confinement was to look at a house with me, below the Berkshire downs. It was too far to travel comfortably in a day, and we spent the night with relatives of hers near Abingdon. We had by now grown so accustomed to one another's company that there seemed nothing odd to us in Lucy proposing me as a guest. Our host and hostess, however, thought it most irregular, and their manifest surprise was a further bond between us. Lucy was by now eight months with child, and at the back of her relatives' concern was the fear that she might be delivered prematurely in their house. They treated her with a solicitude that all too clearly was a rebuke to my own easy-going acceptance of the situation. Try how I might to realize the dangers she ran, I could never feel protective towards Lucy. She looked, we agreed, like Tweedledum armed for battle, and I saw her at this time as preternaturally solid, with an armour of new life defending her from the world. Biologically, no doubt, this was a fallacy, but it was the attitude we jointly accepted, so that we made an immediate bad impression by being struck with *fou rire* in the first five minutes of our visit, when our hostess whispered that she had fitted up a bedroom for Lucy on the ground floor so that she should not be troubled by stairs.

The house we had come to see proved, like so many others, to be quite uninhabitable. Its owner, in fact, was living in his lodge. "Too big for me these days," he said of the house which, when he opened it to us, gave the impression of having been designed as a small villa and wantonly extended, as though no one had remembered to tell the workmen when to stop and they had gone on adding room to room like cells in a wasp-nest. "I never had the money to spend on it," the owner said gloomily; "you could make something of it with a little money."

We went upstairs and along a lightless passage. He had been showing people over this house since 1920, he said, and with the years he had adopted a regular patter. "Nice little room this, very warm in the winter. . . . You get a good view of the

downs here, if you stand in the corner. . . . It's a dry house.
You can see that. I've never had any trouble with damp. . . .
These used to be the nurseries. They'd make a nice suite of
spare bedrooms, dressing-room and bath if you didn't . . . "
and at that point, remembering Lucy, he stopped abruptly
and in such embarrassment that he scarcely spoke until we
left him.

"I'll write to you," I said.

"Yes," he said with great gloom, knowing what I meant. "I
sometimes think the place might do as a school. It's very
healthy."

So we drove back to Lucy's relatives. They wanted her to
dine in bed or, anyway, to go to her room and lie down until
dinner. Instead she came out with me into the evening sunlight, and we sat in what Lucy's relatives called their "blue
garden," reconstructing a life story of the sad little man who
had shown us his house. Lucy's relatives thought us and our
presence there and our whole expedition extremely odd. There
was something going on, they felt, which they did not understand, and Lucy and I, infected by the atmosphere, became,
as it were, confederates in this house which she had known all
her life; in the garden where, as a little girl, she had once, she
told me, buried a dead starling, with tears.

After this expedition Lucy remained in London, spending
more and more of her time indoors. When I finally found a
house to suit me, I was alone.

"You might have waited," said Lucy. It seemed quite natural that she should reproach me. She had a share in my
house. "Damn this baby," she added.

✳　✳　✳　3　✳　✳　✳

In the last week before the birth of her child Lucy began for the first time to betray impatience; she was never, at any time, at all apprehensive — merely bored and weary and vexed past bearing by the nurse who had now taken up residence in the house. Roger and Miss Meikeljohn had made up their minds that she was going to die. "It's all this damned pre-natal care," said Roger. "Do you realize that maternal mortality is higher in this country than it's ever been? D'you know there are cases of women going completely bald after childbirth? And permanently insane? It's worse among the rich than the poor, too."

Miss Meikeljohn said: "Lucy's being so wonderful. She doesn't *realize*."

The nurse occupied herself with extravagant shopping lists. "Does *everyone* have to have all these things?" Lucy asked, aghast at the multitude of medical and nursery supplies which began to pour into the house. "Everyone who can afford them," said Sister Kemp briskly, unconscious of irony. Roger found some comfort in generalizing. "It's anthropologically very interesting," he said, "all this purely ceremonial accumulation of rubbish — like turtle doves brought to the gates of a temple. Everyone according to his means sacrificing to the racial god of hygiene."

He showed remarkable forbearance to Sister Kemp, who brought with her an atmosphere of impending doom and accepted a cocktail every evening, saying, "I'm not really on duty *yet*," or "No time for this *after the day*."

She watched confidently for The Day, her apotheosis, when Lucy would have no need for Roger or me or Miss Meikeljohn, only for herself.

"I shall call you Mrs. Simmonds until The Day," she said, "After that you will be my Lucy." She sat about with us in the drawing-room, and in Lucy's bedroom where we spent most of the day, now; like an alien, sitting at a café; an alien anarchist, with a bomb beside him, watching the passing life of a foreign city, waiting for his signal from the higher powers, the password which might come at once or in a very few days, whispered in his ear, perhaps, by the waiter, or scrawled on the corner of his evening newspaper — the signal that the hour of liberation had come when he would take possession of all he beheld. "The fathers need nearly as much care as the mothers," said Sister Kemp. "No, not another, thank you, Mr. Simmonds. I've got to keep in readiness, you know. It would never do if baby came knocking at the door and found Sister unable to lift the latch."

"No," said Roger. "No, I suppose it wouldn't."

Sister Kemp belonged to a particularly select and highly paid corps of nurses. A baby wheeled out by her, as it would be daily for the first month, would have to access to certain paths in the Park where inferior nurses trespassed at the risk of cold looks. Lucy's perambulator would thus be socially established, and the regular nurse, when she took over, would find her charge already well known and respected. Sister Kemp explained this, adding as a concession to Lucy's political opinions, "The snobbery among nurses is terrible. I've seen many a girl go home from Stanhope Gate in tears." And then, *esprit de corps* asserting itself, "Of course, they ought to have known. There's always Kensington Gardens for *them*."

Once Sister Kemp had attended a house in Seamore Place, in nodding distance of Royalty, but the gardens there, though supremely grand, had been, she said, "dull," by which we understood that even for her there were close circles. Roger was delighted with this. "It's like something out of Thackeray," he said and pressed for further details, but Lucy was past taking relish in social survivals; she was concerned only with the single, physical fact of her own exhaustion. "I hate this baby already," she said. "I'm going to hate it all my life."

Roger worked hard at this time, in the mornings at his detective story, in the afternoons at his committee for Spanish aid. Miss Meikeljohn and I tried to keep Lucy amused with increasingly little success. Miss Meikeljohn took her to concerts and cinemas where, now, she allowed Lucy to buy the seats, as extreme comfort was clearly necessary for her. I took her to the Zoo, every morning at twelve o'clock. There was a sooty, devilish creature in the monkey house named Humboldt's Gibbon which we would watch morosely for half an hour at a time; he seemed to exercise some kind of hypnotic fascination over Lucy; she could not be got to other cages. "If I have a boy I'll call him Humboldt," she said. "D'you know that before I was born, so Aunt Maureen says, my mother used to sit in front of a Flaxman bas-relief so as to give me ideal beauty. Poor mother, she died when I was born." Lucy could say that without embarrassment because she felt no danger in her own future. "I don't care how disagreeable it's going to be," she said. "I only want it soon."

Because of my confidence in her, and my resentment of the proprietary qualms of Roger and Miss Meikeljohn, I accepted her attitude; and was correspondingly shocked when the actual day came.

Roger telephoned to me at breakfast time. "The baby's be-gun."

"Good," I said.

"What d'you mean, good?"

"Well, it is good, isn't it? When did it start?"

"Last night, about an hour after you left."

"It ought to be over soon."

"I suppose so. Shall I come round?"

He came, yawning a great deal from having been up all night. "I was with her for an hour or two. I always imagined people stayed in bed when they were having babies. Lucy's up, going about the house. It was horrible. Now she doesn't want me."

"What happened exactly?"

He began to tell me and then I was sorry I had asked. "That nurse seems very good," he said at the end. "The doctor didn't come until half an hour ago. He went away again right away. They haven't given her any chloroform yet. They say they are keeping that until the pains get worse. I don't see how they could be. You've no conception what it was like." He stayed with me for half an hour and read my newspapers. Then he went home. "I'll telephone you when there's any news," he said.

Two hours later I rang up. "No," he said, "there's no news. I said I'd telephone you if there was."

"But what's happening?"

"I don't know. Some kind of lull."

"But she's all right, isn't she? I mean they're not anxious."

"I don't know. The doctor's coming again. I went in to see her, but she didn't say anything. She was just crying quietly."

"Nothing I can do, is there?"

"No, how could there be?"

"I mean about lunch or anything. You don't feel like coming out?"

"No, I ought to stay around here."

The thought of the lull, of Lucy not speaking, but lying there in tears, waiting for her labour to start again, pierced me as no tale could have done of cumulative pain; but beyond my sense of compassion I was not scared. I had been smoking a pipe; my mouth had gone dry, and when I knocked out the smouldering tobacco the smell of it sickened me. I went out into Ebury Street as though to the deck of a ship, breathing hard against nausea, and, from habit more than sentiment, took a cab to the Zoo.

The man at the turnstile knew me as a familiar figure. "Your lady not with you to-day, sir?"

"No, not to-day."

"I've got five myself," he said.

I did not understand him and repeated foolishly, "Five?"

"Being a married man," he added.

Humboldt's Gibbon seemed disinclined for company. He sat hunched up at the back of his cage, fixing on me a steady and rather bilious stare. He was never, at the best of times, an animal who courted popularity. In the cage on his left lived a sycophantic, shrivelled, grey monkey from India who salaamed for titbits of food; on his right were a troupe of patchy buffoons who swung and tumbled about their cage to attract attention. Not so Humboldt's Gibbon; visitors passed him by — often with almost superstitious aversion and some such comment as "Nasty things"; he had no tricks, or, if he had, he performed them alone, for his own satisfaction, after dark, ritualistically, when, in that exotic enclave among the stucco terraces, the prisoners awake and commemorate the jungles where they had their birth, as exiled darkies, when their work is done, will tread out the music of Africa in a vacant lot behind the drug-store.

Lucy used always to bring fruit to the ape; I had nothing, but, to deceive him, I rattled the wire and held out my empty fingers as though they held a gift. He unrolled himself, revealing an extraordinary length of black limb, and came delicately towards me on toes and finger-tips; his body was slightly pigeon-chested and his fur dense and short, his head spherical, without the poodle-snout of his neighbours — merely two eyes and a line of yellow teeth set in leather, like a bare patch worn in a rug. He was less like a man than any of his kind, and he lacked their human vulgarity. When, at short range, he realized that I held nothing for him he leapt suddenly at the bars and hung there, spread out to his full span, spiderish, snarling with contempt; then dropped to the floor and, turning about, walked delicately back to the corner from which I had lured him. So I looked at him and thought of Lucy, and the minutes passed.

Presently I was aware of someone passing behind me from the salaaming monkey to the troupe of tumblers, and back again, and at either side peering not at the animals but at me. I gazed fixedly at the ape, hoping that this nuisance would pass. Finally a voice said, "I say."

I turned and found Arthur Atwater. He was dressed as I had seen him before, in his raincoat, though it was a fine, warm day, and his soft grey hat, worn at what should have been a raffish angle but which, in effect, looked merely lopsided. (He explained the raincoat in the course of our conversation, saying, "You know how it is in digs. If you leave anything behind when you go out for the day, someone's sure to take a fancy to it.") "It is Plant, isn't it?" he said.

"Yes."

"Thought so. I never forget a face. They call it the royal gift, don't they?"

"Do they?"

"Yes, that and punctuality. I'm punctual, too, It's a curious thing because you see, actually, though I don't make any fuss about it in the position I'm in, I'm descended from Henry VII." There seemed no suitable answer to this piece of information so, since I was silent, he added suddenly, "I say, you do remember me, don't you?"

"Vividly."

He came closer and leant beside me on the rail which separated us from the cage. It was as though we stood on board ship and were looking out to sea, only instead of the passing waters we saw the solitary, still person of Humboldt's Gibbon. "I don't mind telling you," said Atwater, "I've had a pretty thin time of it since we last met."

"I saw you were acquitted at the trial. I thought you were very fortunate."

"Fortunate! You should have heard the things the beak said. Things he had no right to say and wouldn't have dared say to a rich man, and said in a very nasty way, too — things I shan't forget in a hurry. Mr. Justice Longworth — *Justice*, that's funny. Acquitted without a stain! — innocent! Does that give me back my job?"

"But I understood from the evidence at the trial that you were under notice to go anyway."

"Yes. And why? Because sales were dropping. Why should I sell their beastly stockings for them anyway? Money — that's all anyone cares about now. And I'm beginning to feel the same way. When do you suppose I had my last meal — my last square meal?"

"I've really no idea, I'm afraid."

"Tuesday. I'm hungry, Plant — literally hungry."

"You could have saved yourself the sixpence admission here, couldn't you?"

"I'm a Fellow," said Atwater with surprising readiness.

"Oh."

"You don't believe that, do you?"

"I have no reason not to."

"I can prove it; look here — Fellow's tickets, two of them." He produced and pressed on my attention two tickets of admission signed in a thin, feminine hand.

"My dear Atwater," I said, "these don't make you a Fellow; they've merely been given you by someone who is — not that it matters."

"Not that it matters! Let me tell you this; D'you know who gave me these? — the mother of a chap I know; chap I know well. I dropped round to see him the other evening, at the address I found in the telephone book. It was his mother's house as it happened. My pal was abroad. But, anyway I got talking to the mother and told her about how I was placed and what pals her son and I had been. She seemed a decent old bird. At the end she said, 'How very sad. Do let me give you something,' and began fumbling in her bag. I thought at least a quid was coming, and what did she give me? These tickets for the Zoo. I ask you!"

"Well," I said, with a tone as encouraging as I could manage, for it did seem to me that in this instance he had been unfairly disappointed, "the Zoo is a very pleasant place."

At this suggestion Atwater showed a mercurial change of mood from resentment to simple enthusiasm. "It's wonderful," he said, "there's nothing like it. All these animals from all over the world. Think what they've seen — forests and rivers, places probably where no white man's ever been. It makes you long to get away, doesn't it? Think of paddling your canoe upstream in undiscovered country, with strings of orchids overhead and parrots in the trees and great butterflies, and native servants, and hanging your hammock in the open at night and starting off in the morning with no one to worry you, living on fish and fruit — that's life," said Atwater.

Once again I felt impelled to correct his misconceptions of colonial life. "If you are still thinking of settling in Rhodesia," I said, "I must warn you you will find conditions very different from those you describe."

"Rhodesia's off," said Atwater. "I've other plans."

He told me of them at length, and because they distracted me from thinking of Lucy, I listened gratefully. They depended, primarily, on his finding a man of his acquaintance — a good scout named Appleby — who had lately disappeared as so many of Atwater's associates seemed to have done, leaving no indication of his whereabouts. Appleby knew of a cave in Bolivia where the Jesuits, in bygone years, had stored their treasure. When they were driven out, they put a curse on the place, so that the superstitious natives left the hoard inviolate. Appleby had old parchments which made the matter clear. More than this, Appleby had an aerial photograph of the locality, and by a special process known to himself, was able to treat the plate so that auriferous ground came out dark; the hill where the Jesuits had left their treasure was almost solid black; the few white spots indicated chests of jewels and, possibly, bar platinum.

"Appleby's idea was to collect ten stout fellows who would put up a hundred quid each for our fares and digging expenses. I'd have gone like a shot. Had it all fixed up. The only snag was that just at that time I couldn't put my hands on a hundred quid."

"Did the expedition ever start?"

"I don't think so. You see a lot of the chaps were in the same position. Besides old Appleby would never start without me. He's a good scout. If I only knew where he hung out I should be all right."

"Where used he to hang out?"

"You could always find him at the old Wimpole. He was what our barman called one of the regulars."

"Surely they would know his address there?" I kept talking. As long as I was learning about old Appleby I had only half my mind for Lucy.

"Well, you see, the Wimpole's rather free and easy in some ways. As long as you're a good chap you're taken as you come and no questions asked. Subs. are paid by the months; you know the kind of place. If you're shy of the ante, as we used to call it, the doorman doesn't let you in."

"And old Appleby was shy of the ante?"

"That's it. It wasn't a thing to worry about. Most of the

chaps one time or another had been shown the door. I expect it's the same at your club. No disgrace attached. But old Appleby's a bit touchy and began telling off the doorman good and proper, and then the secretary butted in and, to cut a long story short, there was something of a schmozzle."

"Yes," I said, "I see." And even as I spoke all interest in Appleby's schmozzle faded completely away and I thought of Lucy, lying at home in tears, waiting for her pain. "For God's sake, tell me some more." I said.

"More about Appleby?"

"More about anything. Tell me about all the chaps in the Wimpole. Tell me their names one by one and exactly what they look like. Tell me your family history. Tell me the full details of every job you have ever lost. Tell me all the funny stories you have ever heard. Tell my fortune. Don't you see, I want to be *told?*"

"I don't quite twig," said Atwater. "But if you are trying to hint that I'm boring you . . . "

"Atwater," I said earnestly, "I will pay you just to talk to me. Here is a pound, look, take it. There. Does that look as though I was bored?"

"It looks to me as though you were balmy," said Atwater, pocketing the note. "Much obliged all the same. It'll come in handy just at the moment, only as a loan, mind."

"Only as a loan," I said, and we both of us lapsed into silence, he, no doubt, thinking of my balminess, I of Lucy. The black ape walked slowly round his cage raking the sawdust and nut shells with the back of his hand, looking vainly for some neglected morsel of food. Presently there an excited scurry in the cage next to us; two women had appeared with a bunch of bananas. "Excuse me, please," they said and pushed in front of us to feed Humboldt's Gibbon; then they passed on to the grey sycophant beyond, and so down all the cages until their bag was empty. "Where shall we go now?" one of them said. "I don't see the point of animals you aren't allowed to feed."

Atwater overheard this remark; it worked in his mind so that by the time they had left the monkey house, he was in another mood. Atwater the dreamer, Atwater the good scout, and Atwater the underdog seemed to appear in more or less regular sequence. It was Atwater the good scout I liked best, but one clearly had to take him as he came. "Feeding animals while men and women starve," he said bitterly.

It was a topic; a topic dry, scentless and colourless as a pressed flower; a topic on which in the school debating society one had despaired of finding anything new to say — "The motion before the House is that too much kindness is shown to animals, proposed by Mr. John Plant, Head-master's House" — nevertheless, it was something to talk about.

"The animals are paid for their entertainment value," I said. "We don't send out hampers to monkeys in their own forests" — Or did we? There was no knowing what humane ladies in England would not do — "We bring the monkeys here to amuse us."

"What's amusing about that black creature there?"

"Well, he's very beautiful."

"Beautiful?" Atwater stared into the hostile little face beyond the bars. "Can't see it myself." Then rather truculently, "I suppose you'd say he was more beautiful than me."

"Well, as a matter of fact, since you raise the point ..."

"You think that thing beautiful and feed it and shelter it, while you leave me to starve."

This seemed unfair. I had just given Atwater a pound; moreover, it was not I who had fed the ape. I pointed this out.

"I see," said Atwater. "You're paying me for my entertainment value. You think I'm a kind of monkey."

This was uncomfortably near the truth. "You misunderstand me," I said.

"I hope I do. A remark like that would start a roughhouse at the Wimpole."

A new and glorious idea came to me. "Atwater," I said, cautiously, for his oppressed mood was still on him. "Please do not take offence at my suggestion but, supposing I were to pay — as a loan, of course — would it be possible for us, do you think, to lunch at the Wimpole?"

He took the suggestion quite well. "I'll be frank with you," he said. "I haven't paid this month's sub. yet. It's seven and sixpence."

"We'll include that in the loan."

"Good scout. I know you'll like the place."

The taxi driver, to whom I gave the address "Wimpole Club," was nonplussed. "Now you've got me," he said. "I thought I knew them all. It's not what used to be called the Palm Beach?"

"No," said Atwater, and gave more exact directions.

We drove to a mews off Wimpole Street ("It's handy for chaps in the motor business Great Portland Street way," said Atwater). "By the way, I may as well explain, I'm known as Norton at the club."

"Why?"

"Lots of the chaps there use a different name. I expect it's the same at your club."

"I shouldn't be surprised," I said.

I paid the taxi. Atwater kicked open a green door and led me into the hall where a porter, behind the counter, was lunching off tea and sandwiches.

"I've been out of town," said Atwater. "Just dropped in to pay my subscription. Anyone about?"

"Very quiet," said the porter.

The room into which he led me was entirely empty. It was at once bar, lounge and dining-room, but mostly bar, for which a kind of film-set had been erected, built far into the room, with oak rafters, a thatched roof, a wrought-iron lantern and an inn-sign painted in mock heraldy with quartered bottles and tankards.

"Jim!" cried Atwater.

"Sir." A head appeared above the bar. "Well, Mr. Norton, we haven't seen you for a long time. I was just having my bit of dinner."

"May I interrupt that important function and give my friend here something in the nature of a snorter" — this was a new and greatly expanded version of Atwater the good scout. "Two of your specials, please, Jim." To me, "Jim's specials are famous." To Jim, "This is one of my best pals, Mr. Plant." To me, "There's not much Jim doesn't know about me." To Jim, "Where's the gang?"

"They don't seem to come here like they did, Mr. Norton. There's not the money about."

"You've said it." Jim put two cocktails on the bar before

us. "I presume, Jim, that since this is Mr. Plant's first time among us, in pursuance of the old Wimpole custom, these are on the house?"

Jim laughed rather anxiously. "Mr. Norton likes his joke."

"Joke? Jim, you shame me before my friends. But never fear. I have found a rich backer; if we aren't having this with you, you must have one with us."

The barman poured himself out something from a bottle which he kept for the purpose on a shelf below the bar, and said, "First to-day," as we toasted one another. Atwater said, "It's one of the mysteries of the club what Jim keeps in that bottle of his." I knew; it was what every barman kept, cold tea, but I thought it would spoil Atwater's treat if I told him.

Jim's "special" was strong and agreeable.

"Is it all right for me to order a round?" I asked.

"It's more than all right. It's perfect."

Jim shook up another cocktail and refilled his own glass.

"D'you remember the time I drank twelve of your specials before dinner with Mr. Appleby?"

"I do, sir."

"A tiny bit spifflicated that night, eh, Jim?"

"A tiny bit, sir."

We had further rounds; Jim took cash for the drinks — three shillings a round. After the first round, when Atwater broke into his pound note, I paid. Every other time he said, "Chalk it up to the national debt," or some similar reference to the fiction of our loan. Soon Jim and Atwater were deep in reminiscence of Atwater's past.

After a time I found my thoughts wandering and went to telephone to Victoria Square. Roger answered. "It seems things are coming more or less normally," he said.

"How is she?"

"I haven't been in. The doctor's here now, in a white coat like an umpire. He keeps saying I'm not to worry."

"But is she in danger?"

"Of course she is, it's a dangerous business."

"But I mean, more than most people?"

"Yes. No. I don't know. They said everything was quite normal, whatever that means."

"I suppose it means she's not in more danger than most people."

"I suppose so."

"Does it bore you my ringing up to ask?"

"No, not really. Where are you?"

"At a club called the Wimpole."

"Never heard of it."

"No. I'll tell you about it later. Very interesting."

"Good. Do tell me later."

I returned to the bar. "I thought our old comrade had passed out on us," said Atwater. "Been sick?"

"Good heavens, no."

"You look a terrible colour, doesn't he, Jim? Perhaps a special is what he needs. I was sick that night old Grainger sold his Bentley, sick as a dog. . . ."

When I had spent about thirty shillings Jim began to tire of his cold tea. "Why don't you gentlemen sit down at a table and let me order you a nice grill?" he asked.

"All in good time, Jim, all in good time. Mr. Plant here would like one of your specials first just to give him an appetite, and I think rather than see an old pal drink alone, I'll join him."

Later, when we were very drunk, steaks appeared which

neither of us remembered ordering. We ate them at the bar with, at Jim's advice, great quantities of Worcester sauce. Our conversation, I think, was mainly about Appleby and the need of finding him. We rang up one or two people of that name, whom we found in the telephone book, but they disclaimed all knowledge of Jesuit treasure.

It must have been four o'clock in the afternoon when we left the Wimpole. Atwater was more drunk than I. Next day I remembered most of our conversation verbatim. In the mews I asked him: "Where are you living?"

"Digs. Awful hole. But it's all right now I've got money — I can sleep on the Embankment. Police won't let you sleep on the Embankment unless you've got money. Vagrancy. One law for the rich, one for the poor. Iniquitous system."

"Why don't you come and live with me. I've got a house in the country, plenty of room. Stay as long as you like. Die there."

"Thanks, I will. Must go the Embankment first and pack."

And we separated, for the time, he sauntering unsteadily along Wimpole Street, pass the rows of brass plates, I driving in a taxi to my rooms in Ebury Street, where I undressed, folded my clothes, and went quietly to bed. I awoke, in the dark, hours later, in confusion as to where I was and how I had got there.

The telephone was ringing next door in the sitting-room. It was Roger. He said that Lucy had had a son two hours ago; he had been ringing up relatives ever since. She was perfectly well; the first thing she had asked for when she came round from the chloroform was a cigarette. "I feel like going out and getting drunk," said Roger. "Don't you?"

"No," I said. "No, I'm afraid not," and returned to bed.

✻ ✻ ✻ 4 ✻ ✻ ✻

When I got drunk I could sleep it off and wake in tolerable health; Roger could not; in the past we had often discussed this alcoholic insomnia of his and found no remedy for it except temperance. After telephoning to me he had gone out with Basil; he looked a wreck next morning.

"It's extraordinary," he said. "I've got absolutely no feeling about this baby at all. I kept telling myself all these last months that when I actually saw it, all manner of deep-rooted, atavistic emotions would come surging up. I was all set for a deep spiritual experience. They brought the thing in and showed it to me. I looked at it and waited — and nothing at all happened. It was just like the first time one takes hashish — or being 'confirmed' at school."

"I knew a man who had five children," I said. "He felt just as you did until the fifth. Then he was suddenly overcome with love; he bought a thermometer and kept taking its temperature when the nurse was out of the room. I daresay it's a habit, like hashish."

"I don't feel as if I had anything to do with it. It's as though they showed me Lucy's appendix or a tooth they'd pulled out of her."

"What's it like? I mean, it isn't a freak or anything?"

"No, I've been into that; two arms, two legs, one head, white — just a baby. Of course, you can't tell for some time if it's sane or not. I believe the first sign is that it can't take hold of things with its hands. Did you know that Lucy's grandmother was shut up?"

"I had no idea."

"Yes. Lucy never saw her, of course. It's why she's anxious about Julia."

"Is she anxious about Julia?"

"Who wouldn't be?"

"How soon can you tell if they're blind?"

"Not for weeks, I believe. I asked Sister Kemp. She said, 'The very idea' and whisked the baby off as if I wanted to injure it, poor little brute. D'you know what Lucy calls Sister Kemp now? — Kempy."

"It's not possible."

It was true. I went in to see her for five minutes and twice during that time she said "Kempy." When we were alone for a minute I asked her why. "She asked me to," said Lucy, "and she's really very sweet."

"Sweet?"

"She was absolutely sweet to me yesterday."

I had brought some flowers, but the room was full of them. Lucy lay in bed; slack and smiling. I sat down by her and held her hand. "Everyone's been so sweet," she said. "Have you seen my baby?"

"No."

"He's in the dressing-room. Ask Kempy to show you."

"Are you pleased with him?"

"I love him. I do really. I never thought I should. He's such a *person*."

This was incomprehensible.

"You haven't gone bald?" I said.

"No, but my hair's terrible. What did you do yesterday?"

"I got drunk."

"So did poor Roger. Were you with him?"

"No," I said, "it was really very amusing." I began to tell her about Atwater, but she was not listening.

Then Sister Kemp came in with more flowers — from Mr. Benwell.

"How sweet he is," said Lucy.

This was past bearing — first Sister Kemp, now Mr. Benwell. I felt stifled in this pastry-cook's atmosphere. "I've come to say good-bye," I said. "I'm going back to the country to see about my house."

"I'm so glad. It's lovely for you. I'm coming to see it as soon as I'm better."

She did not want me, I thought; Humboldt's Gibbon and I had done our part. "You'll be my first guest," I said.

"Yes. Quite soon."

Sister Kemp went with me to the landing. "Now," she said, "come and see something very precious."

There was a cradle in Roger's dressing-room, made of white stuff and ribbons, and a baby in it.

"Isn't he a fine big man?"

"Magnificent," I said, "and very sweet . . . Kempy."

POSTSCRIPT

The date of this child's birth was August 25, 1939, and while Lucy was still in bed the air-raid sirens sounded the first false alarm of the Second World War. And so an epoch, my epoch, came to an end. Intellectually we had foreseen the event, and had calmly discussed it, but our inherited habits continued to the last moment.

Beavers bred in captivity, inhabiting a concrete pool, will, if given the timber, fatuously go through all the motions of damming an ancestral stream. So I and my friends busied ourselves with our privacies and intimacies. My father's death, the abandonment of my home, my quickening love of Lucy, my literary innovations, my house in the country — all these had seemed to presage a new life. Ths new life came, not by my contrivance.

Neither book — the last of my old life, the first of my new — was ever finished. As for my house, I never spent a night there. It was requisitioned, filled with pregnant women, and through five years bit by bit befouled and dismembered. My friends were dispersed. Lucy and her baby moved back to her aunt's. Roger rose from department to department in the office of Political Warfare. Basil sought and found a series of irregular adventures. For myself plain regimental soldiering proved an orderly and not disagreeable way of life.

I met Atwater several times in the course of the war — the Good-scout of the officer's club, the Under-dog in the transit-camp, the Dreamer lecturing troops about post-war conditions. He was reunited, it seemed, with all his legendary lost friends, he prospered and the Good-scout predominated. To-day, I believe, he holds sway over a large area of Germany. No one of my close acquaintance was killed, but all our lives, as we had constructed them, quietly came to an end. Our story, like my novel, remained unfinished — a heap of neglected foolscap at the back of a drawer.

1947

❁ ❁ ❁ ❁ ❁ ❁ ❁ ❁ ❁ ❁ ❁ ❁ ❁ ❁ ❁

TACTICAL
EXERCISE

J OHN VERNEY MARRIED ELIZABETH IN 1938, BUT IT WAS NOT
until the winter of 1945 that he came to hate her steadily and
fiercely. There had been countless brief gusts of hate before
this, for it was a thing which came easily to him. He was not
what is normally described as a bad-tempered man, rather the
reverse; a look of fatigue and abstraction was the only visible
sign of the passion which possessed him, as others are possessed by laughter or desire, several times a day.

During the war he passed among those he served with as a
phlegmatic fellow. He did not have his good or his bad days;
they were all uniformly good or bad; good in that he did what
had to be done, expeditiously without ever "getting in a flap"
or "going off the deep end"; bad from the intermittent, invisible sheet-lightning of hate which flashed and flickered deep
inside him at every obstruction or reverse. In his orderly room
when, as a company commander, he faced the morning procession of defaulters and malingerers; in the mess when the
subalterns disturbed his reading by playing the wireless; at
the Staff College when the "syndicate" disagreed with his

solution; at Brigade H.Q. when the staff-sergeant mislaid a file or the telephone orderly muddled a call; when the driver of his car missed a turning; later, in hospital, when the doctor seemed to look too cursorily at his wound and the nurses stood gossiping jauntily at the beds of more likeable patients instead of doing their duty to him — in all the annoyances of army life which others dismissed with an oath and a shrug, John Verney's eyelids drooped wearily, a tiny grenade of hate exploded and the fragments rang and ricocheted round the steel walls of his mind.

There had been less to annoy him before the war. He had some money and the hope of a career in politics. Before marriage he served his apprenticeship to the Liberal party in two hopeless by-elections. The Central Office then rewarded him with a constituency in outer London which offered a fair chance in the next general election. In the eighteen months before the war he nursed this constituency from his flat in Belgravia and travelled frequently on the Continent to study political conditions. These studies convinced him that war was inevitable; he denounced the Munich agreement pungently and secured a commission in the Territorial Army.

Into this peacetime life Elizabeth fitted unobtrusively. She was his cousin. In 1938 she had reached the age of twenty-six, four years his junior, without falling in love. She was a calm, handsome young woman, an only child, with some money of her own and more to come. As a girl, in her first season, an injudicious remark, let slip and overheard, got her the reputation of cleverness. Those who knew her best ruthlessly called her "deep."

Thus condemned to social failure, she languished in the

ballrooms of Pont Street for another year and then settled down to a life of concert-going and shopping with her mother, until she surprised her small circle of friends by marrying John Verney. Courtship and consummation were tepid, cousinly, harmonious. They agreed, in face of coming war, to remain childless. No one knew what Elizabeth felt or thought about anything. Her judgements were mainly negative, deep or dull as you cared to take them. She had none of the appearance of a woman likely to inflame great hate.

John Verney was discharged from the Army early in 1945 with a M.C. and one leg, for the future, two inches shorter than the other. He found Elizabeth living in Hampstead with her parents, his uncle and aunt. She had kept him informed by letter of the changes in her condition, but, preoccupied, he had not clearly imagined them. Their flat had been requisitioned by a government office; their furniture and books sent to a repository and totally lost, partly burned by a bomb, partly pillaged by firemen. Elizabeth, who was a linguist, had gone to work in a clandestine branch of the Foreign Office.

Her parents' house had once been a substantial Georgian villa overlooking the Heath. John Verney arrived there early in the morning after a crowded night's journey from Liverpool. The wrought-iron railings and gates had been rudely torn away by the salvage collectors, and in the front garden, once so neat, weeds and shrubs grew in a rank jungle trampled at night by courting soldiers. The back garden was a single, small bomb-crater; heaped clay, statuary and the bricks and glass of ruined greenhouses; dry stalks of willow-herb stood breast high over the mounds. All the windows were gone from the back of the house, replaced by shutters of card and board, which put the main rooms in perpetual darkness. "Welcome to Chaos and Old Night," said his uncle genially.

There were no servants; the old had fled, the young had been conscribed for service. Elizabeth made him some tea before leaving for her office.

Here he lived, lucky, Elizabeth told him, to have a home. Furniture was unprocurable, furnished flats commanded a price beyond their income, which was now taxed to a bare wage. They might have found something in the country, but Elizabeth, being childless, could not get release from her work. Moreover, he had his constituency.

This, too, was transformed. A factory wired round like a prisoner-of-war camp stood in the public gardens. The streets surrounding it, once the trim houses of potential Liberals, had been bombed, patched, confiscated, and filled with an immigrant proletarian population. Every day he received a heap of complaining letters from constituents exiled in provincial boarding-houses. He had hoped that his decoration and his limp might earn him sympathy, but he found the new inhabitants indifferent to the fortunes of war. Instead they showed a sceptical curiosity about Social Security. "They're nothing but a lot of reds," said the Liberal agent.

"You mean I shan't get in?"

"Well, we'll give them a good fight. The Tories are putting up a Battle-of-Britain pilot. I'm afraid he'll get most of what's left of the middle-class vote."

In the event John Verney came bottom of the poll, badly. A rancorous Jewish schoolteacher was elected. The Central Office paid his deposit, but the election had cost him dear. And when it was over there was absolutely nothing for John Verney to do.

He remained in Hampstead, helped his aunt make the beds after Elizabeth had gone to her office, limped to the green-grocer and fishmonger and stood, full of hate, in the queues; helped Elizabeth wash up at night. They ate in the kitchen, where his aunt cooked deliciously the scanty rations. His uncle went three days a week to help pack parcels for Java.

Elizabeth, the deep one, never spoke of her work, which, in fact, was concerned with setting up hostile and oppressive governments in Eastern Europe. One evening at a restaurant, a man came and spoke to her, a tall young man whose sallow, aquiline face was full of intellect and humour. "That's the head of my department," she said. "He's so amusing."

"Looks like a Jew."

"I believe he is. He's a strong Conservative and hates the work," she added hastily, for since his defeat in the election John had become fiercely anti-Semitic.

"There is absolutely no need to work for the State now," he said. "The war's over."

"Our work is just beginning. They won't let any of us go. You must understand what conditions are in this coun-try."

It often fell to Elizabeth to explain "conditions" to him. Strand by strand, knot by knot, through the coalless winter, she exposed the vast net of governmental control which had been woven in his absence. He had been reared in traditional Liberalism and the system revolted him. More than this, it had him caught, personally, tripped up, tied, tangled; wherever he wanted to go, whatever he wanted to do or have done, he found himself baffled and frustrated. And as Elizabeth ex-plained she found herself defending. This regulation was nec-essary to avoid that ill; such a country was suffering, as Britain was not, for having neglected such a precaution; and so on, calmly and reasonably.

"I know it's maddening, John, but you must realize it's the same for everyone."

"That's what all you bureaucrats want," he said. "Equality through slavery. The two-class state — proletarians and officials."

Elizabeth was part and parcel of it. She worked for the State and the Jews. She was a collaborator with the new, alien, occupying power. And as the winter wore on and the gas burned feebly in the stove, and the rain blew in through the patched windows, as at length spring came and buds broke in the obscene wilderness round the house, Elizabeth in his mind became something more important. She became a symbol. For just as soldiers in far-distant camps think of their wives, with a tenderness they seldom felt at home, as the embodiment of all the good things they have left behind, wives who perhaps were scolds and drabs, but in the desert and jungle become transfigured until their trite air-letters become texts of hope, so Elizabeth grew in John Verney's despairing mind to more than human malevolence as the archpriestess and maenad of the century of the common man.

"You aren't looking well, John," said his aunt. "You and Elizabeth ought to get away for a bit. She is due for leave at Easter."

"The State is granting her a supplementary ration of her husband's company, you mean. Are we sure she has filled in all the correct forms? Or are commissars of her rank above such things?"

Uncle and aunt laughed uneasily. John made his little jokes

with such an air of weariness, with such a droop of the eyelids that they sometimes struck chill in that family circle. Elizabeth regarded him gravely and silently.

John was far from well. His leg was in constant pain so that he no longer stood in queues. He slept badly; as also, for the first time in her life, did Elizabeth. They shared a room now, for the winter rains had brought down ceilings in many parts of the shaken house and the upper rooms were thought to be unsafe. They had twin beds on the ground floor in what had once been her father's library.

In the first days of his homecoming John had been amorous. Now he never approached her. They lay night after night six feet apart in the darkness. Once when John had been awake for two hours he turned on the lamp that stood on the table between them. Elizabeth was lying with her eyes wide open staring at the ceiling.

"I'm sorry. Did I wake you?"

"I haven't been asleep."

"I thought I'd read for a bit. Will it disturb you?"

"Not at all."

She turned away. John read for an hour. He did not know whether she was awake or asleep when he turned off the light.

Often after that he longed to put on the light, but was afraid to find her awake and staring. Instead he lay, as others lie in a luxurious rapture of love, hating her.

It did not occur to him to leave her; or, rather, it did occur from time to time, but he hopelessly dismissed the thought. Her life was bound tight to his; her family was his family; their finances were intertangled and their expectations lay together in the same quarters. To leave her would be to start fresh, alone and naked in a strange world; and lame and weary at the age of thirty-eight, John Verney had not the heart to move.

He loved no one else. He had nowhere to go, nothing to do. Moreover he suspected, of late, that it would not hurt her if he went. And, above all, the single steadfast desire left to him was to do her ill. "I wish she were dead," he said to himself as he lay awake at night. "I wish she were dead."

Sometimes they went out together. As the winter passed, John took to dining once or twice a week at his club. He assumed that on these occasions she stayed at home, but one morning it transpired that she too had dined out the evening before. He did not ask with whom, but his aunt did, and Elizabeth replied, "Just someone from the office."

"The Jew?" John asked.

"As a matter of fact, it was."

"I hope you enjoyed it."

"Quite. A beastly dinner, of course, but he's very amusing."

One night when he returned from his club, after a dismal little dinner and two crowded Tube journeys, he found Elizabeth in bed and deeply asleep. She did not stir when he entered. Unlike her normal habit, she was snoring. He stood for a minute, fascinated by this new and unlovely aspect of her, her head thrown back, her mouth open and slightly dribbling at the corner. Then he shook her. She muttered something, turned over and slept heavily and soundlessly.

Half an hour later, as he was striving to compose himself for sleep, she began to snore again. He turned on the light, and looked at her more closely and noticed with surprise, which suddenly changed to joyous hope, that there was a tube of unfamiliar pills, half empty, beside her on the bed table.

He examined it. "*24 Comprimés narcotiques, hypnotiques,*" he read, and then in large scarlet letters, "NE PAS DEPASSER DEUX." He counted those which were left. Eleven.

With tremulous butterfly wings hope began to flutter in his heart, became a certainty. He felt a fire kindle and spread inside him until he was deliciously suffused in every limb and organ. He lay, listening to the snores, with the pure excitement of a child on Christmas Eve. "I shall wake up tomorrow and find her dead," he told himself, as once he had felt the flaccid stocking at the foot of his bed and told himself, "Tomorrow I shall wake up and find it full." Like a child, he longed to sleep to hasten the morning and, like a child, he was wildly, ecstatically sleepless. Presently he swallowed two of the pills himself and almost at once was unconscious.

Elizabeth always rose first to make breakfast for the family. She was at the dressing-table when sharply, without drowsiness, his memory stereoscopically clear about the incidents of the night before, John awoke. "You've been snoring," she said.

Disappointment was so intense that at first he could not speak. Then he said, "You snored, too, last night."

"It must be the sleeping-tablet I took. I must say it gave me a good night."

"Only one?"

"Yes, two's the most that's safe."

"Where did you get them?"

"A friend at the office — the one you called the Jew. He has them prescribed by a doctor for when he's working too hard. I told him I wasn't sleeping, so he gave me half a bottle."

"Could he get me some?"

"I expect so. He can do most things like that."

So he and Elizabeth began to drug themselves regularly

and passed long, vacuous nights. But often John delayed, letting the beatific pill lie beside his glass of water, while knowing the vigil was terminable at will, he postponed the joy of unconsciousness, heard Elizabeth's snores, and hated her sumptuously.

One evening while the plans for the holiday were still under discussion, John and Elizabeth went to the cinema. The film was a murder story of no great ingenuity but with showy scenery. A bride murdered her husband by throwing him out of a window, down a cliff. Things were made easy for her by his taking a lonely lighthouse for their honeymoon. He was very rich and she wanted his money. All she had to do was confide in the local doctor and a few neighbours that her husband frightened her by walking in his sleep; she doped his coffee, dragged him from the bed to the balcony — a feat of some strength — where she had already broken away a yard of balustrade, and rolled him over. Then she went back to bed, gave the alarm next morning, and wept over the mangled body which was presently discovered half awash on the rocks. Retribution overtook her later, but at the time the thing was a complete success.

"I wish it were as easy as that," thought John, and in a few hours the whole tale had floated away in those lightless attics of the mind where films and dreams and funny stories lie spider-shrouded for a lifetime unless, as sometimes happens, an intruder brings them to light.

Such a thing happened a few weeks later when John and Elizabeth went for their holiday. Elizabeth found the place. It belonged to someone in her office. It was named Good Hope Fort, and stood on the Cornish coast. "It's only just been derequisitioned," she said; "I expect we shall find it in pretty bad condition."

"We're used to that," said John. It did not occur to him that she should spend her leave anywhere but with him. She was as much part of him as his maimed and aching leg.

They arrived on a gusty April afternoon after a train journey of normal discomfort. A taxi dove them eight miles from the station, through deep Cornish lanes, past granite cottages and disused, archaic tin-workings. They reached the village which gave the house its postal address, passed through it and out along a track which suddenly emerged from its high banks into open grazing land on the cliff's edge, high, swift clouds and sea-birds wheeling overhead, the turf at their feet alive with fluttering wild flowers, salt in the air, below them the roar of the Atlantic breaking on the rocks, a middle-distance of indigo and white tumbled waters and beyond it the serene arc of the horizon. Here was the house.

"Your father," said John, "would now say, 'Your castle hath a pleasant seat.' "

"Well, it has rather, hasn't it?"

It was a small stone building on the very edge of the cliff, built a century or so ago for defensive purposes, converted to a private house in the years of peace, taken again by the Navy during the war as a signal station, now once more reverting to gentler uses. Some coils of rusty wire, a mast, the concrete foundations of a hut, gave evidence of its former masters.

They carried their things into the house and paid the taxi.

"A woman comes up every morning from the village. I said we shouldn't want her this evening. I see she's left us some oil for the lamps. She's got a fire going too, bless her, and plenty of wood. Oh, and look what I've got as a present from father. I promised not to tell you until we arrived. A bottle of whisky. Wasn't it sweet of him. He's been hoarding his ration for three months . . . " Elizabeth talked brightly as she began to arrange the luggage. "There's a room for each of us. This is the only proper living-room, but there's a study in case you feel like doing any work. I believe we shall be quite comfortable . . . "

The living-room was built with two stout bays, each with a French window opening on a balcony which over-hung the sea. John opened one and the sea-wind filled the room. He stepped out, breathed deeply, and then said suddenly: "Hullo, this is dangerous."

At one place, between the windows, the cast-iron balustrade had broken away and the stone ledge lay open over the cliff. He looked at the gap and at the foaming rocks below, momentarily puzzled. The irregular polyhedron of memory rolled uncertainly and came to rest.

He had been here before, a few weeks ago, on the gallery of the lighthouse in that swiftly forgotten film. He stood there, looking down. It was exactly thus that the waves had come swirling over the rocks, had broken and dropped back with the spray falling about them. This was the sound they had made; this was the broken ironwork and the sheer edge.

Elizabeth was still talking in the room, her voice drowned by wind and sea. John returned to the room, shut and fastened the door. In the quiet she was saying " . . . only got the furniture out of store last week. He left the woman from the village to arrange it. She's got some queer ideas, I must say. Just look where she put . . . "

"What did you say this house was called?"

"Good Hope."

"A good name."

That evening John drank a glass of his father-in-law's whisky, smoked a pipe and planned. He had been a good tactician. He made a leisurely, mental "appreciation of the situation." Object: murder.

When they rose to go to bed he asked: "You packed the tablets?"

"Yes, a new tube. But I am sure I shan't want any tonight."

"Neither shall I," said John, "the air is wonderful."

During the following days he considered the tactical problem. It was entirely simple. He had the "staff-solution" already. He considered it in the words and form he had used in the Army. " . . . Courses open to the enemy . . . achievement of surprise . . . consolidation of success." The staff-solution was exemplary. At the beginning of the first week, he began to put it into execution.

Already, by easy stages, he had made himself known in the village. Elizabeth was a friend of the owner; he the returned hero, still a little strange in civvy street. "The first holiday my wife and I have had together for six years," he told them in the golf club and, growing more confidential at the bar, hinted that they were thinking of making up for lost time and starting a family.

On another evening he spoke of war-strain, of how in this war the civilians had had a worse time of it than the services. His wife, for instance; stuck it all through the blitz; office work all day, bombs at night. She ought to get right away, alone somewhere for a long stretch; her nerves had suffered; nothing serious, but to tell the truth he wasn't quite happy about it. As a matter of fact he had found her walking in her sleep once or twice in London.

His companions knew of similar cases; nothing to worry about, but it wanted watching; didn't want it to develop into anything worse. Had she seen a doctor?

Not yet, John said. In fact she didn't know she had been sleep-walking. He had got her back to bed without waking her. He hoped the sea air would do her good. In fact, she seemed much better already. If she showed any more signs of the trouble when they got home, he knew a very good man to take her to.

The golf club was full of sympathy. John asked if there were a good doctor in the neighbourhood. Yes, they said, old Mackenzie in the village, a first-class man, wasted in a little place like this; not at all a stick-in-the-mud. Read the latest books; psychology and all that. They couldn't think why Old Mack had never specialized and made a name for himself.

"I think I might go and talk to Old Mack about it," said John.

"Do. You couldn't find a better fellow."

Elizabeth had a fortnight's leave. There were still three days to go when John went off to the village to consult Dr. Mackenzie. He found a grey-haired, genial bachelor in a consulting room that was more like a lawyer's office than a physician's, book-lined, dark, permeated by tobacco smoke.

Seated in the shabby leather armchair he developed in more precise language the story he had told in the golf club. Dr. Mackenzie listened without comment.

"It's the first time I've run against anything like this," he concluded.

At length Dr. Mackenzie said: "You got pretty badly knocked about in the war, Mr. Verney?"

"My knee. It still gives me trouble."

"Bad time in hospital?"

"Three months. A beastly place outside Rome."

"There's always a good deal of nervous shock in an injury of that kind. It often persists when the wound is healed."

"Yes, but I don't quite understand . . . "

"My dear Mr. Verney, your wife asked me to say nothing about it, but I think I must tell you that she has already been here to consult me on this matter."

"About her sleep-walking? But she can't . . . " Then John stopped.

"My dear fellow, I quite understand. She thought you didn't know. Twice lately you've been out of bed and she had to lead you back. She knows all about it."

John could find nothing to say.

"It's not the first time," Dr. Mackenzie continued, "that I've been consulted by patients who have told me their symptoms and said they had come on behalf of friends or relations. Usually it's girls who think they're in a family-way. It's an interesting feature of your case that you should want to ascribe the trouble to someone else, probably the decisive feature. I've given your wife the name of a man in London who I think will be able to help you. Meanwhile I can advise plenty of exercise, light meals at night . . . "

John Verney limped back to Good Hope Fort in a state of consternation. Security had been compromised; the operation must be cancelled; initiative had been lost . . . all the phrases of the tactical school came to his mind, but he was still numb after this unexpected reverse. A vast and naked horror peeped at him and was thrust aside.

When he got back Elizabeth was laying the supper table. He stood on the balcony and stared at the gaping rails with eyes smarting with disappointment. It was dead calm that evening. The rising tide lapped and fell and mounted again silently among the rocks below. He stood gazing down, then he turned back into the room.

There was one large drink left in the whisky bottle. He poured it out and swallowed it. Elizabeth brought in the supper and they sat down. Gradually his mind grew a little calmer. They usually ate in silence. At last he said: "Elizabeth, why did you tell the doctor I had been walking in my sleep?"

She quietly put down the plate she had been holding and looked at him curiously. "Why?" she said gently. "Because I was worried, of course. I didn't think you knew about it."

"But have I been?"

"Oh yes, several times — in London and here. I didn't think it mattered at first, but the night before last I found you on the balcony, quite near that dreadful hole in the rails. I was really frightened. But it's going to be alright now. Dr. Mackenzie has given me the name . . . "

It was possible, thought John Verney; nothing was more likely.

He had lived night and day for ten days thinking of that opening, of the sea and rock below, the ragged ironwork and the sharp edge of stone. He suddenly felt defeated, sick and stupid, as he had as he lay on the Italian hillside with his smashed knee. Then as now he had felt weariness even more than pain.

"Coffee, darling."

Suddenly he roused himself. "No," he almost shouted. "No, no, no."

"Darling, what is the matter? Don't get excited. Are you feeling ill? Lie down on the sofa near the window."

He did as he was told. He felt so weary that he could barely move from his chair.

"Do you think coffee would keep you awake, love? You look quite fit to drop already. There, lie down."

He lay down, like the tide slowly mounting among the rocks below, sleep rose and spread in his mind. He nodded and woke with a start.

"Shall I open the window, darling, and give you some air?"

"Elizabeth," he said, "I feel as if I have been drugged." Like the rocks below the window — now awash, now emerging clear from falling water; now awash again deeper; now barely visible, mere patches on the face of gently eddying foam — his brain was softly drowning. He roused himself, as children do in nightmare, still scared, still half asleep. "I can't be drugged," he said loudly, "I never touched the coffee."

"Drugs in the coffee?" said Elizabeth gently, like a nurse soothing a fractious child. "Drugs in the *coffee?* What an absurd idea. That's the kind of thing that only happens on the films, darling."

He did not hear her. He was fast asleep, snoring stertorously by the open window.

1953

✻ ✻ ✻ ✻ ✻ ✻ ✻ ✻ ✻ ✻ ✻ ✻ ✻ ✻ ✻

LOVE
AMONG THE RUINS

Despite their promises at the last election, the politicians had not yet changed the climate. The State Meteorological Institute had so far produced only an unseasonable fall of snow and two little thunderbolts no larger than apricots. The weather varied from day to day and from county to county as it had done of old, most anomalously.

This was a rich, old-fashioned Tennysonian night.

Strains of a string quartet floated out from the drawing-room windows and were lost amid the splash and murmur of the gardens. In the basin the folded lilies had left a brooding sweetness over the water. No gold fin winked in the porphyry font and any peacock which seemed to be milkily drooping in the moon-shadows was indeed a ghost, for the whole flock of them had been found mysteriously and rudely slaughtered a day or two ago in the first disturbing flush of this sudden summer.

Miles, sauntering among the sleeping flowers, was suffused with melancholy. He did not much care for music and this was his last evening at Mountjoy. Never again, perhaps, would he be free to roam these walks.

Mountjoy had been planned and planted in the years of which he knew nothing; generations of skilled and patient husbandmen had weeded and dunged and pruned; generations of dilettanti had watered it with cascades and jets, generations of collectors had lugged statuary here; all, it seemed, for his enjoyment this very night under this huge moon. Miles knew nothing of such periods and processes, but he felt an incomprehensible tidal pull towards the circumjacent splendours.

Eleven struck from the stables. The music ceased. Miles turned back, and as he reached the terrace, the shutters began to close and the great chandeliers were one by one extinguished. By the light of the sconces which still shone on their panels of faded satin and clouded gold, he joined the company dispersing to bed through the islands of old furniture.

His room was not one of the grand succession which lay along the garden front. Those were reserved for murderers. Nor was it on the floor above, tenanted mostly by sexual offenders. His was a humbler wing. Indeed he overlooked the luggage porch and the coal bunker. Only professional men visiting Mountjoy on professional business and very poor relations had been put here in the old days. But Miles was attached to this room, which was the first he had ever called his own in all his twenty years of Progress.

His next-door neighbour, a Mr. Sweat, paused at his door to say good-night. It was only now after twenty months' proximity, when Miles's time was up, that this veteran had begun to unbend. He and a man named Soapy, survivals of another age, had kept themselves to themselves, talking wistfully of cribs they had cracked, of sparklers, of snug bar-parlours where they had met their favourite fences, of strenuous penal days at the Scrubs and on the Moor. They had small use for the younger generation; crime, calvinism and classical music were their interests. But at last Mr. Sweat had taken to nodding, to grunting, and finally, too late for friendship, to speaking to Miles.

"What price the old strings tonight, chum?" he asked.

"I wasn't there, Mr. Sweat."

"You missed a treat. Of course nothing's ever good enough for old Soapy. Made me fair sick to hear Soapy going on all the time. The viola was scratchy, Soapy says. They played the Mozart just like it was Haydn. No feeling in the Debussy pizzicato, says Soapy."

"Soapy knows too much."

"Soapy knows a lot more than some I could mention, schooling or no schooling. Next time they're going to do the Grosse Fugue as the last movement of the B flat. That's something to look forward to, that is, though Soapy says no late Beethoven comes off. We'll see. Leastways, me and Soapy will; *you* won't. You're off tomorrow. Pleased?"

"Not particularly."

"No, no more wouldn't I be. It's a funny thing but I've settled down here wonderful. Never thought I should. It all seemed a bit too posh at first. Not like the old Scrubs. But it's a real pretty place once you're used to it. Wouldn't mind settling here for a lifer if they'd let me. The trouble is there's no security in crime these days. Time was, you knew just what a job was worth, six months, three years; whatever it was, you knew where you were. Now what with prison commissioners and Preventative Custody and Corrective Treatment they can keep you in or push you out just as it suits them. It's not right.

"I'll tell you what it is, chum," continued Mr. Sweat. "There's no understanding of crime these days like what there was. I remember when I was a nipper, the first time I came up before the beak, he spoke up straight: 'My lad,' he says, 'you are embarking upon a course of life that can only lead to disaster and degradation in this world and everlasting damnation in the next.' Now that's talking. It's plain sense and it shows a personal interest. But last time I was up, when they sent me here, they called me an 'antisocial phenomenon'; said I was 'maladjusted.' That's no way to speak of a man what was doing time before they was in long trousers, now is it?"

"They said something of the same kind to me."

"Yes and now they're giving you the push, just like you hadn't no Rights. I tell you it's made a lot of the boys uncomfortable your going out all of a sudden like this. Who'll it be next time, that's what we're wondering?

"I tell you where you went wrong, chum. You didn't give enough trouble. You made it too easy for them to say you was cured. Soapy and me got wise to that. You remember them birds as got done in? That was Soapy and me. They took a lot of killing too; powerful great bastards. But we got the evidence all hid away tidy and if there's ever any talk of me and Soapy being 'rehabilitated' we'll lay it out conspicuous.

"Well, so long, chum. Tomorrow's my morning for Remedial Repose so I daresay you'll be off before I get down. Come back soon."

"I hope so," said Miles and turned alone into his own room.

He stood briefly at the window and gazed his last on the cobbled-yard. He made a good figure of a man, for he came of handsome parents and all his life had been carefully fed and doctored and exercised; well clothed too. He wore the drab serge dress that was the normal garb of the period — only certified homosexuals wore colours — but there were differences of fit and condition among these uniforms. Miles displayed the handiwork of tailor and valet. He belonged to a privileged class.

The State had made him.

No clean-living, God-fearing, Victorian gentleman, he; no complete man of the Renaissance; no gentil knight nor dutiful pagan nor, even, noble savage. All that succession of past worthies had gone its way, content to play a prelude to Miles. He was the Modern Man.

His history, as it appeared in multuplet in the filing cabinets of numberless State departments, was typical of a thousand others. Before his birth the politicians had succeeded in bringing down his father and mother to penury; they, destitute, had thrown themselves into the simple diversions of the very poor and thus, between one war and the next, set in motion a chain-reaction of divorces which scattered them and their various associates in forlorn couples all over the Free World. The aunt on whom the infant Miles had been quartered was conscribed for work in a factory and shortly afterwards died of boredom at the conveyer-belt. The child was put to safety in an orphanage.

Huge sums were thenceforward spent upon him; sums which, fifty years earlier, would have sent whole quiversful of boys to Winchester and New College and established them in the learned professions. In halls adorned with Picassos and Legers he yawned through long periods of Constructive Play.

He never lacked the requisite cubic feet of air. His diet was balanced and on the first Friday of every month he was psycho-analysed. Every detail of his adolescence was recorded and microfilmed and filed, until at the appropriate age he was transferred to the Air Force.

There were no aeroplanes at the station to which he was posted. It was an institution to train instructors to train instructors to train instructors in Personal Recreation.

There for some weeks he tended a dish-washing machine and tended it, as his adjutant testified at his trial, in an exemplary fashion. The work in itself lacked glory, but it was the normal novitiate. Men from the orphanages provided the hard core of the Forces, a caste apart which united the formidable qualities of Janissary and Junker. Miles had been picked early for high command. Dish-washing was only the beginning. The adjutant, an orphan too, had himself washed both dishes and officers' underclothes, he testified, before rising to his present position.

Courts martial had been abolished some years before this. The Forces handed their defaulters over to the civil arm for treatment. Miles came up at quarter sessions. It was plain from the start, when Arson, Wilful Damage, Manslaughter, Prejudicial Conduct and Treason were struck out of the Indictment and the whole reduced to a simple charge of Antisocial Activity, that the sympathies of the Court were with the prisoner.

The Station Psychologist gave his opinion that an element of incendiarism was inseparable from adolescence. Indeed, if checked, it might produce morbid neurosis. For his part he thought the prisoner had performed a perfectly normal act and, moreover, had shown more than normal intelligence in its execution.

At this point some widows, mothers and orphans of the incinerated airmen set up an outcry from the public gallery and were sharply reminded from the Bench that this was a Court of Welfare and not a meeting of the Housewives' Union.

The case developed into a concerted eulogy of the accused. An attempt by the prosecution to emphasise the extent of the damage was rebuked from the Bench.

"The jury," he said, "will expunge from their memories these sentimental details which have been most improperly introduced."

"May be a detail to you," said a voice from the gallery. "He was a good husband to me."

"Arrest that woman," said the Judge.

Order was restored and the panegyrics continued.

At last the Bench summed up. He reminded the jury that it was a first principle of the New Law that no man could be held responsible for the consequences of his own acts. The jury must dismiss from their minds the consideration that much valuable property and many valuable lives had been lost and the cause of Personal Recreation gravely retarded. They had merely to decide whether in fact the prisoner had arranged inflammable material at various judiciously selected points in the Institution and had ignited them. If he had done so, and the evidence plainly indicated that he had, he contravened the Standing Orders of the Institution and was thereby liable to the appropriate penalties.

Thus directed the jury brought in a verdict of guilty coupled with a recommendation of mercy towards the various bereaved persons who from time to time in the course of the hearing had been committed for contempt. The Bench reprimanded the jury for presumption and impertinence in the matter of the prisoners held in contempt, and sentenced Miles to residence during the State's pleasure at Mountjoy Castle (the ancestral seat of a maimed V.C. of the Second World War, who had been sent to a Home for the Handicapped when the place was converted into a gaol).

The State was capricious in her pleasures. For nearly two years Miles enjoyed her particular favours. Every agreeable remedial device was applied to him and applied, it was now proclaimed, successfully. Then without warning a few days back, while he lay dozing under a mulberry tree, the unexpected blow had fallen; they had come to him, the Deputy Chief-Guide and the sub-Deputy, and told him bluntly and brutally that he was rehabilitated.

Now on this last night he knew he was to wake tomorrow on a harsh world. Nevertheless he slept and was gently awoken for the last time to the familiar scent of china tea on his bed table, the thin bread and butter, the curtains drawn above the luggage porch, the sunlit kitchen-yard and the stable clock just visible behind the cut-leaf copper beech.

He breakfasted late and alone. The rest of the household were already engaged in the first community-songs of the day. Presently he was called to the Guidance Office.

Since his first day at Mountjoy, when with other entrants Miles had been addressed at length by the Chief Guide on the Aims and Achievements of the New Penology, they had seldom met. The Chief Guide was almost always addressing penological conferences.

The Guidance Office was the former house-keeper's room

stripped now of its plush and patriotic pictures; sadly tricked out instead with standard civil-service equipment, class A.

It was full of people.

"This is Miles Plastic," said the Chief Guide. "Sit down, Miles. You can see from the presence of our visitors this morning what an important occasion this it."

Miles took a chair and looked and saw seated beside the Chief Guide two elderly men whose faces were familiar from the television screen as prominent colleagues in the Coalition Government. They wore open flannel shirts, blazers with numerous pens and pencils protruding from the breast pocket, and baggy trousers. This was the dress of very high politicians.

"The Minister of Welfare and the Minister of Rest and Culture," continued the Chief Guide. "The stars to which we have hitched our waggon. Have the press got the hand-out?"

"Yes, Chief."

"And the photographers are all ready?"

"Yes, Chief."

"Then I can proceed."

He proceeded as he had done at countless congresses, at countless spas and university cities. He concluded, as he always did: "In the New Britain which we are building, there are no criminals. There are only the victims of inadequate social services."

The Minister of Welfare, who had not reached his present eminence without the help of a certain sharpness in debate, remarked: "But I understood that Plastic is from one of our own orphanages . . ."

"Plastic is recognised as a Special Case," said the Chief Guide.

The Minister of Rest and Culture, who in the old days had more than once done time himself, said: "Well, Plastic, lad, from all they do say I reckon you've been uncommon smart."

"Exactly," said the Chief Guide. "Miles is our first success, the vindication of the Method."

"Of all the new prisons established in the first glorious wave of Reform, Mountjoy alone has produced a complete case of rehabilitation," the Minister of Welfare said. "You may or may not be aware that the Method has come in for a good deal of criticism both in Parliament and outside. There are a lot of young hot-heads who take their inspiration from our Great Neighbour in the East. You can quote the authorities to them till you're black in the face, but they are always pressing for all the latest gadgets of capital and corporal punishment, for chain gangs and solitary confinement, bread and water, the cat-o'-nine-tails, the rope and the block, and all manner of new-fangled nonsense. They think we're a lot of old fogeys. Thank goodness we've still got the solid sense of the people behind us, but we're on the defensive now. We have to show results. That's why we're here this morning. To show them results. *You* are our Result."

These were solemn words and Miles in some measure responded to the occasion. He gazed before him blankly with an expression that might seem to be awe.

"You'd best watch your step now, lad," said the Minister of Rest and Culture.

"Photographs," said the Minister of Welfare. "Yes, shake *my* hand. Turn towards the cameras. Try to smile."

Bulbs flashed all over the dreary little room.

"State be with you," said the Minister of Welfare.

"Give us a paw, lad," said the Minister of Rest and Culture, taking Miles's hand in his turn. "And no funny business, mind."

Then the politicians departed.

"The Deputy-Chief will attend to all the practical matters," said the Chief wearily. "Go and see him now."

Miles went.

"Well, Miles, from now on I must call you Mr. Plastic," said the Deputy-Chief. "In less than a minute you become a Citizen. This little pile of papers is *You*. When I stamp them, Miles the Problem ceases to exist and Mr. Plastic the Citizen is born. We are sending you to Satellite City, the nearest Population Centre, where you will be attached to the Ministry of Welfare as a sub-official. In view of your special training you are not being classified as a Worker. The immediate material rewards, of course, are not as great. But you are definitely in the Service. We have set your foot on the bottom rung of the non-competitive ladder."

The Deputy Chief Guide picked up the rubber stamp and proceeded to his work of creation. Flip-thump, flip-thump the papers were turned and stained.

"There you are, Mr. Plastic," said the Deputy-Chief handing Miles, as it were, the baby.

At last Miles spoke: "What must I do to get back here?" he asked.

"Come, come, you're rehabilitated now, remember. It is your turn to give back to the State some of the service the State has given you. You will report this morning to the Area Progressive. Transport has been laid on. State be with you,

Mr. Plastic. Be careful, that's your Certificate of Human Personality you've dropped — a *vital* document."

☼ ☼ ☼ 2 ☼ ☼ ☼

Satellite City, one of a hundred such grand conceptions, was not yet in its teens, but already the Dome of Security showed signs of wear. This was the name of the great municipal edifice about which the city was planned. The eponymous dome had looked well enough in the architect's model, shallow certainly but amply making up in girth what it lacked in height, the daring exercise of some new trick of construction. But to the surprise of all, when the building arose and was seen from the ground, the dome blandly vanished. It was hidden for ever among the roofs and butting shoulders of the ancillary wings and was never seen again from the outside except by airmen and steeplejacks. Only the name remained. On the day of its dedication, among massed politicians and People's Choirs the great lump of building materials had shone fine as a factory in all its brilliance of glass and new concrete. Since then, during one of the rather frequent weekends of international panic, it had been camouflaged and its windows blackened. Cleaners were few and usually on strike. So the Dome of Security remained blotched and dingy, the sole permanent building of Satellite City. There were no workers' flats, no officials' garden suburb, no parks, no playgrounds yet. These were all on the drawing-boards in the surveyor's office, tattered at the edges, ringed by tea-cups;

their designer long since cremated and his ashes scattered among the docks and nettles. Thus the Dome of Security comprised, even more than had been intended, all the aspirations and amenities of the city.

The officials subsisted in perpetual twilight. Great sheets of glass planned to "trap" the sun, admitted few gleams from scratches in their coat of tar. At evening when the electric light came on, there was a faint glow, here and there. When, as often, the power-station was "shedding its load" the officials stopped work early and groped their way back to their darkened huts where in the useless refrigerators their tiny rations were quietly putrefying. On working days the officials, male and female, trudged through cigarette ends round and round, up and down what had once been lift-shafts, in a silent, shabby, shadowy procession.

Among these pilgrims of the dusk, in the weeks that followed his discharge from Mountjoy, moved the exiled Miles Plastic.

He was in a key department.

Euthanasia had not been part of the original 1945 Health Service; it was a Tory measure designed to attract votes from the aged and the mortally sick. Under the Bevan-Eden Coalition the Service came into general use and won instant popularity. The Union of Teachers was pressing for its application to difficult children. Foreigners came in such numbers to take advantage of the service that immigration authorities now turned back the bearers of single tickets.

Miles recognised the importance of his appointment even before he began work. On his first evening in the hostel his fellow sub-officials gathered round to question him.

"Euthanasia? I say, you're in luck. They work you jolly

hard, of course, but it's the one department that's expanding."

"You'll get promoted before you know your way about."

"Great State! You *must* have pull. Only the very bright boys get posted to Euthanasia."

"I've been in Contraception for five years. It's a blind alley."

"They say that in a year or two Euthanasia will have taken over Pensions."

"You must be an orphan."

"Yes, I am."

"That accounts for it. Orphans get all the plums. I had a Full Family Life, State help me."

It was gratifying, of course, this respect and envy. It was well to have fine prospects; but for the time being Miles's duties were humble enough.

He was junior sub-official in a staff of half a dozen. The Director was an elderly man called Dr. Beamish, a man whose character had been formed in the nervous thirties, now much embittered, like many of his contemporaries, by the fulfillment of his early hopes. He had signed manifestos in his hot youth, had raised his fist in Barcelona and had painted abstractedly for *Horizon;* he had stood beside Spender at great concourses of Youth, and written "publicity" for the Last Viceroy. Now his reward had come to him. He held the most envied post in Satellite City and, sardonically, he was making the worst of it. Dr. Beamish rejoiced in every attenuation of official difficulties.

Satellite City was said to be the worst served Euthanasia Centre in the State. Dr. Beamish's patients were kept waiting so long that often they died natural deaths before he found it convenient to poison them.

His small staff respected Dr. Beamish. They were all of the official class, for it was part of the grim little game which Dr. Beamish played with the higher authorities to economise extravagantly. His department, he maintained, could not, on its present allotment, afford workers. Even the furnace-man and the girl who despatched unwanted false teeth to the Dental Redistribution Centre were sub-officials.

Sub-officials were cheap and plentiful. The universities turned them out in thousands every year. Indeed, ever since the Incitement to Industry Act of 1955, which exempted workers from taxation — that great and popular measure of reform which had consolidated the now permanent Coalition Government — there had been a nefarious one-way traffic of expensively State-educated officials "passing," as it was called, into the ranks of the workers.

Miles's duties required no special skill. Daily at ten the Service opened its doors to welfare-weary citizens. Miles was the man who opened them, stemmed the too eager rush and admitted the first half-dozen; then he closed the doors on the waiting multitude until a Higher Official gave the signal for the admission of another batch.

Once inside they came briefly under his charge; he set them in order, saw that they did not press ahead of their turn, and adjusted the television-set for their amusement. A Higher Official interviewed them, checked their papers and arranged for the confiscation of their property. Miles never passed the door through which they were finally one by one conducted. A faint whiff of cyanide sometimes gave a hint of the mysteries beyond. Meanwhile he swept the waiting room, emptied the waste-paper basket and brewed tea — a worker's job, for which the refinements of Mountjoy proved a too rich apprenticeship.

In his hostel the same reproductions of Leger and Picasso as had haunted his childhood still stared down on him. At the cinema, to which he could afford, at the best, a weekly visit, the same films as he had seen free at orphanage, Air Force station and prison, flickered and drawled before him. He was a child of Welfare, strictly schooled to a life of boredom, but he had known better than this. He had known the tranquil melancholy of the gardens at Mountjoy. He had known ecstasy when the Air Force Training School had whirled to the stars in a typhoon of flame. And as he moved sluggishly between Dome and hostel there rang in his ears the words of the old lag: "You didn't give enough trouble."

Then one day, in the least expected quarter, in his own drab department, hope appeared.

Miles later remembered every detail of that morning. It had started in the normal way; rather below normal indeed, for they were reopening after a week's enforced idleness. There had been a strike among the coal-miners and Euthanasia had been at a standstill. Now the necessary capitulations had been signed, the ovens glowed again, and the queue at the patients' entrance stretched halfway round the dome. Dr. Beamish squinted at the waiting crowd through the periscope and said with some satisfaction: "It will take months to catch up on the waiting list now. We shall have to start making a charge for the service. It's the only way to keep down the demand."

"The Ministry will never agree to that, surely, sir?"

"Damned sentimentalists. My father and mother hanged

themselves in their own back-yard with their own clothes-line. Now no one will lift a finger to help himself. There's something wrong in the system, Plastic. There are still rivers to drown in, trains — every now and then — to put your head under; gasfires in some of the huts. The country is full of the natural resources of death, but everyone has to come to us."

It was not often he spoke so frankly before his subordinates. He had overspent during the week's holiday, drunk too much at his hostel with other unemployed colleagues. Always after a strike the senior officials returned to work in low spirits.

"Shall I let the first batch in, sir?"

"Not for the moment," said Dr. Beamish. "There's a priority case to see first, sent over with a pink chit from Drama. She's in the private waiting-room now. Fetch her in."

Miles went to the room reserved for patients of importance. All one wall was of glass. Pressed to it a girl was standing, turned away from him, looking out at the glum queue below. Miles stood, the light in his eyes, conscious only of a shadow which stirred at the sound of the latch and turned, still a shadow merely but of exquisite grace, to meet him. He stood at the door, momentarily struck silent at this blind glance of beauty. Then he said: "We're quite ready for you now, miss."

The girl came nearer. Miles's eyes adjusted themselves to the light. The shadow took form. The full vision was all that the first glance had hinted; more than all, for every slight movement revealed perfection. One feature only broke the canon of pure beauty; a long, silken, corn-gold beard.

She said, with a deep, sweet tone, all unlike the flat conventional accent of the age: "Let it be quite understood that I don't want anything done to me. I consented to come here.

The Director of Drama and the Director of Health were so pathetic about it all that I thought it was the least I could do. I said I was quite willing to hear about your service, but I do *not* want anything *done*."

"Better tell him inside," said Miles.

He led her to Dr. Beamish's room.

"Great State!" said Dr. Beamish, with eyes for the beard alone.

"Yes," she said. "It is a shock, isn't it? I've got used to it by now, but I can understand how people feel seeing it for the first time."

"Is it real?"

"Pull."

"It *is* strong. Can't they do anything about it?"

"Oh they've tried everything."

Dr. Beamish was so deeply interested that he forgot Miles's presence. "Klugmann's Operation, I suppose?"

"Yes."

"It does go wrong like that every now and then. They had two or three cases at Cambridge."

"I never wanted it done. I never want anything done. It was the Head of the Ballet. He insists on all the girls being sterilized. Apparently you can never dance really well again after you've had a baby. And I did want to dance really well. Now this is what's happened."

"Yes," said Dr. Beamish. "Yes. They're far too slap-dash. They had to put down those girls at Cambridge, too. There was no cure. Well, we'll attend to you, young lady. Have you any arrangements to make or shall I take you straight away?"

"But I don't want to be put down. I told your assistant here,

I've simply consented to come at all, because the Director of Drama cried so, and he's rather a darling. I've not the smallest intention of letting you kill me."

While she spoke, Dr. Beamish's geniality froze. He looked at her with hatred, not speaking. Then he picked up the pink form. "Then this no longer applies?"

"No."

"Then for State's sake," said Dr. Beamish, very angry, "what are you wasting my time for? I've got more than a hundred urgent cases waiting outside and you come in here to tell me that the Director of Drama is a darling. I know the Director of Drama. We live side by side in the same ghastly hostel. He's a pest. And I'm going to write a report to the Ministry about this tomfoolery which will make him, and the lunatic who thinks he can perform a Klugmann, come round to me begging for extermination. And then I'll put them at the bottom of the queue. Get her out of here, Plastic, and let some sane people in."

Miles led her into the public waiting-room. "What an old beast," she said. "What a perfect beast. I've never been spoken to like that before even in the ballet-school. He seemed so nice at first."

"It's his professional feeling," said Miles. "He was naturally put out at losing such an attractive patient."

She smiled. Her beard was not so thick as quite to obscure her delicate ovoid of check and chin. She might have been peeping at him over ripe heads of barley.

Her smile started in her wide grey eyes. Her lips under her golden moustachios were unpainted, tactile. A line of pale down sprang below them and ran through the centre of the chin, spreading and thickening and growing richer in colour till it met the full flow of the whiskers, but leaving on either side, clear and tender, two symmetrical zones, naked and provocative. So might have smiled some carefree deacon in the colonnaded schools of fifth-century Alexandria and struck dumb the heresiarchs.

"I think your beard is beautiful."

"Do you really? I can't help liking it too. I can't help liking anything about myself, can you?"

"Yes. Oh, yes."

"That's not natural."

Clamour at the outer door interrupted the talk. Like gulls round a lighthouse the impatient victims kept up an irregular flap and slap on the panels.

"We're all ready, Plastic," said a senior official. "What's going on this morning?"

What was going on? Miles could not answer. Turbulent sea birds seemed to be dashing themselves against the light in his own heart.

"Don't go," he said to the girl. "Please, I shan't be a minute."

"Oh, I've nothing to take me away. My department all think I'm half dead by now."

Miles opened the door and admitted an indignant half-dozen. He directed them to their chairs, to the registry. Then he went back to the girl who had turned away slightly from the crowd and drawn a scarf peasantwise round her head, hiding her beard.

"I still don't quite like people staring," she said.

"Our patients are far too busy with their own affairs to notice anyone else," said Miles. "Besides you'd have been stared at all right if you'd stayed on in ballet."

Miles adjusted the television but few eyes in the waiting-room glanced towards it; all were fixed on the registar's table and the doors beyond.

"Think of them all coming here," said the bearded girl.

"We give them the best service we can," said Miles.

"Yes, of course, I know you do. Please don't think I was finding fault. I only meant, fancy wanting to die."

"One or two have good reasons."

"I suppose you would say that I had. Everyone has been trying to persuade me, since my operation. The medical officials were the worst. They're afraid they may get into trouble for doing it wrong. And then the ballet people were almost as bad. They are so keen on Art that they say: 'You were the best of your class. You can never dance again. How can life be worth living?' What I try to explain is that it's just because I could dance that I *know* life is worth living. That's what Art means to me. Does that sound very silly?"

"It sounds unorthodox."

"Ah, but you're not an artist."

"Oh, I've danced all right. Twice a week all through my time at the orphanage."

"Therapeutic dancing?"

"That's what they called it."

"But, you see, that's quite different from Art."

"Why?"

"Oh," she said with a sudden full intimacy, with fondness, "oh what a lot you don't know."

The dancer's name was Clara.

✿   ✿   ✿   3   ✿   ✿   ✿

Courtship was free and easy in this epoch, but Miles was Clara's first lover. The strenuous exercises of her training, the austere standards of the corps-de-ballet and her devotion to her art had kept her body and soul unencumbered.

For Miles, child of the State, sex had been part of the curriculum at every stage of his education; first in diagrams, then in demonstrations, then in application, he had mastered all the antics of procreation. Love was a word seldom used except by politicians and by them only in moments of pure fatuity. Nothing that he had been taught prepared him for Clara.

Once in drama, always in drama. Clara now spent her days mending ballet shoes and helping neophytes on the wall bars. She had a cubicle in a Nissen hut and it was there that she and Miles spent most of their evenings. It was unlike anyone else's quarters in Satellite City.

Two little paintings hung on the walls, unlike any paintings Miles had seen before, unlike anything approved by the Ministry of Art. One represented a goddess of antiquity, naked and rosy, fondling a peacock on a bank of flowers; the other a vast, tree-fringed lake and a party in spreading silken clothes embarking in a pleasure boat under a broken arch. The gilt frames were much chipped, but what remained of them was elaborately foliated.

"They're French," said Clara. "More than two hundred years old. My mother left them to me."

All her possessions had come from her mother, nearly

enough of them to furnish the little room — a looking glass framed in porcelain flowers, a gilt, irregular clock. She and Miles drank their sad, officially compounded coffee out of brilliant, riveted cups.

"It reminds me of prison," said Miles when he was first admitted there.

It was the highest praise he knew.

On the first evening among this delicate bric-a-brac his lips found the bare twin spaces of her chin.

"I knew it would be a mistake to let the beastly doctor poison me," said Clara complacently.

Full summer came. Another moon waxed over these rare lovers. Once they sought coolness and secrecy among the high cow-parsley and willow-herb of the waste building sites. Clara's beard was all silvered like a patriarch's in the midnight radiance.

"On such a night as this," said Miles, supine, gazing into the face of the moon, "on such a night as this I burned an Air Force Station and half its occupants."

Clara sat up and began lazily smoothing her whiskers, then more vigorously tugged the comb through the thicker, tangled growth of her head, dragging it from her forehead; re-ordered the clothing which their embraces had loosed. She was full of womanly content and ready to go home. But Miles, all male, *post coitum tristis,* was struck by a chill sense of loss. No demonstration or exercise had prepared him for this strange new experience of the sudden loneliness that follows requited love.

Walking home they talked casually and rather crossly.

"You never go to the ballet now."

"No."

"Won't they give you seats?"

"I suppose they would."

"Then why don't you go?"

"I don't think I should like it. I see them often rehearsing. I don't like it."

"But you lived for it."

"Other interests now."

"Me?"

"Of course."

"You love me more than the ballet?"

"I am very happy."

"Happier than if you were dancing?"

"I can't tell, can I? You're all I 've got now."

"But if you could change?"

"I can't."

"If?"

"There's no 'if'."

"Damn."

"Don't fret, darling. It's only the moon."

And they parted in silence.

November came, a season of strikes; leisure for Miles, unsought and unvalued; lonely periods when the ballet school worked on and the death house stood cold and empty.

Clara began to complain of ill health. She was growing stout.

"Just contentment," she said at first, but the change worried her. "Can it be that beastly operation?" she asked. "I heard the reason they put down one of the Cambridge girls was that she kept growing fatter and fatter."

"She weighed nineteen stone," said Miles. "I know because Dr. Beamish mentioned it. He has strong professional objections to the Klugmann operation."

"I'm going to see the Director of Medicine. There's a new one now."

When she returned from her appointment, Miles, still left idle by the strikers, was waiting for her among her pictures and china. She sat beside him on the bed.

"Let's have a drink," she said.

They had taken to drinking wine together, very rarely because of the expense. The State chose and named the vintage. This month the issue was "Progress Port." Clara kept it in a crimson, white-cut, Bohemian flagon. The glasses were modern, unbreakable and unsightly.

"What did the doctor say?"

"He's very sweet."

"Well?"

"Much cleverer than the one before."

"Did he say it was anything to do with your operation?"

"Oh, yes. Everything to do with it."

"Can he put you right?"

"Yes, he thinks so."

"Good."

They drank their wine.

"That first doctor did make a mess of the operation, didn't he?"

"Such a mess. The new doctor says I'm a unique case. You see, I'm pregnant."

"*Clara.*"

"Yes, it is a surprise, isn't it?"

"This needs thinking about," said Miles.

He thought.

He refilled their glasses.

He said: "It's hard luck on the poor little beast not being an orphan. Not much opportunity for it. If he's a boy we must try and get him registered as a worker. Of course it might be a girl. Then" — brightly — "we could make her a dancer."

"Oh, don't mention dancing," cried Clara, and suddenly began weeping. "Don't speak to me of dancing."

Her tears fell fast. No tantrum this, but deep uncontrolled inconsolable sorrow.

And next day she disappeared.

❈ ❈ ❈ 4 ❈ ❈ ❈

Santa-Claus-Tide was near. Shops were full of shoddy little dolls. Children in the schools sang old ditties about peace and goodwill. Strikers went back to work in order to qualify for their seasonal bonus. Electric bulbs were hung in the conifers, and the furnaces in the Dome of Security roared again. Miles had been promoted. He now sat beside the assistant registrar and helped stamp and file the documents of the dead. It was harder work than he was used to and Miles was hungry for Clara's company. The lights were going out in the Dome and on the Goodwill Tree in the car park. He walked the half-mile of hutments to Clara's quarters. Other girls were waiting for their consorts or setting out to find them in the

Recreatorium, but Clara's door was locked. A note, pinned to it, read: *Miles, Going away for a bit. C.* Angry and puzzled he returned to his hostel.

Clara, unlike himself, had uncles and cousins scattered about the country. Since her operation she had been shy of visiting them. Now, Miles supposed, she was taking cover among them. It was the manner of her flight, so unlike her gentle ways, that tortured him. For a busy week he thought of nothing else. His reproaches sang in his head as the undertone to all the activities of the day and at night he lay sleepless repeating in his mind every word spoken between them and every act of intimacy.

After a week the thought of her became spasmodic and regular. The subject bored him unendurably. He strove to keep it out of his mind as a man might strive to control an attack of hiccups, and as impotently. Spasmodically, mechanically, the thought of Clara returned. He timed it and found that it came every 7½ minutes. He went to sleep thinking of her, he woke up thinking of her. But between times he slept. He consulted the departmental psychiatrist who told him that he was burdened by the responsibility of parentage. But it was not Clara the mother who haunted him, but Clara the betrayer.

Next week he thought of her every twenty minutes. The week after that he thought of her irregularly, though often; only when something outside himself reminded him of her. He began to look at other girls and considered himself cured.

He looked hard at other girls as he passed them in the dim corridors of the Dome and they looked boldly back at him. Then one of them stopped him and said: "I've seen you before with Clara," and at the mention of her name all interest in the other girl ceased in pain. "I went to visit her yesterday."

"Where?"

"In hospital, of course. Didn't you know?"

"What's the matter with her?"

"She won't say. Nor will anyone else at the hospital. She's top secret. If you ask me she's been in an accident and there's some politician involved. I can't think of any other reason for all the fuss. She's covered in bandages and gay as a lark."

Next day, December 25, was Santa Claus Day; no holiday in the department of Euthanasia, which was an essential service. At dusk Miles walked to the hospital, one of the unfinished edifices, all concrete and steel and glass in front and a jumble of huts behind. The hall porter was engrossed in the television, which was performing an old obscure folk play which past generations had performed on Santa Claus Day, and was now revived and revised as a matter of historical interest.

It was of professional interest to the porter for it dealt with maternity services before the days of Welfare. He gave the number of Clara's room without glancing up from the strange spectacle of an ox and an ass, an old man with a lantern, and a young mother. "People here are always complaining," he said. "They ought to realize what things were like before Progress."

The corridors were loud with relayed music. Miles found the hut he sought. It was marked "Experimental Surgery. Health Officers Only." He found the cubicle. He found Clara sleeping, the sheet pulled up to her eyes, her hair loose on the pillow. She had brought some of her property with her.

An old shawl lay across the bed-table. A painted fan stood against the television set. She awoke, her eyes full of frank welcome and pulled the sheet higher, speaking through it.

"Darling, you shouldn't have come. I was keeping it for a surprise."

Miles sat by the bed and thought of nothing to say except: "How are you?"

"Wonderful. They've taken the bandages off today. They won't let me have a looking glass yet, but they say everything has been a tremendous success. I'm something very special, Miles — a new chapter in surgical progress."

"But what has happened to you. Is it something to do with the baby?"

"Oh no. At least, it was. That was the first operation. But that's all over now."

"You mean our child?"

"Yes, that had to go. I should never have been able to dance afterwards. I told you all about it. That was why I had the Klugmann operation, don't you remember?"

"But you gave up dancing."

"That's where they've been so clever. Didn't I tell you about the sweet, clever new medical director? He's cured all that."

"Your dear beard."

"Quite gone. An operation the new director invented himself. It's going to be named after him or even perhaps after me. He's so unselfish he wants to call it the Clara Operation. He's taken off all the skin and put on a wonderful new substance, a sort of synthetic rubber that takes grease-paint perfectly. He says the colour isn't perfect, but that it will never show on the stage. Look, feel it."

She sat up in bed, joyful and proud.

Her eyes and brow were all that was left of the loved face. Below it something quite inhuman, a tight, slippery mask, salmon pink.

Miles stared. In the television screen by the bed further characters had appeared — Food Production Workers. They seemed to declare a sudden strike, left their sheep and ran off at the bidding of some kind of shop-steward in fantastic dress. The machine by the bedside broke into song, an old, forgotten ditty: "O tidings of comfort and joy, comfort and joy, O tidings of comfort and joy."

Miles retched unobtrusively. The ghastly face regarded him with fondness and pride. At length the right words came to him; the trite, the traditional sentence uttered by countless lips of generations of baffled and impassioned Englishmen: "I think I shall go for a short walk."

But first he walked only as far as his hostel. There he lay down until the moon moved to his window and fell across his sleepless face. Then he set out, walking far into the fields, out of sight of the Dome of Security, for two hours until the moon was near setting.

He had travelled at random, but now the white rays fell on a signpost and he read: "*Mountjoy* ¾." He strode on with only the stars to light his way till he came to the castle gates.

They stood open as always, gracious symbol of the new penology. He followed the drive. The whole lightless face of the old house stared at him silently, without rebuke. He knew now what was needed. He carried in his pocket a cigarette lighter which often worked. It worked for him now.

No need for oil here. The dry old silk of the drawing-room

curtains lit like paper. Paint and panelling, plaster and tapestry and gilding bowed to the embrace of the leaping flames. He stepped outside. Soon it was too hot on the terrace and he retreated further, to the marble temple at the end of the long walk. The murderers were leaping from the first storey windows, but the sexual offenders, trapped above, set up a wail of terror. He heard the chandeliers fall and saw the boiling lead cascading from the roof. This was something altogether finer than the strangulation of a few peacocks. He watched exultant as minute by minute the scene disclosed fresh wonders. Great timbers crashed within; outside the lily-pond hissed with falling brands; a vast ceiling of smoke shut out the stars and under it tongues of flame floated away into the tree tops.

Two hours later when the first engine arrived, the force of the fiery storm was already spent. Miles rose from his marble throne and began the long walk home. But he was no longer at all fatigued. He strode out cheerfully with his shadow, cast by the dying blaze, stretching before him along the lane.

On the main road a motorist stopped him and asked: "What's that over there? A house on fire?"

"It was," said Miles. "It's almost out now."

"Looks like a big place. Only Government property, I suppose?"

"That's all," said Miles.

"Well hop in if you want a lift."

"Thanks," said Miles, "I'm walking for pleasure."

✾ ✾ ✾ 5 ✾ ✾ ✾

Miles rose after two hours in bed. The hostel was alive with all the normal activity of morning. The wireless was playing; the sub-officials were coughing over their wash-basins; the reek of State sausages frying in State grease filled the asbestos cubicle. He was slightly stiff after his long walk and slightly footsore, but his mind was as calm and empty as the sleep from which he had awoken. The scorched-earth policy had succeeded. He had made a desert in his imagination which he might call peace. Once before he had burned his childhood. Now his brief adult life lay in ashes; the enchantments that surrounded Clara were one with the splendours of Mountjoy; her great golden beard, one with the tongues of flame that had leaped and expired among the stars; her fans and pictures and scraps of old embroidery, one with the gilded cornices and silk hangings, black, cold and sodden. He ate his sausage with keen appetite and went to work.

All was quiet too at the Department of Euthanasia.

The first announcement of the Mountjoy disaster had been on the early news. Its proximity to Satellite City gave it a special poignancy there.

"It is a significant phenomenon," said Dr. Beamish, "that any bad news has an immediate effect on our service. You see it whenever there is an international crisis. Sometimes I think people only come to us when they have nothing to talk about. Have you looked at our queue today?"

Miles turned to the periscope. Only one man waited out-

side, old Parsnip, a poet of the thirties who came daily but
was usually jostled to the back of the crowd. He was a comic
character in the department, this veteran poet. Twice in
Miles's short term he had succeeded in gaining admission,
but on both occasions had suddenly taken fright and bolted.

"It's a lucky day for Parsnip," said Miles.

"Yes. He deserves some luck. I knew him well once, him
and his friend Pimpernell. *New Writing*, the Left Book Club,
they were all the rage. Pimpernell was one of my first patients.
Hand Parsnip in and we'll finish him off."

So old Parsnip was summoned and that day his nerve stood
firm. He passed fairly calmly through the gas chamber on his
way to rejoin Pimpernell.

"We might as well knock off for the day," said Dr. Beamish.
"We shall be busy again soon when the excitement dies
down."

But the politicians seemed determined to keep the excitement up. All the normal features of television were interrupted and curtailed to give place to Mountjoy. Survivors appeared on the screen, among them Soapy, who described how
long practice as a cat burglar had enabled him to escape.
Mr. Sweat, he remarked with respect, had got clear away.
The ruins were surveyed by the apparatus. A sexual maniac
with broken legs gave audience from his hospital bed. The
Minister of Welfare, it was announced, would make a special
appearance that evening to comment on the disaster.

Miles dozed intermittently beside the hostel set and at dusk
rose, still calm and free; so purged of emotion that he made
his way once more to the hospital and called on Clara.

She had spent the afternoon with looking-glass and make-up

box. The new substance of her face fulfilled all the surgeon's promises. It took paint to perfection. Clara had given herself a full mask as though for the lights of the stage; an even creamy white with sudden high spots of crimson on the cheek bones, huge hard crimson lips, eye brows extended and turned up catwise, the eyes shaded all round with ultramarine and dotted at the corners with crimson.

"You're the first to see me," she said. "I was half afraid you wouldn't come. You seemed cross yesterday."

"I wanted to see the television," said Miles. "It's so crowded at the hostel."

"So dull today. Nothing except this prison that has been burned down."

"I was there myself. Don't you remember? I often talked of it."

"Did you, Miles? Perhaps so. I've such a bad memory for things that don't concern me. Do you really want to hear the Minister? It would be much cosier to talk."

"It's him I've come for."

And presently the Minister appeared, open-necked as always, but without his usual smile; grave to the verge of tears. He spoke for twenty minutes. ". . . The great experiment must go on . . . the martyrs of maladjustment shall not have died in vain . . . A greater, new Mountjoy shall rise from the ashes of the old . . ." Eventually tears came — real tears for he held an invisible 'onion — and trickled down his cheeks. So the speech ended.

"That's all I came for," said Miles, and left Clara to her cocoa-butter and face-towel.

Next day all the organs of public information were still

piping the theme of Mountjoy. Two or three patients, already bored with the entertainment, presented themselves for extermination and were happily despatched. Then a message came from the Regional Director, official-in-chief of Satellite City. He required the immediate presence of Miles in his office.

"I have a move order for you, Mr. Plastic. You are to report to the Ministers of Welfare and Rest and Culture. You will be issued with a Grade-A hat, umbrella and brief case for the journey. My congratulations."

Equipped with these insignia of sudden, dizzy promotion, Miles travelled to the capital leaving behind a domeful of sub-officials chattering with envy.

At the terminus an official met him. Together in an official car they drove to Whitehall.

"Let me carry your brief case, Mr. Plastic."

"There's nothing in it."

Miles's escort laughed obsequiously at this risqué joke.

At the Ministry the lifts were in working order. It was a new and alarming experience to enter the little cage and rise to the top of the great building.

"Do they always work here?"

"Not *always*, but very very often."

Miles realised that he was indeed at the heart of things.

"Wait here. I will call you when the Ministers are ready."

Miles looked from the waiting-room window at the slow streams of traffic. Just below him stood a strange, purposeless obstruction of stone. A very old man, walking by, removed his hat to it as though saluting an acquaintance. Why? Miles wondered. Then he was summoned to the politicians.

They were alone in their office save for a gruesome young woman. The Minister of Rest and Culture said: "Ease your feet, lad," and indicated a large leatherette armchair.

"Not such a happy occasion, alas, as our last meeting," said the Minister of Welfare.

"Oh, I don't know," said Miles. He was enjoying the outing.

"The tragedy at Mountjoy Castle was a grievous loss to the cause of penology."

"But the great work of Rehabilitation will continue," said the gruesome young woman.

"A greater Mountjoy will arise from the ashes," said the Minister.

"Those noble criminal lives have not been lost in vain."

"Their memory will inspire us."

"Yes," said Miles. "I heard the broadcast."

"Exactly," said the Minister. "Precisely. Then you appreciate, perhaps, what a change the occurrence makes in your own position. From being, as we hoped, the first of a continuous series of successes, you are our only one. It would not be too much to say that the whole future of penology is in your hands. The destruction of Mountjoy Castle by itself was merely a set-back. A sad one, of course, but something which might be described as the growing pains of a great movement. But there is a darker side. I told you, I think, that our great experiment had been made only against considerable opposition. Now — I speak confidentially — that opposition has become vocal and unscrupulous. There is, in fact, a whispering campaign that the fire was no accident but the act of one of the very men whom we were seeking to serve. That campaign must be scotched."

"They can't do us down as easy as they think," said the Minister of Rest and Culture. "Us old dogs know a trick or two."

"Exactly. Counter-propaganda. You are our Exhibit A. The irrefutable evidence of the triumph of our system. We are going to send you up and down the country to lecture. My colleagues have already written your speech. You will be accompanied by Miss Flower here, who will show and explain the model of the new Mountjoy. Perhaps you will care to see it yourself. Miss Flower, the model please."

All the time they were speaking Miles had been aware of a bulky, sheeted object on a table in the window. Miss Flower now unveiled it. Miles gazed in awe.

The object displayed was a familiar, standard packing-case, set on end.

"A rush job," said the Minister of Welfare. "You will be provided with something more elaborate for your tour."

Miles gazed at the box.

It fitted. It fell into place precisely in the void of his mind, satisfying all the needs for which his education had prepared him. The conditioned personality recognized its proper pre-ordained environment. All else was insubstantial; the gardens of Mountjoy, Clara's cracked Crown Derby and her enveloping beard were trophies of a fading dream.

The Modern Man was home.

"There is one further point," continued the Minister of Welfare. "A domestic one but not as irrelevant as it may seem. Have you by any chance formed an attachment in Satellite City? Your dossier suggests that you have."

"Any woman trouble?" explained the Minister of Rest and Culture.

"Oh, yes," said Miles. "Great trouble. But that is over."

"You see, perfect rehabilitation, complete citizenship should include marriage."

"It has not," said Miles.

"That should be rectified."

"Folks like a bloke to be spliced," said the Minister of Rest and Culture. "With a couple of kids."

"There is hardly time for *them*," said the Minister of Welfare. "But we think that psychologically you will have more appeal if you have a wife by your side. Miss Flower here has every qualification."

"Looks are only skin deep, lad," said the Minister of Rest and Culture.

"So if you have no preferable alternative to offer . . . ?"

"None," said Miles.

"Spoken like an orphan. I see a splendid career ahead of the pair of you."

"When can we get divorced?"

"Come, come, Plastic. You mustn't look too far ahead. First things first. You have already obtained the necessary leave from your Director, Miss Flower?"

"Yes, Minister."

"Then off you both go. And State be with you."

In perfect peace of heart Miles followed Miss Flower to the Registrar's office.

Then the mood veered.

Miles felt ill at ease during the ceremony and fidgeted with something small and hard which he found in his pocket. It proved to be his cigarette lighter, a most uncertain apparatus. He pressed the catch and instantly, surprisingly there burst out a tiny flame — gemlike, hymeneal, auspicious.